ED BELOW

D0130136

Also by alison **allen-gray**

Unique

'genuinely enthralling'
Guardian

'a terrific book—exciting, heartening, intelligent
and all too topical.'
Books for Keeps

'An exciting and imaginative exploration of
modern ethical issues.'
Daily Echo

'Addresses complex ethical and scientific issues
with gravitas and compassion.'
Booktrusted News

Lifegame

alison **allen-gray**

OXFORD
UNIVERSITY PRESS

The author gratefully acknowledges financial assistance from the
Authors' Foundation during the writing of the book. This support
not only speeded the completion of the work but also helped to
rally the spirits on the long trek towards publication.
Thank you all very much.

OXFORD
UNIVERSITY PRESS

Great Clarendon Street, Oxford OX2 6DP

Oxford University Press is a department of the University of Oxford.
It furthers the University's objective of excellence in research, scholarship,
and education by publishing worldwide in

Oxford   New York

Auckland   Cape Town   Dar es Salaam   Hong Kong   Karachi
Kuala Lumpur   Madrid   Melbourne   Mexico City   Nairobi
New Delhi   Shanghai   Taipei   Toronto

With offices in

Argentina   Austria   Brazil   Chile   Czech Republic   France   Greece
Guatemala   Hungary   Italy   Japan   Poland   Portugal   Singapore
South Korea   Switzerland   Thailand   Turkey   Ukraine   Vietnam

Oxford is a registered trade mark of Oxford University Press
in the UK and in certain other countries

British Library Cataloguing in Publication Data

Data available

ISBN: 978-0-19-272843-2

3 5 7 9 10 8 6 4 2

Printed in Great Britain by CPI Cox & Wyman, Reading, Berkshire

Paper used in the production of this book is a natural,
recyclable product made from wood grown in sustainable forests.
The manufacturing process conforms to the environmental
regulations of the country of origin.

In **memory** of my **father**,
with **love** and **gratitude**

Chapter 1

The baby was brought to the Orphanage straight from the car accident that killed his mother. It was 3 a.m. Dead of night in the dead of the winter of the year 112.

Papa Louis winced as his bare feet met the floor tiles. Many times, over the years, the night bell had woken him like this. As Director of the Orphanage he could have left one of his staff to deal with the night arrivals, but that wasn't the way he liked to run things. At Orphanage 206 each new child was welcomed by Papa Louis himself. If welcome was the right word, given the circumstances.

Outside on the icy pavement a lone Officiate Guard, illuminated by the street lamp, was holding the child. Papa Louis took in the spots of blood on the infant's shawl but his glance was tugged immediately to meet the fierce gaze of large, almost-black eyes. The baby could be no more than two months old, but those eyes locked on to Papa Louis, took hold of him, thrusting out their unique challenge upon the world. I'm watching you, they seemed to say. So you'd better not foul up.

Papa Louis took the child and tucked him into the shelter of his arm. He could feel the force of the silent gaze as sure as if it were a beam of heat. The child was still in shock. The silence wouldn't last. Papa Louis knew this from long experience. He turned towards the office. The sooner they could get the official data done, the sooner this lanky, pale-faced Guard would leave and he could concentrate on the child.

'No living relatives,' said the Guard. 'We'll clear out her stuff in the morning.'

He meant that they'd go to the home of the dead woman and dispose of everything. And because there were no living relatives, all the goods would be sold and the proceeds given to the Island State, which would now raise the child. End of story.

'She was killed outright,' he added.

'And the baby is unharmed?' said Papa Louis.

'He was lucky.'

Papa Louis's questioning glance brushed the Guard's eye just long enough to find the usual insolent glare in return. There were many questions he could have asked but there was no point. You never got answers by asking questions, not on this Island. If the Officiate wanted you to know about something, then you'd be told. Otherwise not.

Papa Louis set the baby down carefully in a basket by his desk. As he straightened himself he saw the child's eyes still on him, watching.

He turned to the Guard.

'ID card?' he asked.

'No.'

Papa Louis didn't understand.

'But there must be! Everyone has . . .'

'What's it matter?' said the Guard. 'There's no one to take the kid in, no family left, so it doesn't matter who she was, does it?'

For the first time, Papa Louis noticed something beneath the usual arrogant Officiate manner. And it wasn't just that the Guard was in a hurry to dump the baby and get home. He was desperate to leave.

'How do you know there's no family, if there's no ID?' asked Papa Louis. After all, he didn't like being taken for a complete idiot.

The Guard glanced nervously at the ceiling.

'It's all right,' said Papa Louis, 'the cams are broken.'

The Guard was only a boy, really. Maybe no more than seventeen. Papa Louis smiled, hoping to encourage him. But it was no good. He was frightened.

'Look,' said the Guard, 'forget the ID. He's lucky enough I got him here, all right?'

Papa Louis shivered, and not because of the early morning chill that clung to the drab little office. No, he'd caught the shiver of fear from the Guard. Did the Officiate have a particular interest in this death?

'When you rang the night bell, you said a car crash,' said Papa Louis. 'Is that right?'

The Guard hesitated. Papa Louis waited, sensing that the boy could give him more if he didn't push too hard.

'She'd . . . run off the road. She'd been . . . '

'She'd been what?' asked Papa Louis gently. Was this boy

struggling with his conscience? It looked like it. Maybe even Officiate Guards had a conscience.

'I was the first one there, all right?' said the Guard, twitching a defensive glance at him. 'I saw the baby on the back seat. I got him out and took him to my car.'

'And the mother?'

Now the Guard looked straight at Papa Louis.

'There was a hole in the windscreen . . . '

'She'd been shot?'

The Guard shrugged and threw another nervous glance at the ceiling. 'Then some Senior Officiate turned up and they ordered me away.'

Papa Louis could see that the boy was shaking now. He reached out a hand to his shoulder. He felt shaky himself.

'Did they see the baby?' he asked.

The Guard shook his head.

'You did the right thing,' said Papa Louis. 'But the mother . . . '

The Guard turned to leave. As he reached the door, he said, 'The car's number. It was 734719.'

Papa Louis swung round to the desk and keyed the number into his notepad. When he turned back to thank him, the Guard was gone.

Papa Louis puffed out a long sigh and stared at the child, who was probing the space around him with huge, confused eyes.

'Sorry, fella, no way of knowing your name at the moment. So until I know, we'll call you Fella, how's that?' He bent towards the basket and the baby's eyes found him and locked on to him again. He bounced his arms against the air. And then he started to cry.

Papa Louis lifted him and snuggled him into the crook of his elbow. But this did nothing to soothe him. It made him wriggle and scream, his face scrunched and red.

It was then that he felt something odd about the shape of the child. Something hard, unbending, at the base of his spine. He sat and laid him gently face down over his knees. Fella began to scream. Papa Louis worked quickly, trying to free the child from whatever it was that was hurting him. He pulled at the nappy and saw a plastic bag stuffed into it. He glanced round to check he was alone and then pulled out the bag and opened it.

The moment he saw what was inside, his heart started to pound painfully. A paperbook. Very small, but unmistakably a paperbook. Why hide it in such a place? The mother must have done it. But *why* would she have it? You hardly ever saw a paperbook. Only if it was an instruction manual for a computer or housechore device, and this was neither of these.

This was a completely different kind of thing. No pictures, diagrams, or figures. Just words, words, words. And not ordinary words. It was even hard to be sure that it was Island language, because it was in the old-fashioned style. It was done with a pen held in the hand; yes, it must be! Papa Louis stared at it in astonishment. It was a long, long time since he had seen pen-writing. The words were so densely packed, the shapes of the letters so unfamiliar. He shivered again, so suddenly that the paperbook snapped shut in his hands.

It was this way of writing, with a pen held in the hand, that they used to use in the Downzone in the Time Before. Could it possibly be that Fella's mother had written it? No, it wasn't possible. Perhaps she had found the paperbook and hidden it. But why? You wouldn't hide something like this without reason and you would have no reason unless you could read it. But in Papa Louis's lifetime and even before that, no one had ever been taught to read or write pen-writing on this Island.

The child had fallen quiet. As if he knew that this was a moment on which his whole life turned.

The silence deepened. Papa Louis could hear the white noise in his own head and the fearful pulsing of blood at his temples. He could feel the gentle thud of Fella's tiny heart against his knees and the warmth of this strange little paperbook as he turned it over and over in his hands.

He knew he should hand it in to the Officiate.

Instead, with shaking hands, he locked it in the safe.

And then, that first night of his life with Fella, Papa Louis left the child with Annie, the kindest of the women who worked at the Orphanage. She bathed him and changed his nappy. She tried to feed him. She cuddled and rocked him, but he wouldn't stop crying. Officiate rules said that children were to be drugged if they cried too much, but Papa Louis had never allowed that.

So, while Annie rocked, Papa Louis set out to try and find the other thing that sometimes worked. At least, that's what he told himself he was doing at the time. But really, he went because he was curious. That was what drove him to look up the address where the car was registered. To seek out the place where Fella and his mother had lived.

He took the little van and headed off between the rows of dark tower blocks that surrounded the Orphanage. The dead woman's home, in Blue Boulevard, was in one of the B-grade areas on the other side of town. He found the place after about half an hour of driving round the Boulevards, along rows of identical four-bed detached villas which were as bleak, in their way, as the dark towers of his own E-grade zone. His luck was in. Even though the sun wasn't up yet, there was a light on in one of the neighbouring houses. A woman in a primrose-coloured housecoat opened the door, frowning, shivering in the grey morning.

'Never met her, only seen her once or twice,' she said when asked about the woman next door. She looked suspicious. Papa Louis showed his ID.

'She's dead,' he explained. 'Killed in a car crash. She had a child . . .'

'Nothing to do with us,' said the woman.

Papa Louis looked at her hard little face. Useless to explain what he was after. She was already pushing the door closed.

Well, Louis old pal, he thought, as the door clicked shut in his face, you're just going to have to risk it.

So he went round to the back of the house and broke in. It wasn't hard. He didn't actually have to break anything and there was no alarm system. There was a tiny window open and he managed to get his arm through and open the larger casement below it. He paused to get his breath. He was getting a bit fragile for this sort of thing and it took a few minutes to get his stiff old legs folded up and through the window. At last he was sitting on the draining board.

He never felt good about resorting to this. But it was necessary. The Officiate understood nothing about children who'd lost their parents. They'd 'dispose' of the whole household, having neither the imagination to think nor the heart to care that a child in distress could suck a tiny breath of comfort from the last, lingering scent of its mother. So sometimes he, Papa Louis, Director of Orphanage 206, became a raider of dead people's linen.

There was nothing much to dispose of in this house. As he glanced into each sparsely furnished room looking for some clue as to who or what this woman had been, he saw nothing beyond the usual household equipment. Upstairs he found a nightdress in the bed. He took the pillowcases off the pillows and stuffed one inside the other, along with the nightdress. That should be enough.

He cast a glance around the bare room, which was now being washed by the first light of low winter sun. Suddenly, he could feel the dark gaze of the baby he had left at the Orphanage.

Papa Louis will try to take care of your child, he told the rumpled, empty bed. He'll do his best.

He had just decided to have a more thorough search of the place, when a movement on the edge of his vision made him glance out of the window at the Boulevard below. A large black car had turned into the end of the road and was climbing the hill towards the house.

Papa Louis ran back down the stairs and out through the back door. The garden was completely enclosed at the back by a high fence. He turned down the side alleyway, his only way back to the van. Too late. The car, a luxury Officiate vehicle, had stopped outside the house.

He hunkered down behind the waste bins in the alleyway, his heart racing. An armed guard got out of the front of the car and opened the rear door for a man to emerge. This man was not in uniform. But he must be far, far higher rank than the armed thugs who were driving him.

Papa Louis shrank back as the men approached the house. He heard the splintering of the door as it was broken down.

He waited a few moments more, and then, on shaking legs, hurried down the drive and back to the van.

Lucky that part of the Boulevard was on a steep slope. Lucky he could take the brake off and let the van roll silently away out of sight. Because the very last thing he wanted at that moment was to be heard or seen.

Chapter 2

There was something wrong with Papa Louis. Fella knew it. No matter how hard he tried to push this knowing away, it was no good. Once you know something, you know it.

You could see it in the way Papa Louis had slowed down. The way, when he lifted a baby from its cot, it would take him longer, cost him some pain, to straighten up. It was a movement Fella was so used to, perhaps the most typical of his movements, sweeping a child into his arms, that it was easy to see the change. And the change in colour. His skin was slowly fading to yellowish-grey.

Fella blinked at the tears that were blurring the tower blocks ahead of him. He wiped the back of his hand across his eyes but more tears came, and more.

He could not imagine a world without Papa Louis in it.

Some of the women at the Orphanage weren't so bad. They did their best to be nice to the kids, but it was Papa Louis who stood between them and the Officiate. Everyone knew that they were luckier here than in most State

Orphanages. They were never drugged, for one thing. Just as well, because if anyone ever tried to drug *him* they'd end up in a pretty drowsy state themselves.

Fella swung his leg back and took a vicious kick at a beer can lying on the pavement, sending it clattering along the hot, cracked concrete.

'Hey!' A voice called out behind him.

Great! Now he'd be reported for littering or uncalm behaviour. He turned. No, not some smug little Officiate informer. It was Grebe. He just had time to wipe his eyes again without it being too obvious. Then she was next to him, grinning.

But in a heartbeat the grin had gone and her eyes had widened in alarm.

'Fella? What's wrong?'

He never had been able to hide anything from Grebe. His oldest, his best friend. Still, he didn't want this intrusion. The way he felt about Papa Louis was the most private thing in his life. Probably the only private thing in his life. He couldn't explain it, even to Grebe. He shrugged and quickened his pace. Papa Louis would be waiting for him down by the river.

She walked with him in a silence that was like a silk scarf wrapped around a rock. Fella knew that she was considering whether to try another angle to the question. No question came, and he was glad. It seemed she'd decided just to walk beside him for a while. There was something about the way she had to take extra-long paces to keep up that made him smile inside, despite his misery.

'Guess what?' she said.

This made him smile outright, took him straight back to those stupid childhood games they used to play, where they would boast to each other about imaginary things they'd done, or they would pretend that they weren't really who they were but someone else with a much more exciting life. Except sometimes these games had upset Fella because he didn't even know who he was to begin with.

'Go on. Guess what?' She nudged her shoulder against his arm.

'What?'

'My father has bought my mother a new speedcar. Because it's my birthday soon.'

'Kind of him. What's he bought you?'

'Don't know. But anyway, listen. The speedcar is the wrong colour. My mother says it won't go with any of her jewellery.'

'No!' Fella slapped a hand to his forehead in horror. '*Whatever* is she going to *do*?'

'Don't know. The trauma is so severe she's taken to her bed. She may never recover.'

Fella grinned down at her.

'Is that true?'

'No. She hasn't taken to her bed. But they did have a very noisy row about it.'

Grebe's parents were B-grade, so they could afford to buy almost anything they wanted but they weren't allowed the travel perks of the A-graders. It was this, Fella assumed, that caused Grebe's mother to have regular tantrums. Over the years, listening to Grebe's stories about her parents had sometimes made Fella grateful to be an orphan. Except, not really. Because *his* parents wouldn't have been like Grebe's, would they?

The thing about being an orphan was that you could create parents in your own imagination—and over the years Fella's creations had been many and elaborate. They'd had to be. He didn't even have a letter, which all the other Orphanage kids did. The letter would arrive, as soon as your information had been processed, to tell you why you're in a State Orphanage. Your parent/parents was/were killed/died on a certain date. The Island State would now accommodate all your needs. But he'd never had a letter.

There'd been a car crash, that's all he knew. Many times he had questioned Papa Louis and sometimes he'd thought he'd seen something in the old man's eyes. Something like hesitation or pain. But Papa Louis had always said no, he knew nothing about who Fella's parents were. And Fella had always believed him.

'So, anyway, this stupid birthday . . . ' said Grebe.

'It's not so stupid. As soon as you're sixteen you can leave the Attainment Centre.'

Grebe shot him a sad look. No need to say it. The Attainment Centre was a nightmare but what came next would probably be worse.

'I don't think they'll give me B-grade work,' said Grebe, 'I'm not clever enough. It'll be C if I'm lucky.'

Fella reached down and laced his fingers through hers, stroking his thumb across the fine bones of her hand. Tiny, fragile hand. Like a bat's wing.

'What would you like for your birthday?' he said. 'Any present you want.' He flung out his free arm with a flourish. 'You choose.'

'Yeah, well. That's what we all want, isn't it?' she said. 'To choose.'

She squeezed his hand and they fell silent for a while.

'So anyway, this stupid birthday,' she said again. 'My parents are hiring the Dome at the end of our Boulevard. All their horrible friends are coming and they've insisted on inviting loads of horrible people from my set at the Attainment Centre even though I hate them all and they'll play their horrible music and take loads of tabbacaseed and alco with their horrible friends and it'll all be just . . . just . . .'

' . . . totally unpleasant,' he said.

'Yes. Will you come?'

'Of course.'

'Thank you.'

Quickly, she sprang onto tiptoe and brushed a butterfly kiss onto his cheek. In the instant that her face touched his, he became aware that his cheek was still wet with the last of his tears. It was the first time in all the years they'd known each other she'd ever done anything like this and he watched, puzzled, as she ran off down the street. Taking some of his tears with her, he supposed.

His heart was thudding. He huffed out a sigh and turned towards the intersection at the top of the Orphanage road. There was a rough patch of ground at the bottom of the Orphanage playing field, near the river, and it was here that

Papa Louis had asked to meet him after Attainment Centre this afternoon. They'd often met there when they wanted to talk because the only audiocam in that area had broken and the Officiate had so far failed to notice this. No, there was nothing unusual in Papa Louis's suggestion to meet, not in the suggestion itself. But still Fella was afraid.

Slowly, he approached the concrete Guard hut that over-looked the intersection. A tram had just unloaded a group of giggling girls. Good. This meant that the Guards would have something more entertaining to do than ask him his name.

He hung back as the arrival of the girls, some of them not much older than him, brought the Guards out of the hot darkness of the hut. These girls didn't seem to mind the men leering at them. They met the crude remarks with shrill laughter. One of them produced her ID card from her bra, jiggling her generous breasts in their too-tight top right under the men's eyes. The girls reckoned they knew where the power lay, thought Fella, but they were wrong.

He was almost clear of the hut when the familiar jeer came.

'Oi! Noper boy!'

It was what all the Orphanage kids had to live with. To be branded a Noper, the lowest of the low people, 'no-hopers'. You just had to find a way of showing that the insult didn't touch you.

Fella turned to smile at the Guard. It was one of the older ones. Clearly there weren't enough girls to go round.

'Name!' bellowed the Guard.

Fella passed this way every day on his way back from the Attainment Centre. The Guards knew his name very well but he gave it again, trying to steady his rage.

'Fella who?'

Now the first Guard had attracted a couple of others who, with some of the girls, were staring at him.

'Just Fella,' he said.

'What kind of name is that?'

'*My* name.'

He waited while they all amused themselves with this. Sometimes it was his hair that displeased them. Boys were not supposed to have long hair. Worse than this, if you were Orphanage scum, boy or girl, you were supposed to have your head shaved. But Papa Louis's head shaver never seemed to be working properly. Five years ago, when Fella was ten, some women had been sent in to shave all the kids in the Orphanage. It was the first time in his life that Fella had felt like killing someone. Although not the last.

'Got a lot of hair for a Noper,' said the first Guard. 'Least he's got plenty of *something.*'

The others laughed again, with less enthusiasm this time. They were more interested in the girls, and Fella saw that his tormentor had lost his audience.

'Get lost, you hairy Noper,' said the Guard. 'But be good. We're watching you.'

Papa Louis was sitting on the bench down by the water's edge. Fella paused to steady himself, taking in the bony hunch of shoulder under the faded summer shirt, the body that had been slowly shrinking day by day as his own had been growing. The old man was staring out across the dank, weed-clogged river. His lips were moving in a silent mutter and from time to time he gave a tiny shake of his head and tapped at something on his lap. Fella couldn't see what it was. He gave a gentle cough and Papa Louis turned.

'Ah!' He raised a stiff arm and patted the bench beside him.

As Fella sat he saw that the thing on Papa Louis's lap was a tiny brown paperbook. He frowned a question across at the yellowed old eyes. Papa Louis caught his hand and squeezed it.

So he'd been right. Something big was about to happen. All day long, trapped in the throttling heat of the Attainment Centre, he'd known it. And now a queasy feeling stirred in his stomach. Was this it? The thing that every orphan longs for and fears, about to be revealed? And why now? Fella pushed the answer away, heart racing, and stared at the paperbook.

'Fella, this may make you very angry with me,' said Papa Louis.

'How could I ever be angry with you?' He was trying to sound lighthearted and failing.

'Give it a go,' said Papa Louis. 'You're angry with everyone else!'

'That's because everyone else is an idiot!'

Papa Louis laughed and spluttered out a few painful coughs. Fella heard the wheeze way down in the old man's lungs and his own chest tightened in fear.

'Fella, I am truly sorry for what I have to tell you. This . . . ' he patted the paperbook again, ' . . . this is rightfully yours.'

That was all Fella needed to hear. He snatched at the paperbook and, for a second, felt the resistance in Papa Louis's hands. But then it was in his own hands, and open.

'It was hidden on you when you were brought to me and I have kept it hidden all your life,' said Papa Louis. 'I'm sorry.'

Here it was, thought Fella, his own secret history about to crack open.

Except it didn't. It couldn't, because he couldn't read a word of these strange, uneven lines with their muddles of mis-shaped letters. The meaning of this took a couple of seconds to hit.

'It's another language! Is it?'

But it couldn't be. Other languages didn't exist any more because other peoples didn't exist any more.

'Fella, you know it can't be that,' said Papa Louis. 'No, it's our own language, I think. But this is pen-writing—the old way of doing it, with a pen held in the hand.'

'What, you mean . . . like from the Time Before? So . . . who could have written it?'

His hands had started to tremble. Fear and anger were welling up. Fear for all the things he didn't know and anger at Papa Louis for keeping them from him.

'I'm sorry, Fella,' said Papa Louis, 'I've been a fool to keep it all these years and do nothing! I should have tried to discover its meaning. I don't know who wrote it. We'd need to try and read it. And I think we could, given time . . . '

The old man's face was lit up with eagerness and suddenly all the rage that had built up inside Fella dissolved. The paperbook didn't matter, nor who wrote it. They were not going to be given time to read it. Not together. The baked rosettes of lichen on the bench swam before his eyes. He blinked back the tears.

'Why didn't you give it to me before?'

Papa Louis's eyes wandered towards the rusting audio-cam that stood a little further down the riverbank.

'I was afraid to, Fella. I thought at the time that it might have been because of this paperbook that your mother was murdered.'

The word sliced through him. 'Murdered?'

'Yes, Fella. I believe she was murdered and that it was done on the orders of someone very high up. I am sorry that

I have kept this thought from you, that I have kept the paperbook from you. But I didn't think either would do you any good.'

'What d'you mean? Why murdered?'

'When your mother's car ran off the road, the Guard who brought you in thought . . . ' Papa Louis hesitated. 'He thought it wasn't an accident. And then, while it was still just about dark, I went to find your house. I wanted to get something that might comfort you, a toy or . . . or something of your mother's. You were in such a terrible state. But, Fella, I wasn't the only one there. There was a car, someone of very high rank. They broke down the door. I only just managed to get clear.'

'So . . . even though they'd killed her, they still didn't get what they wanted, is that what you're saying? You think they were looking for this?'

'At the time I did. I came back here and buried it by the yew hedge. It's been buried for over fifteen years. I was so terrified that one day they'd come looking for it. But they never have. So they couldn't have known about it.'

Fella didn't know what he felt more: pride that his mother had done something to anger the Officiate or rage that she had got herself killed and left him alone. He felt both.

'So why did they want her dead?' he said.

Papa Louis's hand came to rest with his own on the paperbook. 'Perhaps this will tell us.'

'You think she wrote it herself? In pen-writing? She couldn't have!'

'We'll try and find out, shall we? Together. But, Fella, no one must ever know that we have this.'

Fella turned the paperbook over and over in his hands and felt the fear rise inside him.

'Of course not. No one will ever know.'

Grebe leaned back slowly from the desk and turned her head to see if the girl at the screen to her right had finished the Task. No, she hadn't. In fact, she was looking hopefully in the direction of Grebe's screen. But then she saw who was sitting there and looked away in disgust. No good trying to copy from Grebe. Everyone knew Grebe was an idiot.

She turned to look to her left, slowly again, in case the Attainment Director prowling around the centre of the circular room caught the movement. They were supposed to stay facing their screens, facing the circular wall, until Task Time was over. The girl to her left had finished the Task and was examining her perfectly painted fingernails. Her badge showed that she was a B-grader.

Grebe rubbed her aching head and looked at her screen again. It was a Task about the Downzone and it was really important to get every question right because your work grade would depend, amongst other things, on having a perfect knowledge of Island State history.

She thought she had got most of it right. It had been drummed into them since State Nursery. Island time had begun when selected people were brought across the Outer-sea from the nearest land mass, known as the Downzone. That was 128 years ago. Correct. But then, any idiot who knew what year it was now would know that. Shortly after the arrival of those lucky settlers, the Downzone had suf-fered a bio-chemical attack. There had been no survivors. Estimated timescale for decontamination: two thousand years was the best guess the Officiate scientists could make, although even they admitted that nobody knew for certain when the Downzone would be pronounced safe.

Grebe felt a familiar tightening in her throat. She sat up straight and took a deep breath. This always happened when she thought about the Downzone—she got all wor-ried about breathing, conscious of her lungs working, afraid that something would happen to stop them work-ing. Ever since they were little, they'd been taught about what would happen to a human being if they set foot in the Downzone. It wouldn't happen at first. Or rather, at first you wouldn't know about it, because it was in the air and you couldn't see it coming. But slowly, slowly, the poi-sons in the air would close down all the systems in your body. Your brain would start to feel muzzy and because you couldn't think straight, you couldn't form words. Then you'd forget the words altogether. Your eyes would begin to itch and this was the stage at which, although there would be no outward sign yet, your nervous system and your liver would be starting to pack up. Eventually, some desperate message would try to get through to the lungs to tell them to keep breathing. But there'd be no nerves left to tell the muscles to work the bellows. And in any case it was the breathing that had done for you in the first place. Just breathing the air with its hidden dose of death.

Fella always said there was a whole history to do with the Downzone that they weren't being told, and Grebe could see what he meant, although she worried when he talked like this. For example, said Fella, they'd never been told why the Downzone was attacked or who attacked it. He had once told her that they had 'a duty to be curious'. Grebe had asked what the word 'curious' meant and he had laughed.

Where *was* Fella? That was what Grebe was curious about right now. He hadn't come to the Attainment Centre today. Where *was* he, what was he doing? He'd been strange yesterday—distracted. She had looked for him this morning as she always did. Not in an obvious way, but there were ways of seeing people without looking as if you're looking. Anyway, she didn't have to look. A room without Fella was an empty room. She could feel it.

Suddenly the voice sounded through the earpieces, 'Task Time over. Attainers, switch off your screens.'

So that was it. She would have got some of the questions wrong, she knew. All the stuff about the protective shields that had been put up to keep the contamination out of the Island's air zone, for a start. She just couldn't remember the facts and figures.

They must have been given permission to leave, although Grebe hadn't heard it, because chairs were being scraped back, kids were hurrying to the door. The Attainment Director was looking in her direction.

'Greta, I see you're so dedicated to your Tasks that you don't want to leave them!' he jeered.

She jumped up and followed the last few people out of the door. Were sarcasm and a big mouth prerequisites for being an Attainment Director? Prerequisite. Where did that word come from? One of Fella's words, undoubtedly. Undoubtedly one of Fella's. It wasn't in their Word File.

Neither was 'undoubtedly'.

Walking fast along the corridor with her head down, Grebe didn't notice Miss Trazler until the shrill, toneless voice cut into her thoughts.

'Greta! Just the person I was looking for! I was rather worried about Fella,' she said. 'He's been absent today, I see. Do you know why?'

Grebe kept her face neutral. Any change, any little flicker of expression, would be detected and dissected. Miss Trazler's sharp jaw was tucked almost onto her collar bone as she peered down, waiting for an answer.

'I know you two are very close,' she added. 'If there's something wrong with Fella, I'm here to help and . . . well, you know you can always talk to me, don't you, Greta?'

Yes. Like you could have a polite exchange with a starving boa constrictor and ask it to go easy on the squeezing. Grebe smiled. A warm but regretful smile. Grebe the actress. She was getting good at this.

'I'm sorry, Miss. I don't know anything about it. Really.'

'He doesn't talk to you about what he's up to? About his feelings?' she asked. 'That surprises me, Greta.'

Grebe felt herself blush.

'Perhaps our Fella has a secret girlfriend?'

Trazler had a horrible, concerned half-smile, as if to say that she understood what poor teenage girls go through. But there was mockery underneath it. She knew what she was doing. Grebe's face was now so red she could feel the heat.

'I need to get to my next Task Time, Miss,' she mumbled.

'Yes, of course,' said Trazler. 'Off you go, Greta.'

Grebe hurried away, keeping her head down while she fought with the tears. She hated herself when she let people see inside her.

She reached the corner of the corridor and hit the main flow of chattering, jostling kids coming from the other direction, heading for the next Task Time. She got pushed to the side and slammed against the wall, as usual, which didn't improve her temper. She was a boiling kettle of rage. And as well as raging at Trazler and at herself, she suddenly found she was angry with Fella too. How should *she* know where he was? He hadn't told her anything. Part of her hoped that Trazler would send out the truant patrols and then he'd be back in the Attainment Centre by the end of the afternoon.

The crowd ahead of her stopped suddenly. There was a bottleneck around the doors and an Attainment Director was bellowing sarcastic remarks about common sense, letting people out of the taskroom first. People started pushing from behind. Grebe turned, about to lash out at whoever it was jabbing her in the back. She stopped herself in time. It was one of the A-grade girls, three times Grebe's size and leader of a gang you didn't mess with. She jabbed again and Grebe tried to move out of the way but the crowd was so thick now there was nowhere to go.

The Attainment Director was shouting. Shouting at people to be quiet, to file into the room quietly and sit quietly. The crowd pushed forward and, just as Grebe drew level with the Attainment Director, he bellowed again, right into her ear.

'QUIET!'

'Quiet yourself!' muttered Grebe.

And the Attainment Director drew back his fist and punched her in the head.

'SIT DOWN AND SHUT UP!'

Although her head was pulsing with pain, she managed to lurch towards the guy and dig her fingernails into his face, meaning, with all her strength, to hurt. She was pulled off him, pulled backwards from the whole scene as the man fell and a couple of the beefier boys closed in on him, throwing some hard, accurate punches before the siren started to wail and the Guards turned up.

Grebe slid her keycard through the reader and, as slowly and silently as she could, pushed the front door open. She stepped into the scent of the tabbacaseed burner that her parents kept on the marble hall table. She listened. It seemed as if she was in luck—the house felt empty.

She moved silently up the stairs and into her bathroom. Here too there was a smell—a clean linen smell—and the neatly folded towels and sparkling porcelain told her that the cleaner had been in. She turned on the taps to fill her spa, then sat on the loo seat and leant her head back, staring through the window at the hot sky. She'd thrown up twice on the way home but the sick, dizzy feeling was beginning to ease now. If she stayed still for a while it would be all right, but what would never be all right was the anger.

She was angry with herself too. She had broken her own code of keeping her mouth shut and her head down. Grebe the obedient, Grebe the invisible. It was the only way to survive.

Was it the punches to the stomach that had made her throw up, or was it the shock of it? She'd heard about the security guards beating people up but she thought they only did it to the older boys who stepped out of line. Now she knew. Anyone was a target, even a—what was it they'd called her?—even a 'half-witted little runt'. They knew they could get away with it. Nobody believed what kids said.

Forcing her stiff limbs to move, she peeled off her clothes. Then she swirled some bodywash into the churning water of the spa and stepped in, sinking into the fizzing, buffeting warmth.

What was it that had pushed her to break her own code? She smacked an angry hand into the suds. She knew. It wasn't just Fella not being there today. It wasn't just the birthday party.

For the first time that day, she made herself think about it, the really bad thing. The really bad thing was the Pairing. Her parents had been talking about Pairing her with some horrible boy called Stephen, a son of some friends of theirs, and presenting them to the Officiate for marriage. She'd tried to tell herself that it might not happen, but deep down she knew her mother was determined, because this Stephen came from what she called a 'really good family'. Grebe shivered violently, despite the hot water that swirled around her. It would be the end of everything. She punched at the water again. Where *was* Fella? Didn't he *care*?

Well, how could he, when she hadn't had the guts to tell him?

It was Fella who'd given her the name Grebe when they

were little because of the stupid tuft of hair that stood up on her head. It was like the tufty bit on a grebe's head, he said. A grebe was a bird, apparently. She had no idea how Fella knew this, but all that mattered was that the name had stuck. She drew a suddy hand out of the water and grabbed the tuft of hair. There it still was, refusing to lie down.

She heard her parents' car draw up in the drive and the front door open. Within minutes they'd order their food and the screens would go on. Her mother was on the fourth level of some lottery game and was about to win, so she believed, a great sum of money.

Grebe sank down in the spa until the bubbles played round her chin. She wasn't going to be Paired, ever. Unless it was to Fella. Suddenly, hot tears were rolling down her face and all she wanted was for the swirling waters of the spa to wash her away somewhere. She didn't care where.

Chapter 6

Fella felt as though he'd been sitting there on the floor forever, staring up through the bathroom skylight. Behind him was the empty dormitory, where he slept each night along with the other boys he'd known all his life. Beyond the skylight the sun branded a ragged hole in the bright blue, just the same as it had through all the summers of his fifteen years. Except that nothing was the same. Everything about his life had changed because of the paperbook. He squeezed the hard cover between his hands. Everything had changed.

It had been slow going at first, picking his way with each pen-written word, trying to find meaning, to hear the voice of whoever it was that had written it. He wanted to believe that it was his mother. But if he believed *that* . . . he shivered, jolting himself out of his trance, and opened the paperbook again. He must go back over it, the small part of it he'd managed to read, just to make sure he'd understood. He rubbed his sweat-stung eyes and turned back to the first page.

April 28

It's been a long day and it feels as though I've travelled back in time or to another planet, although, in fact, the journey itself is easy—just half an hour in a high-speed train under the sea and you're here. But I suppose I've travelled back in time in a sense. It's the year 112 here.

We left home via the underground railway terminus beneath our Parliament Hill. It's breathtaking—it's a shame more people don't get to see it. The great steel and marble caverns that house the platforms are like underground cathedrals and the trains are the last word in luxury.

My fellow travellers were all security-cleared for secondment work on the Island too. I had a bit of chit-chat with some of the other women, although nothing about where we were going—it seems to be understood that we don't talk about any of that. Anyway, it's great to have a conversation of any kind without being recognized and stared at. I still can't believe the new identity is working! But I don't want to push my luck—have packed plenty of hair dye and contact lenses. Am getting quite used to blonde and blue!

The whole train thing is fascinating. We all know that goods flow from the Island to us, and vice-versa, on the underground railway system. But I find it hard to believe that you could move all these goods around, as well as our own people, without the Islanders noticing or questioning that movement. Presumably all the train drivers on these routes are ours. Will try to find out.

We were warned that the weather may be worse here than on the mainland because we're further north. It's certainly vile right now—rain, rain, rain. It deadens the spirits, makes me wonder if it was such a good idea to come here. But I must stay focused—I have to find out what Silas is <u>really</u> doing with his business interests on this Island.

April 30
Well, to continue the 'first impressions' gleaned yesterday, I suppose the first big shock, once we reached the city, was the architecture. At home we're so used to living with layer upon layer of our own history reflected in our buildings. Here there's nothing older than 113 years old—they began construction a year before the people were brought here. Most of the buildings are much newer than that, of course. A lot of concrete—I suppose it's cheap. And everything seems to be laid out on a grid system. I found myself longing for the road to curve, but it never did.

According to the information given to us in our Security Clearance briefing, just five thousand people were placed here by our government 112 years ago in a programme to combat overcrowding and social problems on the mainland. These would have been settled in what is now this main city. They were then told that they'd been the last to get out before their *homeland was obliterated by a bio-chemical attack. And they accepted that—believing that they were the lucky survivors.*

Fella gasped in a deep breath. *'Believing that they were the lucky survivors.'* Again, his thoughts swirled with this phrase and all the things it meant. They'd been lied to. There *were* other people beyond the Island. The writer of this—whoever it was—came from the Downzone! And the really big idea, the one that sent a fizz of fear and excitement right through him—perhaps he himself could get there . . . *just half an hour in a high-speed train under the sea.* The words chimed in his head again and again.

He slapped the paperbook shut and sprang to his feet. Papa Louis would be as excited as he was. Perhaps Papa Louis could come too . . . plans drew themselves in broad, reckless strokes in his mind as he hurried down the stairs and along the hot corridors to Papa Louis's office. Papa Louis could be made well again . . .

Papa Louis wasn't in his office.

'Where is he?' Fella snapped at the secretary.

'Not here. He was called out. You should be at the Attainment Centre.'

'I'm sick.'

He ran back down the corridor and out onto the recreation area, a sweltering expanse of tarmac on which stood the rusty skeletons of two climbing frames. In his younger days, Papa Louis used to give the frames a fresh coat of paint every spring. And in his younger days Papa Louis would have seen to it that every scrap of the litter that now fringed the tarmac was picked up. Never mind. Things could change now. Fella had no idea how. All he knew was that a feeling of hope surged through his limbs as he ran down to their meeting spot. It might be that Papa Louis was there, waiting for him, waiting to hear what the paperbook said. He'd read far enough to believe that it was possible to get off this Island—and the paperbook would tell him more. It would show him the way, he was sure.

He rounded the tall shrubs that marked the end of the playing field and slid to a stop on the baked earth, seeing that the bench where they had sat down by the river only yesterday was empty. A stab of disappointment and anger. Where *was* he?

He swept a last glance around the little patch of wasteland and was about to leave but something stopped him. He turned back and stared at the pole that supported the broken audiocam. The thing that had snagged his attention was a wire, slender and shiny, that snaked up the pole from the ground to the base of the cam itself. A tiny pulse of panic squeezed his heart. Had that wire been there yesterday? He held his breath and heard, in the hot summer stillness, the familiar faint hum that told him the thing was working.

He pushed the paperbook deep down into his pocket, backed off from the audiocam and set off to find Grebe.

Chapter 7

F ella climbed up onto the flat roof below Grebe's room and eased himself onto the sill of her open window. Still he wasn't sure. How could it be that you'd be on your way to see someone, intending to tell them something . . . and then when you got there it didn't seem like such a good idea? The whole thing was too big, such a wild hope. Grebe would think he was crazy. She wouldn't believe him, even if he showed her the paperbook. She'd say it was just one of his fantasies.

Anyway, it didn't matter, because he could see that she wasn't in the room. He'd made up his mind to leave when he heard sloshing and splashing and a yelped 'Who is it?'

She must have caught the movement or sound of him through the open bathroom door. Fella glanced away as he half-saw a bathrobe being put on.

'It's only me. Finish your bath, I'll wait,' he called.

'No, it's all right! Hang on!' She sounded cross, and he was sorry about that. But also not sorry, because now he felt decided. He did need to talk.

She came huffing out from the bathroom, the bathrobe bundled round her skinny frame and a huge towel piled on her head. What he could see of her face looked red.

'What is it?' she said. 'Couldn't you . . . ?'

. . . Use the front door like a normal person? They both knew that he couldn't, because, unlike normal people, he was Orphanage scum and therefore not the sort of person her parents wanted her to mix with. Call first? Yes, he should have called first . . .

'Sorry,' he said, 'I should have called first.'

She swept past him, heading towards the little kitchen area at one end of the room that always looked huge and luxurious to Fella.

'Drink of something?' she said.

'Yeah, anything cold. Thanks.'

Fella sat on the bed to think while Grebe found some glasses. So much had happened inside him since Papa Louis handed him the paperbook that it was hard to know where to start telling her. But he had to tell her. Things would be easier, with Grebe to share them with.

And then, as she bent down to get ice out of the fridge, the huge towel on her head flopped forward and began to unfold. She put up a hand to rescue it but not before Fella caught a glimpse of something.

'Grebe, what's happened?'

It was a wound of some sort. He moved towards her and she lurched away, winding the towel back in place.

'It's all right! Sit down and I'll bring you—'

'Let me see!'

He grabbed her and pulled her towards him. She shrank back and instinctively he tightened his grasp on her wrist.

'Ow! Don't!'

She struggled again, then gave up and, to his dismay, burst into tears. They stood for a few pounding heartbeats. And then he moved his hand from her wrist, sliding it gently into her hand, pulling her hand round behind his back and wrapping his arms around her. She hugged against his chest, sobbing, and he rocked her gently. It was all he could think of to do.

Soon her sobbing subsided into irregular sniffles but he could still feel his heartbeat pounding angrily against her temple. She must be able to feel it too.

'Who hurt you?' he asked into the damp towel.

She pulled away from him and sat on the bed. She was shaking.

'One of the Attainment Directors.'

'What . . . he hit you?'

She nodded.

'Will you let me look?'

As he sat beside her on the bed, she raised her hand to the towel and he helped her. Damp curls tickled onto his hands from the folds of cloth as they unwound it. And at last he saw the cut and the dark, puffy bruise on the side of her head.

'Why?'

'I answered him back. I thought he wouldn't hear.'

She must have seen the twitch of a frown cross his brow because then came a torrent of explanation.

'I'd had a horrible day and . . . things on my mind, you know, about this birthday thing. And my parents are planning to . . . I just felt . . . ' Her grey-blue eyes were huge and full of tears in her pale face. 'I just felt like . . . so *trapped*! So *angry*!'

He moved to catch her hand but she waved it away from him.

'I don't want my life mapped out for me! I don't want to be Paired with some idiot just so I can live in a B-grade house, and I know it sounds ungrateful because that's what everybody else wants and I'm supposed to be lucky because I've got a lot of *things* . . . ' She swiped an arm miserably in the direction of the telescreen and entertainment terminal that stood at the end of the room. 'But I want . . . I want *more* than this, Fella!'

One part of this had caught and was playing over and over in his mind: '*Paired with some idiot* . . . ' He suddenly found that he didn't know what to say. A silence fell.

Then she sprang to her feet and began sloshing cordial and water into glasses and sending ice cubes slithering across the worktop.

'Grebe.'

'What?'

Now it seemed she was angry with him. He hesitated, not knowing how to say it.

'*WHAT?*' She *was* angry with him.

'Grebe,' he said, 'we're going to leave this Island. You and me together. I think I know a way to do it.'

She swung round to face him, eyes wide and shining and

a pink flush spreading up her cheeks. Her lips parted in an almost silent gasp.

There was a heat spreading through him too and he didn't know what he was feeling. The nearest he could get was that he felt, at that moment, as if they were staring straight into each other's hearts.

Chapter 8

'Don't say things you don't mean!' said Grebe. 'I'm not. I know for certain there's a way off this Island. At least, there used to be.'

'What makes you think that?'

He reached into his pocket. 'Papa Louis gave me this . . . hang on, you're not bugged in this room are you?'

'Of course not. My parents can't even be bothered to listen to what I say to *them*, let alone what I say to anyone else. What *is* that?'

'A paperbook. It was with me—hidden—when I was taken to the Orphanage. Papa Louis found it. And then he buried it in the Orphanage garden. He was terrified they'd come looking for it.'

'They?'

'The Officiate. He thinks the Officiate murdered my mother.'

'Murdered? Why?'

'Because she knew things—things written in here.'

He handed her the paperbook. She opened it and frowned.

'But, Fella . . . how can you read this? It's . . . I can't *begin* to see what it means . . . ' She flicked through a few pages, then turned back to the inside cover. 'This is the only bit I can understand, the numbers. 6661. What does that mean?'

'I don't know. But look again, Grebe, this is pen-writing. She came from . . . ' He hesitated, ' . . . from a place where they could still write with a pen held in the hand.'

'You mean, you think your mother did this pen-writing?'

'I don't know. I thought at first . . . I suppose I *hoped* it was my mother. But . . . '

He hadn't articulated the 'but' until now. Grebe came and sat beside him on the bed.

'But what?'

'She doesn't mention anything about having a son, so I think it can't be her.'

'Maybe it was written before you were born.'

'I hadn't thought of that! You could be right! It starts in the year 112.'

'And you were born at the end of that year. Have you read all of it?'

'No, only a few pages.'

'Well, then!'

'But I've read enough to know that, whoever she was, she didn't come from this Island. She came under the sea, in a train. It only took half an hour! Half an hour between here and the Downzone!'

'The *Downzone*? Don't be stupid!'

'I know it's hard to believe, but—'

'It's impossible! And how could a train run under the sea? You mean the Outersea? But it's contaminated, you know that! Survival time for a human following contact with the water is less than two hours and . . . '

'Oh, don't start quoting all that Officiate nonsense, Grebe. Just listen to me. The Downzone can't be as far away as we think. It's somewhere to the south of here. And if *she came* on a train, then—'

'A train can't go under the sea!'

'Well, it did. And if she came here, it means that we could go there. If we . . . if we can find where the train is.'

He knew how lame it sounded.

'And how are we going to do that?' said Grebe. 'And anyway, the Downzone . . . '

'I don't know, but we've got to try! Why are you just finding difficulties?'

'I'm not. But you've got to *think*, Fella! How do you know this pen-writing is true?'

'What do you mean?'

'It could be . . . just made up!'

'It's not made up! Now *you're* being stupid!'

'You're the one who's always saying we should question things! Fella, I'm just saying you should read all of it before you decide what to do.'

Part of him knew she was right but part of him was angry. He wanted so much for her to believe and hope like he did.

'Anyway,' she said, 'what about the contamination? We'd die. We know that the Downzone—'

'Grebe, we *don't* know! We don't really know for ourselves. We're just supposed to accept what the Officiate tells
us! Oh, what's the point? You're not going to listen anyway.
It's not worth the effort for you. Perhaps you *ought* to be
Paired with an idiot!'

He snatched at her hand as she sprang off the bed but
he couldn't reach her, any more than he could snatch the
words back. The bathroom door slammed behind her just as
he got to it.

'Grebe . . . '

'Go away!'

'Please!'

'Go to the Downzone and get yourself killed! Why would
I care? I *hate* you!'

He stood trembling, staring at the door for a few blank
moments. Then he climbed back out of the window onto
the flat roof and from there clumsily lowered himself to the
ground. A lump of pain was tightening in his chest. She
couldn't have meant it?

He didn't know.

But somehow, something had got lost between them. He
did know that.

Chapter 9

F ella pressed his aching shoulders back against the bathroom wall. He let the paperbook rest on his outstretched legs and re-focused his eyes on the skylight. When he'd asked, again and again, that evening, where Papa Louis was, they'd told him he was still out— nobody knew where—and so the only thing he could do was carry on with his task. And now the day's harsh sun had been replaced by a pale moon hanging in the inky night. He blinked and rubbed his eyes.

Grebe had been right. He'd been angry with her because he knew she was right about the paperbook. He should finish reading it before he made up his mind. So here he was—way into the night it must be now, reading the words illuminated by the circle of a beamlight. It hurt him to read it, but he knew he must keep going.

May 1

My new home is in a 'B' grade area of the City. Each wretched house is the same, row upon row, block upon

45

block. But if the 'B' grade area is architecture to deaden the soul, the place my taxi drove through to get here positively torments it—clusters of harsh rectangular towers, thirty or more storeys high, with no sign of any human imprint save the bins of stinking rubbish crowded at their feet. How can anyone bear it? No flowers, no trees, no children playing—where would they play?—not even any graffiti, for goodness' sake! No, these people don't have it in them to scribble their protests on walls or anywhere else.

Tomorrow I begin work at the hospital, or the medi-centre as they call it here. Of course I still worry that someone will recognize me, but I'm trying to put that aside. Actually, I'm just being paranoid. Not even I can recognize myself with blonde hair and blue eyes!

I won't be working in the same unit that Silas has funded, but there should be opportunities for me to look around and try to get a feel of what's going on there. Except that I'm already feeling it will be hard to make the sort of friendships that could lead to useful information. Out on my driveway this evening, I called hello to a neighbour. She looked as though I were hurling some terrible insult. No chance of lobbing a smile over the back garden fence, either—it's a good head or two taller than I am.

May 4
Work OK—routine nursing stuff. The medi-centre is reasonably well-equipped, although nothing like as

good as we have at home. We can recognize our own people because of the blue uniforms we all have to wear, and these 'bluecoat' colleagues from home are friendly in a cool, polite kind of way—but the Islanders are downright strange. These people seem to feel so little for each other. I find myself asking what it is they really care about and I suppose it can be summed up in the words that the Officiate is so fond of: possession status.

I can see why we have done this to the Islanders. We have focused all their energies onto the attainment of possessions. And we have done this so that they will fight amongst themselves and not ask any big questions. This wretched Island is rigorously controlled by the Officiate. They're all-powerful here, or so they think. When our people come over on secondment for major projects, it seems that we're just slotted in as another level of the Officiate. We're answerable to ourselves, but never questioned by them—and, of course, they've no idea where we're from.

Yes, the social controls are obvious. What is less obvious is how they damp-down the enquiring mind. Maybe medication. But is it really possible to kill the capacity to think across the whole population? It's a fascinating experiment.

Fella felt a surge of anger. *He* wasn't a part of this experiment and he never had been. How dare she talk about 'experiments', let alone 'fascinating' ones!

And what was so important that she'd come here in the first place? Something to do with this Silas person. But she obviously hated the Island, she was used to a much better life. He flicked back to the last page and a shiver caught him. She was right about one thing. The medication. Except he and Grebe had managed to fool everybody over that. They'd never swallowed their pills. Did that mean they weren't part of the 'experiment'?

Angrily, he read on.

May 5

Terrible shock today. Dr Farl has turned up at the medi-centre. The very last person—apart from Silas—that I want to see. So far I've only seen him from a distance. What the hell is he doing here? Surely he can't have found out that I'm here—only Carys knows. I must keep calm. I'm here for a purpose—to find out exactly what Silas is funding and why. Farl would never recognize me at a distance, and I'll make sure he never gets close.

May 6

Was working in the children's unit today. Child with broken arm. Mother couldn't care less. Toddler in tow with stinking nappy. What sort of people are they here? No more sign of Farl.

May 7

Farl was following me all day today, watching. It was terrible, wondering if he knew. And then I realized that he did know. He came to look at a patient I was dealing with. All he said was, 'Could we call up this child's records, nurse?' But it was the way he looked at me. I saw that he recognized me. My change of appearance didn't fool him. How could it? The man is obsessed with me.

I made sure I was never alone with him and I left early in case he tried to catch me as I was going off shift.

Fella leaned back. His eyes were aching, but he must keep going, he must find out why this Farl man was following her. He blinked down at the paperbook, which had fallen closed on his lap. He picked it up and was searching for the page he'd just left when he heard a noise from the darkened dormitory beyond.

He killed the beamlight and stuffed the paperbook into his pocket, bracing himself to fight if necessary.

A familiar whisper rasped across from the bathroom doorway. With a rush of relief, Fella switched on the beamlight again. He leapt up to help Papa Louis as he lowered himself painfully to sit on the bath stool.

'Where have you *been*? I've—'

Papa Louis placed a hand on his arrn. 'Never mind now. How's it going?'

'Good. And bad. She's from the Downzone.'

There was a rasp of breath, a pause, before Papa Louis said, 'But . . . Fella, that can't be!'

'It can. It's all so simple. Just imagine that you're told one lie and everything you think you know is built on that lie.'

'A lie?'

'The Downzone. There are still people there and they're controlling us through the Officiate. There never was a bio-chemical attack.'

Papa Louis said nothing for long, thoughtful moments. Fella was frightened. Papa Louis had always known what to do or say, how to protect the children in his care. But now the rules had changed.

'I thought it would be something . . . dangerous,' said the old man at last, 'something they didn't want us to know. But *this* . . . '

'I know it's hard to believe,' said Fella.

Papa Louis shook his head. 'It's a shock. But, no. It's not hard to believe. Not when you really think about how things are on this Island. But *why*?'

'That's the point. We're trained not to think or to ask. She says so in here. And there's this man called Farl—I think he's from the Downzone too. She doesn't like him, it sounds like she's afraid of him . . . '

'Fella . . . say that name again.'

'A guy called Farl. She didn't want him to recognize her, but—'

'Farl? Are you sure?' Papa Louis pulled the paperbook from his hands. 'F-a-r-l? Show me.'

Fella leaned over and found the name. 'Farl. There. Why?'

'Does she describe him?'

'No. Only that he's called *Doctor* Farl.'

Fella felt a sudden tension pass through Papa Louis's shoulder into his own as the old man let out a moan.

'Why? Have you heard of him?'

'I hadn't,' said Papa Louis, 'until today. Today I've spent most of my time in an Officiate cell. Then, when they thought they'd kept me waiting long enough, I was taken to see Dr Farl.'

'The same Dr Farl?'

'We have to assume so,' said Papa Louis, 'because he was asking lots of questions—about babies that had been brought here during the wintermonths of 112.'

Chapter 10

Fella felt a cold bead of fear slip down his spine.

'So . . . why?' he said. 'He's looking for *me*?'

'It seems so,' sighed Papa Louis.

Fella gripped the paperbook. 'Why now? Is it to do with *this*?'

'I don't know. Farl is from the Downzone, you said?'

'I think so, because she knew him.'

'But it was the Officiate who arrested me today,' said Papa Louis.

'The Downzoners *control* the Officiate!' said Fella. 'They use them to do their work, listen . . . ' He flicked through the paperbook to find the place. 'She says that the Downzoners are answerable only to themselves and the Officiate have no idea where they're really from. Listen.'

Papa Louis groaned and shook his head as Fella stopped reading. 'So we don't really know who or what we're dealing with here . . . '

A terrible thought slid into Fella's mind.

'Whoever wrote this says that Farl was obsessed with her.

If it *is* my mother's writing, and then she was murdered, then . . . maybe Farl was involved . . . '

' "Obsessed", she says?' Papa Louis frowned. 'He *might* be the type . . . I don't know. I didn't like the man. There *was* something . . . I just didn't trust him. He was very formal, abrupt. He asked about the babies. I said there were five that came in in the winter of 112, which there were. There was a lot of probing about the dates and times they were brought in, and by whom. I think I've managed to buy us some time, because I said I couldn't remember, that I'd have to look up all the details he'd asked for, and report back to him in the morning. He wanted information about all the mothers particularly.'

'But there *is* no information about my mother,' said Fella. 'There's only this.'

'Yes, and even the pages you've managed to decipher already make it a very dangerous thing to have.' Papa Louis's watery eyes glistened in the dark. 'Have you found anything to suggest that it *was* your mother who wrote all this?'

Fella struggled with a feeling that was something like he imagined homesickness to be, although he had never known a real home. And there was another feeling—he didn't want to be disloyal to Papa Louis.

'There's no reason to think so,' he said. 'Because she doesn't mention me.'

'Oh.' Papa Louis seemed surprised; perhaps disappointed too.

'Grebe says that it might have been written before I was born, but—'

'You've told Grebe about this?'

'Yes. But . . . go on, what about Farl? What does he actually know, do you think?'

'Well,' Papa Louis sighed, 'if he does know about the paperbook, he was hiding it well. But I don't see how he could know. Even if he's been using the Officiate to spy, he wouldn't have picked up on the paperbook, because that cam down by the river is broken, that's why I chose there for us to meet.'

Fella tried to re-picture that meeting by the river. But the truth was he hadn't looked at the audiocam himself. He'd been too interested in what Papa Louis had to tell him.

'That audiocam has been mended,' he said.

'*What*? Are you sure?'

'Yes. I saw it today. But I don't know *when* it was mended. But Farl *could* know about the paperbook. He must do, mustn't he? Otherwise why the interest in me?'

Papa Louis sighed. The long, defeated sigh of a tired man. It was bad, Fella knew it. And Papa Louis wasn't going to pretend otherwise. He could feel the old man thinking and after a moment he said, 'Fella, two things are clear. You've got to finish reading all this paperbook. And—for whatever reason—this Farl man will probably come looking for you and we don't know what his intentions are. So you've got to get out, to somewhere you won't be found.'

There was only one place he could think of.

'There's my old den in the concrete dump. You know, over at the perimeter of Tower Zone Three. Grebe and I used to go there a lot when we were kids.' The memory shot through him with a pang, stirring up the misery of their quarrel. 'There are only a couple of audiocams and I know how to work round them. Sometimes there are drones in that area, but you're all right if you can hide. I don't think the heat sensors work through concrete that thick.'

'Good. How shall I get a message to you? Grebe?'

Without Papa Louis, there was only Grebe. But could he be sure of her, after what he'd said? Yes. No matter what, he could be sure of Grebe. He nodded.

'All right, I'll send Grebe with a message,' said Papa Louis. 'You've got to find out if the paperbook says anything more about Farl.'

As Fella was closing the paperbook, something caught his eye.

'Look,' he said, 'it mentions him again here.'

May 8

I've just about managed to stop shaking sufficiently to write. Farl came to the house. He says I must leave immediately. Silas knows I'm here and he doesn't like it.

Why should I believe him, I asked—he may have his own reasons for wanting me home. He may just be trying to frighten me by saying that Silas knows—it might not be true. He said that Silas did know, and that that should frighten me. I told him not to threaten me. I asked him how Silas knew—had he been the one to tell him? After all, he used to work for Silas. Then, of course, he lost his temper and all the old stuff came out

about me being stubborn and selfish. I told him to get
out. I don't like being told what to do—by Silas or
anyone else.

   He's just sent a text, giving me one last chance to go
back home with him. He says I must meet him
tomorrow night at a place called The Glass House. It's
on the south coast of this Island and there's a tunnel
and travel pod to get us home. I don't know what to
do. I don't trust him.

Fella stopped, staring at those words *to get us home.*
'This is it, Papa Louis!'
'Shhh . . . !' Papa Louis put a hand out. 'Who is this Silas
person?'

'I don't know! She was investigating him. But the *Glass
House*, Papa Louis!'
'She was frightened of Silas knowing she was here,' mur-
mured Papa Louis, 'and she didn't trust Farl . . . '
'The *Glass House*, Papa Louis!' cried Fella, impatient
now. 'There's a tunnel! A way off the Island! On the south
coast . . . '
But Papa Louis was already hauling himself to his feet.
Fella leapt up to help him, holding out an arm. The old man
swayed and Fella took his weight for a second or two until
he steadied. How had Papa Louis become so light and he so
strong?
'Oh, Fella!' he said. 'What a mess! I wish . . . '
'You wish you hadn't given me the paperbook?'
'I wish I'd looked at it myself, years ago!'

Fella knew what Papa Louis meant by this and he felt a burning in his eyes. He was *not* going to let it be too late for Papa Louis. There was still a chance.

'But, Papa Louis, at least we have it now. It'll show us the way off the Island and we can get you proper help! They're cleverer than us in the Downzone—they have much better medi-centres, she says so in here!'

Papa Louis patted his arm. 'One step at a time. You get out to your den while it's still dark. Stay hidden there until I send a message. I'm going to see if I can find a way to this Glass House . . . '

'How?'

'We'd need to make up a Travel Disc. I've done it once or twice before—the Officiate lets me have access to a TD-writing computer if children have to transfer from one Orphanage to another and a map is needed.'

'No, Papa Louis, it's too dangerous!'

'I've done it before. I'll be careful, I'll make up a good story, don't worry! Now, you must take whatever you need from the kitchens. No—on second thoughts, I'll come with you and pack up some food.'

'Go to bed, Papa Louis. I can get the stuff.'

'Huh!' Fella knew the wry smile, though he couldn't see his face. 'You'll leave here with nothing but cakes and biscuits. No, I'm going to make sure you've got all you need.'

Slowly they made their way through the sleeping Orphanage, along corridors and down staircases that Fella had known all his life; through all the familiar smells of floor polish, dirty kids, disinfectant, and the lingering breath of that night's supper. It was like travelling back through the life they had shared. And, as Fella took the gentle weight of the old man leaning on his arm, an overwhelming sadness flooded through him. As if this was the beginning of goodbye.

Chapter 11

Great splats of rain began to fall and Grebe looked up to see that the sky had turned dirty grey and drained of light, making the tower blocks up ahead look black in comparison. This was where people who couldn't even make D-grade had to live. The flats were quite nice inside, apparently, and no one had to make do without anything essential, like housechore devices, entertainment centres, and computers. So it couldn't be that bad. Even so, those grim blocks made her feel that she ought to be grateful . . .

She was trying not to think about what she would say to Fella. She'd tried to plan it all out in her head but she was so afraid of making things worse. She should just say she was sorry without trying to explain about the Pairing and how it made her feel, because she couldn't explain that without explaining how she felt about Fella. And she couldn't explain. Not to him.

She had been so stupid. She hadn't thought about what that paperbook meant to him and how it must feel for him to find some sort of link with his mother at last.

He hadn't come to the Attainment Centre again today. Was it because he wanted to avoid her? Suddenly she longed just to see him. Just to say sorry. That was all she needed to do. She began to run against the rain. It was a bit early in the season, but this felt like the first of the summer storms. Why did people moan about the summer storms? It was only wind and water and thunder and lightning. And it felt good, running hard against the oncoming wetness, gasping in gusts of cold air and water, lungs pumping, eyes squinting, boots slapping down onto wet pavement. She felt as though she could run for ever.

She couldn't, though, because her body just wasn't up to it. Now she had a stitch and it still hurt where the security guards had kicked her stomach and ribs. She stopped and bent double, her hands resting on her knees.

A medi-van sizzled past on the wet road and, as her eyes followed it, she saw that it was pulling into the Orphanage driveway, where two Officiate cars were already parked. There was a light on in Papa Louis's office, which was on the ground floor by the door and, as she drew nearer, loping with the pain of the stitch, she saw that there were people moving around in there. Some of them were carrying boxes.

The double doors slid open for her as she approached and she saw two Officiate Guards waiting inside, either side of Papa Louis's office door.

'Do you live here, girl?' said one.

'I've just come to see . . . '

'Yes, she lives here,' said Papa Louis, appearing in the

doorway. 'Rather early back from the Attainment Centre, girl. Why is that?'

He seemed so tired, so frail. He also looked stern, and Papa Louis was not a stern man. He was looking at her really hard.

'Umm . . . Attainment Director off sick . . . ' she said. She was trembling and she saw that Papa Louis was too.

'Freddy isn't here, I'm afraid,' he said, still holding her gaze tightly. 'I expect you'll find him at the usual old place.' Papa Louis narrowed his eyes. She sensed he dared not say more. The *old* place? Suddenly, she understood. Fella was at the den they first went to all those years ago when they were little. In the concrete dump.

A tall man stepped into the doorway behind Papa Louis. He had shiny skin stretched tight over a thin face and small, bright eyes that looked straight at her.

'This is Dr Farl. He's come to check over our records. And then . . . I have to go away for a while, I'm afraid,' said Papa Louis.

Grebe could hardly breathe with fear. They were taking Papa Louis. Papa Louis gazed at her for a split second more and then, with a faint smile, he reached out and patted her on the shoulder.

'Better make yourself useful. I don't think anyone's remembered to feed the rabbits today. Run along to the kitchen and get some food for them. Put it right inside the hutch—there's a storm coming.' He hesitated, smiling. 'Don't worry, girl. All will be well.'

Grebe opened her mouth but nothing came out. She

could sense that the man called Farl was watching her. And then someone shouted. At first she thought it must be Farl, because Papa Louis never shouted. But he was shouting now.

'DON'T look at me like that, girl! Do as you're told!'

And she was off down the corridor, not able to think of anything beyond the fact that she must do exactly as Papa Louis said. She remembered where the kitchen was and knocked on the door. No one answered. So she went in anyway and disturbed a huddle of people at one end of the room—women kitchen workers. Two of them spun round to face her, and she could see that they had been crying. Others still were.

'I've come to get the rabbit food,' she said.

'What d'you mean?' sniffed one bulgy-eyed woman.

'Papa Louis asked me to get rabbit food,' she said, trying to keep her voice level. She was going to blow this one, and there was an audiocam pointing straight at her.

A younger woman shuffled to the front, blowing her nose.

'Yes, of course, come on, girl.' She grabbed Grebe's hand and squeezed it hard, adding, with a distinct note of defiance, 'Whatever Papa Louis asks for, we're happy to give.'

She led Grebe across the kitchen and, opening a cupboard, handed her some carrots. They were a little way away from the audiocam now.

'Just do whatever he told you, whoever you are,' whispered the woman. She nodded towards an outside door. 'The hutch is at the bottom of the lawn.'

Grebe stumbled out into the heavy afternoon. The rain was still falling, the sky still grey and dull. The grass ahead of her seemed to have sucked up all the light there was and was bright, almost luminous green. Way in the distance she heard the first crack of thunder.

She crossed the lawn, trying to look purposeful. The thud of her heart almost took her breath away. They were taking Papa Louis. This would destroy Fella. Papa Louis had sent her out here for a reason. She mustn't mess things up.

Suddenly the sky quivered with white light and there was a peal of splitting, tearing crashes directly above. The rain pelted harder. She hurried forward, slithering on the wet grass, because now she could see the rabbit hutch. Her fingers fumbled with the little door latch as two fat white rabbits scrabbled at the wire mesh. She opened the door and gave the rabbits the carrots. She heard their tiny crunching noises as her hand explored the hutch. There was something at the back. It felt like a plastic bag.

She knew what she must do next, even though she had no idea where the audiocams were. Trembling, she got herself as close to the hutch as she could, grabbed the bag and shoved it down the front of her shirt, shivering at the coldness against her skin.

She fastened the hutch door, then hurried away, following the perimeter fence until at last she found a gap in the vertical steel girders. Once off the Orphanage premises she ran in the direction of Tower Zone Three until the pain tearing at her side forced her to stop.

She had come to the edge of a shopping mall. Advertising

hoarding flashed bright colours into the storm, their bullying voices muffled by the rain. A woman ran across the vehicle park towards a family wagon. Two kids, trailing behind her, were fighting over a package, which split and fell onto the puddled tarmac. The woman yelled. The kids began to scream at each other. And then Grebe saw, parked a little way from the family wagon, a mobile audiocam unit. She turned and forced herself to walk away at a normal pace. A constant stream of traffic swept past her but she dared not turn to see if the mobile unit was following her.

At last she peeled off into the road that led to Tower Zone Three. It was a dangerous area for any outsider, let alone someone like her. She wondered if she ought to get rid of her boots and jacket, both expensive items that would attract attackers. But with this storm building, she needed both. No, she'd just have to keep her eyes open and be ready to run. She could just remember the route, she thought—you skirted round the largest tower, crossed the canal by the footbridge, then headed out into the wasteland where the great blocks of concrete had been dumped.

She glanced behind her. Nothing following on the road. Ahead, an empty pavement. She took a deep breath and walked on, keeping her head down against the pelting rain.

Chapter 12

F ella had been about eight years old when he first discovered the dump. The blocks of concrete left over from the building of Tower Zone Three had been scattered from cranes, like a jumble of giant, misshapen children's bricks.

To a desperate kid longing for a space away from the bickering and bullying of the Orphanage it was perfect. Lowering himself down one day into a deep fissure between two blocks, he had discovered a concrete cave and made it his own. He had levelled the earth and put wood down to make a floor. He'd brought candles and food. He'd brought Grebe. It had been years since he had last been here. Yes, probably the last time was when Grebe was with him.

The sun had just begun to bleed over the horizon beyond Tower Zone Three as he reached the jagged sea of concrete blocks. It was a vast area, stretching out into the Flatlands beyond the city, where nobody ever went. He scanned the silent peaks and shadows, smelt the familiar dank smell. He knew what he was looking for. From where he stood now he should be able to see three triangles, the middle one slightly higher than its neighbours. There they were.

As soon as he entered the cave, the deep-remembered smell of cold concrete and old wood switched back time for him. He was once again his eight-year-old self, remembering the excitement and fear of first discovering it. The remembering made him sick with longing for the life he might have had. He had been a miserable kid then, completely alone, escaping into worlds of his own invention. Maybe he'd been living in the wrong world all along and he'd been right to try and imagine himself out of it.

But he couldn't afford to feel sorry for himself. There was work to do. He swung his beamlight around the cave and found, to his amazement, that everything was much the same as he remembered it, only smaller. At the end of the cave was the slab of concrete that made a good seat. Years ago he'd brought a blanket and . . . yes, here it was still, musty and dirty, but still where he'd left it. He emptied his backpack and arranged the food Papa Louis had packed up for him. Biscuits and cakes—but also bread, cheese, tinned meat and fish, a cold chicken pie, tomatoes, fruit and bottles of juice and water. There was another blanket, too. Papa Louis had insisted on putting it in, and he'd been right. It was dawn now and it was cold down here. Fella knew he should try and sleep, but he could not. He wriggled his back against the wall. He lit two large candles, dug out the paperbook, and began again.

May 9

I made sure I was out all afternoon and evening in case

Farl came for me. He'll be long gone now. But I'm staying here until I'm clear in my mind exactly what's happening at the medi-centre. I won't let Silas or Farl dictate my life. I'm a qualified nurse. I want to do something good with my life, not just be a rich man's trophy. And, besides, I don't trust either of them.

May 16
The strain of keeping my eyes and ears open to everything during this last week has been truly exhausting. I have never felt so tired in my life and, on top of this, I've had a bout of sickness. It may be a reaction to all the inoculations we have to have before coming here. There's another thing that's making me feel tired and I think it's to do with having no one to talk to.

I have managed to discover that the unit Silas is funding is called the Special Surgical Unit. Only the staff who have clearance to work there are allowed in and so far it's been impossible to get any information about what the special surgery entails.

May 17
Something disturbing happened today. I was on my way to the children's ward in my own unit when a harassed looking young surgeon dashed up to me and, seeing my blue uniform, asked what level of clearance I had. I showed him my amber badge. This clearly wasn't what he wanted, but he said, 'Well, there's an emergency in

the Special Surgical Unit. You'll have to assist. There's a shortage of staff. Follow me.'

This was such a fortuitous opportunity. The very unit that Silas has funded. From what I could tell, going down in the lift, the unit is quite a way underground.

He directed me to the scrub area and by the time I'd got scrubbed up and gowned, he'd already brought the patient into Theatre. She was a little girl of about five, and she had some sort of infected growth in the neck.

'Sorry.' He gave me a half-smile. 'I can't use Islander nurses for this and the few we have of our own are forever going off sick at weekends. Can't blame them really—they want to get back home and see their families.'

He was moving quickly, making his incision, swabbing the blood and pus. I couldn't see how this would be classified as an emergency. Then I saw the transfusion bags.

'Blood poisoning?' I asked.

'Yes. It shouldn't have happened, but . . . forceps, please.'

He began to search the wound. When he withdrew the forceps I saw that they were holding a tiny disc of metal. He scrutinized it carefully under the light. 'Must have been a faulty microchip. It's started to break down inside the body. Saline, please.'

I handed him the saline and he quickly flushed out the wound and closed it up.

Then he loaded up a chip implanter and began to

pinch and pull the skin on the other side of the child's
neck. At last he was satisfied that he'd found a good
site. He pushed the implanter in.

'What's the chip for?' I asked.

'So we can track her.'

'Why?'

'Just for general health monitoring, I suppose.'

'Does everybody on this Island have a tracking chip,
then?'

He looked at me and I couldn't quite read his
expression. Irritation and fear. Then he said, 'You're
amber clearance. You'll have been told everything you
need to know. Thank you for your help.'

So—some people on this Island are implanted with a
tracking chip. Maybe everybody is. Why? And do they
know they are chipped?

Fella stopped reading, his heart pounding with anger and
fear. Instinctively, he reached his hands up to his neck. He
couldn't feel anything. He wiped his eyes. He must carry on.

May 18

Imagine the outcry at home if we had cameras and
microphones built into every street lamp, as they do
here. So easy—if you can wire for light, you can wire for
camera and voice pick-up. Remarkably, the population
of this Island seems to accept this encroachment on
privacy. But then, they know nothing else.

I've not been able to get any further in finding out

*about the chipping of individuals, although the Island is
of course geared up for satellite navigation—many
Islanders from B-grade upwards have this on their cars. I
believe some have autodrive too, so that a vehicle can
actually drive itself. So if you can do all this with sat.
nav., I guess you can easily track anything with a chip
wherever it goes. Do they actually do this for
everybody? What the hell would be the point in that? To
give Officiate employees something to do? To ingrain
the culture of fear?*

May 19

*I had what may turn out to be a stroke of luck today.
The surgeon who replaced the little girl's chip seems to
have taken a fancy to me. We had coffee in the
underground café that serves the Special Surgical Unit.*

*His name is Alex Wingford and he's worked as a
surgeon in the unit for two months. He had a lot to say
about how impressed he is with the equipment and
facilities. He spoke of a generous anonymous
benefactor. It almost amused me to know that he was
talking to the anonymous benefactor's incognito wife.*

Fella frowned and read that last line again. It meant that
the man she was spying on was her own husband! His heart
pounded faster as he realized what this could mean. This
Silas could be his father. Just thinking about it made him feel
panicky. It didn't feel real. And it might not be. He drew the
blanket round him and continued reading.

I could sense that Alex had asked to meet me for a reason, and pretty soon it emerged. He was embarrassed that he'd had to call me in to help with the operation the other day.

'It's not what I normally do,' he said. 'To be honest, I was afraid of messing it up.'

'But you are a surgeon?' I asked.

He seemed uncomfortable with the question. All he would say was, 'I'm a paediatrician. My job here is to place the chips in the babies.'

It was clear that he felt he'd said too much, so I tried to smooth things, win his confidence.

'A wonderful profession,' I said, 'working with children.'

He said yes, it was. And then he said he was looking forward to going back home.

I think this is an uneasy man, a man who wants out for some reason. But I dared not push too much at that meeting. He's asked if he can see me again.

Fella leaned back against the cold concrete and raked over what he knew about medi-centres. Not much. When you were little you went to the out-clinic to have some nurse stick needles in your arm so that you didn't get diseases. If you cut yourself badly you got a needle in the bum. Nobody had ever explained why. He'd had toothache and Papa Louis had taken him to a medi-centre dentist who'd said, 'This won't hurt', but it did.

If a woman wanted a baby she had to go to the medi-centre but not all women were allowed babies, so they had to wait until they were called in for the treatment. This much Fella had learned from Grebe, whose mother had had the treatment. There'd been lots—probably around twenty—of children he'd known from the Orphanage who'd gone to the medi-centre after an accident or because of illness and had never come back. And old people, so he'd heard, were taken there to die.

The candles guttered as he stared into the darkness. He felt as though the space around him was closing in, as if the concrete were moving imperceptibly towards him and would crush him. He felt a scream rising inside him. Not a real scream, more like his heart and mind and every little bit of his being was screaming, unheard except by him. And this straining, silent sound was unbearable.

He took a deep breath. He must stay strong. He must keep his mind strong. Maybe he had a chip in his neck. Maybe Farl or the Officiate would find him. But whatever was going to happen to him in the future, while he was still free he must keep trying.

His eyelids were becoming heavy but he knew he mustn't sleep just yet. He dug out some water and the chicken pie from his backpack and ate and drank, trying as he did so to imagine this woman. Who *was* she? If she wasn't his mother, then why had she stuffed this paperbook down the back of his nappy and given him all this trouble?

But then, if she *was* his mother, perhaps he'd been in trouble all his life. He shivered, trying to shake off the thought: *They know about the paperbook. And they'll come after it.*

Once more, he forced himself to concentrate. He shifted

position, wrapped the blanket tighter around him and picked up the paperbook again.

May 24

Today I saw Alex again. It was in the grounds of the medi-centre. He was sitting on the wall of a little fountain, staring into the spray of water. I went up to him, with the intention of teasing him about the fact that I'd not heard from him since his promise to call me.

When he turned to me I saw that his eyes were puffy and red. And he'd clearly been drinking. He had the wild, despairing look of someone on the very edge. He's leaving the medi-centre, he said. They're sending him back home.

'Who is?' I asked him. 'You mean, you've been dismissed from the Special Surgical Unit?'

At that, he began to cry. Silently. It reminded me of the way you might scream in a dream and no sound comes.

I sat beside him but he immediately leaped up. His face was terrible, stricken with a depth of anguish that I've never seen on anyone before.

He said that on no account should I let anyone know that he and I knew each other, and that I should leave the Island as soon as possible and never come back. I tried to ask him why but he was adamant that he could say no more. 'Just go, just get the hell out of this evil place!'

I reached out to him again, but he ran from me and I dared not follow.

I've been wary ever since I arrived here, but now it's more than that. The look of absolute terror, the anguish on Alex's face really shook me. He was a broken man—but what's broken him? It can't just be because they've sacked him—it's something else. Something to do with his work at the Unit. Maybe Farl was right, maybe I should just leave. I certainly feel frightened enough to leave, to choose not to know. But that's the point. You can choose to know, or you can choose not to know. Whatever it is, I choose to <u>know</u>.

Chapter 13

The day was darkening fast and Grebe found it hard to keep her eyes open against the stinging needles of rain. The thunder was sinking lower and nearer, the unseen explosions slamming around the sheer walls of the tower blocks behind her. At least the weather might mean there'd be no drones patrolling.

She almost had the canal in sight when suddenly she caught the movement of three or four figures between her and the bridge. She had just passed a clump of bent and broken saplings. She turned back and darted into what little shelter they offered. Had they seen her? The dark figures began to run in her direction, heads down. Now she could make out the shapes through the rain. Officiate Guards. Helmeted, equipment bunched at their waists. Things for hitting, gassing, binding—and shooting. It was too late to run. In any case there was nowhere to run to. They kept coming. She could hear the squelch of their boots, the rasp of their breathing. She clung onto the dying young tree in front of her.

And then they turned. They were heading for the tower blocks.

Grebe struggled to unscramble her thoughts. It wasn't so unusual for Officiate Guards to patrol the Tower Zones. It need not be anything to do with us, she told herself. She watched until they were swallowed into the rain. And then she forced her stiff fingers to let go of the tree, and headed towards the bridge and the concrete dump beyond.

She was snagging her clothes as she slid down the rain-lashed concrete surfaces. She should slow down, because you could easily lose your footing on the green slime and trap an ankle in the dark crevasses between the blocks. But she wanted to get there before dusk fell, before she lost sight of the three triangles, just as she remembered them, drawn against the darkening sky.

The last of the light died as she reached the entrance to Fella's den. She flapped in her wet pockets to find her key-card and switch on the tiny beamlight attached to it. Carefully, she lowered herself down into the shaft between two blocks. There was nothing beneath her feet and she had no option but to let go and hope.

She hit the ground, her boots making a gritty scrape, and immediately swept the beamlight around the cave.

'Fella?'

No answer. She stepped forward.

'Fella? You there?'

Had she got it wrong? No. The feeble beam of light was picking out an old blanket on a wooden platform. And beside this blanket a newer one, huddled into a familiar shape. She let the light wander over it for a second. She didn't want to startle him. She didn't want to wake him at all, knowing what she knew.

She crept forward and knelt beside him. Now she could see his sleeping face, the blanket bunched up under his chin. He looked so peaceful. She let her eyes wander over the thick mass of illegal hair, the eyelids covering those dark, intelligent eyes. Long black eyelashes. Nose. Lips. For a moment she thought she wouldn't tell him about Papa Louis. She was afraid he couldn't bear it. Papa Louis was old, he was sick. And sick old people never came back from medi-centres.

She saw a tiny movement pulse across his eyelids. He opened his eyes and blinked. She glanced the beamlight at her own face.

'It's only me.'

'Grebe!'

He hauled himself up onto an elbow and she smelt the warmth of him.

'What time is it?'

'Don't know. Just after sunset.'

'I was reading. Grebe, there's just so much in the paper-book to tell you! But the really incredible thing is—I've found my mother! I mean, I know she's dead, so I can never really find her. But in a way I have. I can read and I can hear her voice. It's *her*! She wrote it!'

He shone his beamlight into her face and she shot an arm up. 'Don't!'

'Sorry. Isn't it great, though? It's the *best* thing! Listen, listen!'

He rummaged in a backpack to find candles, and lit them. Then he reached down into the blanket and pulled out the paperbook.

'Where is it? Here! Listen.'

May 28

The last few days have been full of anxiety—firstly there were my worries about Alex and those images of our last meeting. But in the end, I had to put my thoughts about him to one side and face some other facts. It's not just that I haven't been sleeping well—the sickness has returned. And it can't be a reaction to the inoculations because I had all those a week before I came here.

So I took the plunge and pinched some pregnancy tests from the store cupboard.

There's going to be a baby. I've taken three tests and they can't all be wrong. At first I didn't know how I felt about it. Shocked, I suppose. Then happy, then frightened, then joyful, I think.

I've been trying to calculate and I think it will be born around the end of October.

I'll be long gone from here by then.

'You see, it *is* her!' he cried.

'What's October?' asked Grebe.

'I don't know, I think it must be a term for a time of year, like April and May that she uses, but—'

'Does she say who your father is? Is it this Alex man?'

She could see, in the circle of candlelight, a flicker of

disappointment cross his face. Then he looked up. She could see he was annoyed and the last thing she wanted was another quarrel.

'I'm sorry,' she said.

'I guess it's this Silas guy, her husband.'

He fell silent and Grebe felt awful. Why had she mentioned the word father? Now, of all times.

'I think it's brilliant you can read that,' she said, trying to sound cheerful, 'I don't know how you can.'

Fella shrugged. 'I was really slow at first, but I'm getting faster. It's great that it's her, though, isn't it?'

'It's wonderful, Fella. It means . . . you've found someone!'

He was silent again, staring ahead. Then he looked at her brightly. She couldn't bear it because she knew what was coming.

'Papa Louis said he'd send you. Has he found out any more about the Glass House? Oh, but you don't know about it, do you? There's this place on the south coast. I think we could get to it. Well, we've *got* to get to it because that's where the tunnel is. I want Papa Louis to come too, because I'm sure we can find someone there to make him better. Maybe this Silas could help, he's got something to do with medi-centres . . . Grebe, what's the matter?'

She found that she was crying.

'They've taken him, Fella. I'm sorry.'

He was silent for a moment, then, seeming to disbelieve her, said, 'Where?'

'The medi-centre.'

'What do you mean? No! Who told you that?'

'I saw. The medi-van was there, and Papa Louis told me, because he wanted you to know. "All will be well," he said. There were some Officiate guards and this awful man, Dr Farl . . . '

Fella leapt up. The paperbook fell from the blanket and slapped onto the floor.

'I've got to get him out of there!'

'Fella, no! Just think about it. Papa Louis wants you to stay out of the way. He couldn't say, but I *know* he does! Look, he left you this package. I think it's really important.'

Fella didn't even look at the plastic bag she was holding out to him. He was staring into the blackness with a vicious expression that frightened her. She began to tear open the package, in the desperate hope that it would contain some sort of answer. As her hands found the familiar disc shape inside, she felt a stab of dismay. What use was an old-fashioned CD when they had nothing to play it on? Then she saw it wasn't a CD. It was smaller—a TD. Even more disappointing. You couldn't use a Travel Disc without some sort of vehicle.

'Fella?' She held the disc out to him, but he didn't seem to see it or her. As she slid it back into her pocket, some part of her mind wondered how Papa Louis had got hold of a Travel Disc when only A-graders were allowed them. But what mattered to her now was keeping Fella calm.

'Describe this Farl,' he said.

'Horrid small eyes . . . shiny skin . . . frightening. Taller than . . . very tall.'

'What exactly did he say?'

'He didn't say anything,' said Grebe, shivering as she remembered the man's eyes. 'But he looked . . . as if he wanted to squeeze all the thoughts out of me. You mustn't go near him, *please.*'

There was a silence.

'Farl knew my mother,' said Fella. 'They were both from the Downzone. Maybe I can persuade him to help us.'

'No! He didn't look like the kind of man you'd ask for help. And Papa Louis wants you to stay away, please believe me, Fella! Look—what were you saying about this place you want to find, where the tunnel is?' She showed him the TD again. 'Papa Louis wanted me to give you this. Please . . . '

'What if they kill him? It'll be because of me and I never said goodbye. I'm going to find him!'

'Fella, who do you trust? Farl or Papa Louis?'

'That's a stupid question!'

'It isn't!' cried Grebe, angry at her own sense of helplessness. She just wasn't making him understand. She sensed danger, but she couldn't say exactly how or why. 'This is serious. It's because of the paperbook, it must be! And Papa Louis was frightened—frightened for *you*, I mean. He wants to protect you.'

Fella wasn't listening. He'd picked up the paperbook and now he was flashing his beamlight around the cold concrete walls.

'All right,' she said. 'You say this Farl knew your mother. But he didn't—or couldn't—save her from getting killed.

And if he didn't help her, why would he help you or Papa Louis? Fella?'

He was in the far end of the den, standing on an outcrop of concrete. He reached up towards the roof and Grebe saw him stuff the paperbook into a slit between the roof and the wall. He jumped down and turned to face her.

'Listen,' he said, 'I'm going to the medi-centre. I have to see Papa Louis. The paperbook will be safe hidden here, just in case.'

'In case of what?'

'In case I get caught.'

'Fella, you *will* get caught!'

'I have to see him. I'll meet you back at your place.'

'Promise me you won't go near Dr Farl!' she cried.

But he was already hauling himself up out of the den towards the night sky. His legs swung, then his feet scrabbled a hold on the concrete and he gave a last push and was gone.

Grebe stood a moment in the guttering candlelight. Then she turned to face the back of the den and ran her own tiny beam of light along the top of the wall.

Chapter 14

Papa Louis could feel the voice of his grandmother—faint at first, then coming within the grasp of his hearing, recognizably the cheerful, gossipy music of her voice. 'Not like here,' she was saying, as she always loved to say, and always with the sad little shake of her head, the pursing of lips.

He lost her again.

What do you mean, Grandma? What do you mean, 'Not like here'?

'My city,' she said, 'the city where I was born.'

Ah yes, thought Papa Louis. Grandma always liked to talk about how she was born in the Downzone, how she came over the Outersea with her parents when she was a little girl.

His mind blanked. Then he saw a dark-eyed baby with blood on his shawl. A little boy crying for his mother.

'Not like here.'

There was Grandma again. He must hold on to her this time. What do you mean, Grandma?

'Oh, Louis boy, there were such beautiful buildings! All gone now. Poison falling from the sky. The fires! How *lucky* we were to be chosen to come here before it happened! But now we can never go back . . . '

Papa Louis struggled, trying to pull himself back to his right mind, his right way of thinking. There was something he needed to remember. About travel . . .

The baby! The boy, Fella. He must travel to the Outersea, to the place called the Glass House. Papa Louis couldn't remember how or why, but he knew the boy must go, and go quickly. There was someone hunting him. A man with pale skin, and eyes like . . . eyes like . . . tiny, cruel eyes.

Papa Louis began to call out to his grandma. If only she would stop talking, just for a moment, and listen. Save the boy! Save the little boy called Fella. It was important. He must make her listen. Grandma could show the boy how to get home . . .

Here she was. At last! He could feel her holding his arm, pressing it down.

'Not like here' . . . was that what she was saying? It didn't sound like her any more.

'Here,' said the woman's voice, 'just here.'

There was a tiny, sharp coldness on his arm and Papa Louis slept again.

Chapter 15

F ella braced his back against the wet bark as the branches around him swayed in the wind. A couple of floors up, in the main block of the Care Centre, there was a flat roof, and, from the height of this tree, he could see glass doors opening out onto it. It was a possible way in. Possibly his only way in. But the drainpipes and window ledges would be hopelessly slippery in this weather.

He hesitated, listening to the surging wind and the drumming of rain. The canopy of leaves was keeping most of it off him for now. There was something comforting about trees. They grew how they wanted to, one of the few things over which the Officiate had no control. Except, of course, they could be cut down. His mind was wandering. He couldn't even keep focused on the paperbook. Nothing mattered except seeing Papa Louis.

Most of the rooms in the building were lit up. It might even be that one of the rooms lit up was *his* room. Fella had no way of knowing. He'd have to go in blind and he would probably be caught.

At least they'd never find the paperbook.

Somebody had just opened one of the glass doors that led onto the flat roof. This was the best chance he was going to get. He shifted himself into position and, as quietly as he could, lowered himself towards the sodden ground.

Chapter 16

Grebe hauled herself up, bracing her knees against the sharp concrete, and at last reached the open air. It was still raining heavily. It should have been pitch dark by now, but the skyline was glowing with the overspill of light from Tower Zone Three and this helped her pick out the dark shapes ahead. Carefully, she began to feel her way over the blocks, heading for where she thought the bridge must be. It was slow going, blinking the rain out of her eyes as she tried to focus on her feet for fear of slipping. She mustn't lose her sense of direction, though. She stopped to look up and as she did so she thought she caught a movement way ahead of her. Could it be Fella? Perhaps, but only if he'd been slow or got lost. She lay flat against the tilted block ahead of her and then inched herself up to look again. Nothing.

No! There *was* something. Her heart pounded against the concrete as she watched. A head had bobbed up above the jagged skyline, then another. A beam of light washed over the blocks some fifty metres or so to her left. Then there was a startled shout—a cry of pain, perhaps—and the light disappeared.

Chapter 17

Papa Louis heard a faint click, but he did not open his eyes or turn his head to see if this was indeed the door being opened by the Care Deliverer who, sooner or later, would be sent to speed up the process begun by the disease and end his life. This would be done by altering the mix of stuff that went into him through the needle in his arm. It was expensive to keep a sick old man alive and anyway, there was no point. The Island State could squeeze no more usefulness out of Papa Louis.

Perhaps there was no one in the room after all. The silence had deepened again.

And then, the faintest of whispers.

'Papa Louis?'

How Fella had found him was beyond all imagining. Papa Louis turned his head and opened his eyes onto the boy's anxious face, close to his own in the darkened room.

'Fella. Go! Not safe . . . !' he whispered.

'Listen, Papa Louis,' whispered Fella, 'it *is* my mother. And we're going to try to get home. I think we can.'

Papa Louis wanted to say something. As it formed in his mind, it didn't seem much. But it was the sum of everything he knew, the best he could do.

'Trust the goodness inside you, Fella,' he said. 'Goodness is more powerful than evil. It *always* is.'

He thought he heard the boy whisper *thank you*. They found each other's hands and Papa Louis squeezed as tight as he could and as he did it seemed that he took in a breath. A deep, deep breath.

Chapter 18

Even as Fella returned the squeeze he could feel Papa Louis's grip loosening. But he held on to him still, because he wanted Papa Louis to know that he was there right up to the end. And also because he couldn't bear to let go of him. He suddenly felt completely alone and he needed Papa Louis's strength, somehow, to flow into him.

The door to the room was flung open and light seared across the bed. Fella saw the old man's head lolled to one side and, as whoever it was behind him approached, he managed to slide his finger onto his wrist. There was no pulse and Fella felt exhilarated, triumphant.

They hadn't got to him. At the end it was just himself and Papa Louis. And he could let go now, because the strength Papa Louis had to give was already in him. It had been flowing into him all his life.

A woman's voice asked, 'Is this the boy, Dr Farl?'

'Yes.'

Fella turned to see the tall, pale man in the doorway. He walked towards him and met his disdainful gaze. 'I came to thank him,' he said.

Chapter 19

Grebe watched as two men, silhouetted against the orange glow, moved across to where their friend had fallen. He had fallen, she was certain, because now she could hear shouts of pain. Easy to snap an ankle in terrain like this. She waited, feeling the sharp edges of the paperbook pressing against her abdomen. She had recognized the shapes of the two silhouettes, their helmets, their belts of weapons. They surely would have no reason to be out here on the dump unless somehow they knew about Fella's den. Or perhaps other kids from the Tower Zone had dens here. Maybe it was nothing to do with Fella. Either way, she was glad she'd taken the paperbook.

She waited until all the men had dipped out of sight. Then, with the moaning of the injured Guard still carrying on the wind, she slowly began to move towards the edge of the dump.

Chapter 20

Fella held Farl's gaze. It was boring into him, examining his face in detail. He must keep his expression steady, he mustn't give anything away.

'Quite understandable that you would wish to say goodbye,' said Farl. 'Mr Morelli was well liked at the Orphanage, I believe.'

Fella turned back to the bed where, already, the person lying there didn't look like Papa Louis any more. Or rather, it *looked* like Papa Louis, but it wasn't him any more. It was confusing. He turned back to Farl.

'I wouldn't say that he was well liked,' he said, 'I'd say that everyone loved him.'

'Quite,' said Farl. 'I'd like you to come with me, please.'

'Why?'

'I don't believe I have to give a reason,' said Farl, 'but since you enquire, I'm going to be sorting out a few things at Orphanage 206 which is, I understand, where you live. I thought you might appreciate a lift home.'

He signalled to the nurse to open the door.

'Thank you,' said Fella.

As he followed Farl down the long, shiny corridors, Fella's mind was struggling to make a plan. Farl had come up to the ward alone, but he probably wouldn't have driven here alone. This journey through the medi-centre would almost certainly end at a vehicle full of Guards. He would have to break free before they got outside. He scanned the corridor. Doors to left and right—so many doors. But would any of them lead him to an escape route? The place was like one of those mazes in a computer game. You could walk into a dead end and that would be it.

But suddenly it happened and he had no time to think. A bell pinged loudly just to his right and an elevator door opened. A guy pushed a tea trolley out from the elevator and Fella grabbed it and swung it round, with all his strength, into Farl. The hot water container tipped and fell. There was a noise, half scream, half roar. As Fella jumped into the elevator he had a vague sense that Farl had buck-led at the waist and the tea guy had gone to help him. He hit the lowest of the buttons and, as the doors closed, Farl looked up.

As he leaned back against the closed doors, Fella's legs nearly gave way beneath him, and not because of the sud-den lurch of the elevator. It was because of the look that Farl had shot at him as the doors had closed. A look of pure frus-tration and venomous anger. Papa Louis had been right. This man was very, very determined to catch him.

Suddenly he turned and retched, searing spasms in his stomach pumping stuff out of him onto the gleaming floor of the elevator. As if his body was trying to pump out the fear.

Seconds later the elevator doors opened again and, for a heartbeat of terror, Fella thought he had gone nowhere.

But no, this was a new corridor, pale pink walls and dimmer lighting. Slowly, he stepped out of the elevator, looked to left and right and listened. Save for the hum of the dimmed strip lighting, there was a deep silence in the corridor. He scanned the ceiling line. There would be some sort of audiocam device, he was sure, although they wouldn't look like the streetlamp audiocams outside. He saw that there were round discs fitted to the ceiling at intervals that might be audiocams or might be sprinklers. Either way, his only hope was to get out as soon as he could.

He set off to his right, searching for anything that looked like a way out. After a few metres the corridor opened out on one side into a semi-circular area with soft, pinkish light-ing. There were bright, comfortable sofas, toys, and a toddler-sized table with chairs. The area was empty and Fella had almost passed it when he heard something. A sniff. He spun round, scanning the sofas in panic. Then he saw two chil-dren close together at one edge of the semi-circle. A boy of about twelve and a younger girl. They looked even more ter-rified than he was. He stared at them a second more. They seemed almost unreal, so blank and stiff were their faces. And then the boy called out.

'Hey, help us, will you? We shouldn't be here!'

'What do you mean?' Fella swung a brief look over his

shoulder, then approached the children. The boy's eyes were huge with terror, his voice wavering.

'My mum and dad don't know I'm here. They never said anything about me needing a check-up. I'm not ill!' He nodded towards the girl, who had started to cry. 'She's not, either. I was at the Attainment Centre. And then this man came and said I had to go with him. They made me get in a van. They said I'd gotta come here.' The boy swallowed hard, fighting his tears. 'But there's nothing *wrong* with me! I just wanna go home. *Please!*'

Then Fella saw the girl's eyes widen at something behind him. He swung round to see a woman in a blue uniform.

The woman shrieked and made a grab for Fella. He ducked out of her way and ran down the corridor. Seconds later the pulsing scream of a siren filled the air.

Fella ran on down the corridor. Beyond the sound of the siren he thought he could hear doors banging, and shouts. But the faster he ran, the slower he seemed to be moving. He knew he must find the darkness amidst all this light that would tell him where an external door or window was, but he could see nothing that looked like a way out. In fact, in the few moments of tight fear that he had been running, he had seen no window at all. He skidded at a crossroads. Halfway down the corridor to his right he saw a door opening, someone coming out. He swung left and, as he did so, saw a staircase behind a glass door. He dragged the door open and began sprinting up the steps. One flight, two . . . The light spilling from the corridor below was gradually fading as he went higher. They hadn't switched the lights on further up. Perhaps no one bothered with the stairs. Good. He got into a rhythm, bounding up the flights, swinging himself round each landing, bounding upwards again into deepening darkness, searching for a door. And then the echo of his footfall began to deaden. The air was changing, becoming thicker and mustier. He could barely see ahead of him now. But even though he couldn't see, he guessed.

No! He pulled himself up just in time, at the top of the last flight, legs shaking, and put out a hand. The wall was nearer than he thought. It grazed his knuckles. He searched blindly along it. The exit was sealed. Concrete blocks, it felt like.

He turned, leaning against the concrete, grabbing the handrail to steady his dizziness as he peered back down the stairwell to the spot of light below. From way down there, the muffled pulse of the siren was probing up towards him. And there was no option but to go back.

Or was there? He could wait here, in the hope that they'd give up. But no, if the medical staff called the Officiate in, they'd never give up. And here he'd be trapped. He had to go back down and get out. And quickly. He put out a foot to feel for the first step and set off, gaining speed as the light strengthened.

Back at the bottom, he paused, listening for sounds beneath the siren. Beyond the glass door the corridor was empty, and . . . why hadn't he seen it before? . . . opposite was an elevator. He closed his hand around the door handle and pulled gently. He stuck his head out. To left and right the corridor was clear. He bounded through the door and reached for the elevator button. He waited, scanning the empty, screaming corridor. If there was someone in this elevator he'd have to run again, but now he knew that there was nowhere to go. Nowhere but up. Suddenly there was movement at the end of the corridor to his right. Two men in dark uniform. They'd seen him and were running towards him. The ping of the elevator almost stopped his heart. The doors slid open. No one inside. He leapt in and his shaking hands found the up button. Long, long seconds passed until the doors slowly slid to pinch out the siren's scream.

How far up to go? He tried to remember how many flights of steps he'd gone up before he reached the dead end . . .

And then the elevator shuddered, the ping sounded again, and the door opened on to a couple of young nurses. They screamed as he pushed past them and ran. There was no siren sounding here and there was a difference in the air. Beneath the overlay of disinfectant was something fresher, a wet, night-air smell. He saw that he was again at a crossroads and, feeling the fresh air to his right, he turned and ran and at last saw a window at the very end. With his legs heavy and almost failing, he reached it, flung it open, and jumped out.

He hit soggy ground sooner than he expected, rolled down a steep bank and landed in some sort of prickly shrub. He picked himself up immediately. Could he still hear the wail of the siren way underground, or was it just the white noise of fear that had rushed in to fill his head?

He turned and ran, and kept running, through unfamiliar, rain-soaked streets, until his footfall stamped out the memory of the siren's scream.

Chapter 21

Grebe slipped in through the back door into the kitchen. She poured herself a glass of water and leaned back against the sink, her trembling hand resting on the paperbook that was still stuffed down the front of her trousers.

Suddenly the door to the hall opened and her mother appeared. Grebe saw her expression flash from surprise to anger.

'Where've you *been*?' she cried, 'Greta, you're *filthy*! That was a new outfit! How much do you think it cost? It's ruined!'

Grebe turned and sloshed the remainder of her water back into the sink.

'You won't have noticed, Mother, but there's been a storm going on for hours outside. I can wash these clothes. No great tragedy.'

'"No great—" How *dare* you! CLIVE!'

Her mother always applied to her father for back-up. It was pathetic. In any case, he wouldn't bother to come, however much she shrieked. He'd be at his screen and nothing short of his trousers being on fire would move him—and perhaps not even that. Grebe banged the glass down on the sink and headed for the door.

'No one will take you with that attitude, you know,' snapped her mother. 'Only the best girls get Paired to people like Stephen.'

'Then let him have one of the best girls, because I don't want him!'

'It doesn't matter what you want. In a year's time you'll be Paired and off our hands—and not a moment too soon. Selfish little vixen! My health won't stand much more.'

She went across to the table, on which stood an ornate tabbacaseed burner. Grebe watched as her long, slender fingers reached for the tabbacaseed box and began feeding the seeds into the neck of the burner. She seemed to have forgotten that Grebe was there. As her mother picked up the lighter, Grebe slipped into the hallway. Just as she turned towards the stairs, she saw a jewelled fob lying on the hall table. The speedcar key. So it must be still here—the retailers hadn't come to collect it yet. Grebe glanced back to see her mother inhaling deeply from the burner's tube. Then she picked up the fob and slipped silently out of the front door.

The speedcar sat on the driveway. The rain drumming on its roof was shimmering in the light reflected from the nearest audiocam. Grebe supposed it wouldn't matter if she was seen. No reason why she shouldn't go and sit in her mother's car for a while. Anyway, it shouldn't take long to check out the TD. But she must check it out. Whatever was on it, Papa Louis had thought it was important. She slid the keycard into the speedcar's door, opened it and climbed into a sleek interior that smelt of new leather and her mother's sickly perfume. The entertainment console seemed easy enough to use. There was a slot for TDs. Grebe switched on the electrical circuits, pulled Papa Louis's plastic bag from inside her shirt, and posted the disc. Instantly the console screen lit up and Grebe saw a message that must have been keyed in by Papa Louis himself. She quietly closed the speedcar door, dimmed the overhead light, slid down in the seat and stared at the screen, which said:

TO USE THIS YOU'RE GOING TO NEED A VEHICLE WITH AUTODRIVE. THE NEW BLUE VAN HAS AUTODRIVE. JUST STEAL IT. HIGHLIGHT THE TITLE OF THIS ROUTE, THEN SELECT AUTODRIVE. SAFE JOURNEY. ALL MY LOVE GOES WITH YOU. PAPA.

Grebe breathed a wobbly sigh and touched the icon to get the next page. What she was now looking at was a map, she knew that much. But it took a few moments for her to make sense of it, to realize which line was the route they must follow and which was the outline of the Island itself; which were the cities and where—she shuddered—where was the Outersea. The route line snaked towards the bottom of the screen, where the brown mass of the Island ended and the blue mass of Outersea began.

The Outersea that still carried the poison from the Downzone attacks.

No matter what Fella said, she was afraid of that mass of blue. The Inseas were fine. An A-grade girl in her group at the Attainment Centre had travelled to one of the Inseas and had a holiday there with her family. They'd even walked in the very edge of the water because, of course, the Inseas weren't poisoned. But if water from the Outersea touched you . . .

A suddenly-seen movement in the darkness outside made her scream. A face at the window of the speedcar. The face had disappeared and a fist rapped at the glass before she realized who it was.

'Fella!'

She leaned over and opened the passenger door. He flumped into the seat beside her. He was soaked through. He looked terrified. What she wanted to do was throw her arms round him, but something stopped her. Instead, she shrieked.

'You nearly killed me!'

'Sorry,' he said. 'Look—I can't stay long.'

'What d'you mean? Where are you going now?'

'I don't know. It's not safe for me to be anywhere. Farl is after me. We need to get to the Glass House somehow, but . . . '

'The one on the south coast?' she said. 'Near the Outersea?'

'Yes, but—'

'Shut up and look!'

She pointed, and Fella stared at the map on the screen.

'The TD!' he cried. 'He *did* it!

'Yes!' she said. 'I told you before and you wouldn't listen! I don't know *how* he did it . . . '

'He took a terrible risk . . . '

'Because he so badly wanted you to get there. Look, that's the south coast there, isn't it? And this speedcar has autodrive, so we could go there now.'

And then Fella leaned across and flung his arms round her, holding her so tight she thought he would crush her.

'Papa Louis is dead!' he sobbed.

She felt the heave of his chest and heard the stifled howl. And she sobbed with him.

'It's not so scary as you think it's going to be, once you get used to it, is it?' said Grebe. She didn't sound convinced, thought Fella.

They had been making their way out of the city for almost half an hour in Grebe's mother's speedcar, which was driving itself along the TD route.

The traffic lights ahead had just turned from amber to red and, once again, Fella braced himself in anticipation. But, once again, the speedcar slowed and stopped at the lights. It had put itself in the left-hand lane, so they would be turning left towards the southern outskirts of the city. Fella had never been this far away from the Orphanage before.

He glanced across at Grebe and saw her delicate profile, pale against the blaze of city lights outside. Her slightly upturned nose, the strange upturn of blonde curls in the middle of her fringe. It was as though the two of them were wrapped up together in a private world and no one from outside could get to them. He liked it. He wanted it to stay like this. But he was worried about Grebe. This wasn't her mess. And she shouldn't be running away from her parents like this.

'Grebe,' he said, 'you know you don't have to come with me. I mean . . . there's a lot for you here on this Island and I don't want . . . '

He saw the wetness in her eyes as she turned to face him.

'I won't come if you don't want me to,' she said.

'It's not that!' he said, because it wasn't. He *did* want her to come, because nothing seemed to mean anything unless she was there with him. 'It's just that . . . we'll never be able to come back. And your parents . . . your whole *life* . . . '

'I don't care!'

'Yes, but we don't know what we're going to find, and—oh, NO!'

'What?'

'The paperbook!' He felt a surge of panic. How could he have forgotten about it?

Grebe was wriggling about in her seat. She seemed to be undoing the zip of her trousers.

'We'll have to go back!' he cried.

'There!' She slapped the paperbook into his lap. Disbelieving, he picked it up and held it to the light. He felt its warmth. He looked across at her and saw a set to her jaw that looked very much like smugness.

'Why do people call you stupid?' he said.

'Because I look stupid and if you look stupid, people

think you *are*,' she said. 'Don't knock it—it has its advantages.'

He reached across to her hand. 'Thank you.'

'You're very welcome. And I *am* coming with you . . . ' she hesitated, 'because whatever happens is bound to be better than what my parents had planned.'

He waited. He thought he knew already. Something she had said before about being Paired with an idiot. It was the sort of thing her parents would do to her. He couldn't think of a single thing to say that would sound like what he meant.

Eventually she said, 'I can see you're full of curiosity, so I'll tell you . . . '

'A Pairing,' he said.

'Yes. And the guy's a Noper. A B-grade Noper but a Noper all the same. So anything would be better than that.'

He lurched towards her as the speedcar took a sudden sharp right. He steadied himself on the dashboard and looked out through the rain. Outside there were just a few more streetlights ahead, then darkness. He glanced down at the TD screen. The pulsing route line had grown shorter. They were leaving the city behind.

F ella tried to study the landscape outside as they sliced through the night. But the rain battering at the speedcar's windscreen was blurring the dark shapes that he thought might be trees and hills. There were no lights, which meant no people. He had never, ever, looked out at a night with no lights in it, and he was frightened and excited at the same time.

'This storm should have blown out by now,' said Grebe, hunkering down in her seat. 'But it's getting worse, isn't it?'

It was true. Every now and then a sharp gust of wind buffeted the speedcar but that didn't matter. It held the road perfectly; it felt safe and comfortable inside.

They must be almost two hours away from the city now. Farl and the nightmare in the medi-centre felt like part of a past life. And for the first time, Fella began to feel that it might really be possible to live another, different sort of life. It was something to do with being out of the city, being away from everything he had ever known, travelling through a new landscape, even though he couldn't see it properly. But everywhere he travelled, for as long as he lived, he knew he would take Papa Louis with him. So, in a sense, he hadn't died. The thought made him feel stronger. He lay back in his seat and looked at the map screen.

'We can't be far away now,' he said.

Grebe was squinting through the streaking rain.

'See those trees on the horizon?' she said. 'They're really thrashing about. Do you think the summer storms are worse out here in the country than they are in the city? Oooh!' She flinched as a small branch hit the windscreen.

'It'll be all right,' said Fella. 'This speedcar is top of its class, isn't it? Your father wouldn't have dared give your mother anything less.'

'No.'

'Seriously, though. Aren't you going to miss them at all?'

'No . . . '

'But . . . ?'

'But . . . I suppose I feel the same as you. I miss the parents I might have had. I think parents should care about their children—the way Papa Louis cared about you. They didn't care about me, that's all. And why should you love people who don't love you?'

'But they must have—' He stopped suddenly as her head turned sharply away from him.

He had better shut up. What did he know about parents and families anyway? And suddenly this thought pulled another one into the foreground of his mind. Something that had been floating in the background ever since he escaped from the medi-centre.

'Grebe . . . '

'Yes?' She turned back to him.

'There were these two kids in the medi-centre, a boy and a girl. I couldn't stay, I couldn't talk to them properly because this woman was going to catch me. But the boy said that he'd been made to go there and his parents didn't know where he was.'

'Who made him go?' said Grebe.

'He didn't say. Just "a man". Must be Officiate. But why would they take children to the medi-centre without their parents knowing? I think—from what the boy said—that they'd told him he needed a check-up. But if he did, why do it like that? And the boy said there was nothing wrong with him.'

'There must have been, or else why did they take him there? Anyway, thank goodness you weren't caught!'

'Yes . . . ' Suddenly he realized something. 'That woman, the nurse who nearly caught me with the kids. She was wearing a blue uniform! That means she wasn't an Islander nurse—she was from the Downzone!'

'How do you know?'

'From something my mother said in the paperbook. They have special blue uniforms to let Downzoners know who the other Downzoners are.'

'So . . . Downzoner people were looking after these children?'

'Yes. But why not tell the parents? Those poor kids were really frightened.'

Grebe shrugged. 'Don't know. People just do what they want, don't they? Nobody cares about kids, they—'

She stopped dead with a gasp and pointed out of the window into the dark. But now it wasn't all dark out there. Now there was something down below them, something glistening silver and black. And it was moving, swelling and shifting as if it was alive. There was a strange sort of energy in the movement that Fella had never seen before. It heaved and rolled and glistened for a long, long way beyond them until it disappeared into dead black.

'The Outersea!' whispered Grebe.

And somewhere beyond that blackness, out across that heaving mass of water, was the Downzone. Fella's heart was racing as he felt the speedcar slow and turn to head down towards it.

Chapter 24

The speedcar made its way slowly along a narrow road that zigzagged down and down towards the mass of moving water. It was a long way, and steep. There was a sudden crash of thunder and, way out across the water, lightning sent shards of brightness fracturing through the black. Fella glanced at Grebe and saw that she was holding herself rigidly back against the seat.

'It'll be all right,' he said. 'We're nearly there.'

'That water . . . it looks so *angry*!' she said. 'And anyway—where? Where *is* this glass place?'

'I don't know.'

And for the first time since they'd selected the autodrive back there outside Grebe's house, Fella wondered whether Papa Louis had got it right. He could see no glass house—no building at all—in the darkness ahead.

The speedcar gave a lurch and the noise of the tyres changed. They were now on a rougher road and, looking out to his left, Fella could see that the water was now only just below eye level. Grebe didn't seem to have seen it.

She was still staring ahead. Suddenly she said, 'What's that?'

'That's it! It must be!' he cried.

They were slowly bumping towards something dark and angular that reared up into the sky. For a split second, lightning pierced the blackness again—and they saw it. A round glass structure sitting right on the edge of the water.

The speedcar stopped.

Fella looked across at Grebe. Then he opened his door and got out.

The rain-soaked wind tore at his hair and swirled it around his head and over his eyes. He brushed it aside and looked up to see the steel frame of the building, the churning Outersea, flecked with white, reflected in the great black panes of glass.

And the sound! The smell!

Grebe got out of the speedcar and came to stand close.

'What's that noise?' she shouted.

'I think it's the water. It must be—look, the water moving in and out is making that sort of . . . roaring and crunching sound on the shore.' He took a beamlight from his pocket and began to examine the huge metal door to the house.

'Fella, suppose there's someone in there?'

She clung tighter to him, almost blown over by the wind that snatched her words.

'Doesn't look as if there is,' he yelled. 'Anyway, we've got to try . . . '

'How are we going to get in?'

He hadn't thought about it. Something so important and they hadn't even thought!

'Look there,' she pointed. 'It's a keypad door. It's really old-fashioned. They used to do it by remembering four numbers—a code. Press the keys and you're in. If you know the numbers.'

'But we don't.'

Fella swung the beamlight upwards, scanning the glass walls for any sign of a way in. The wind was sending a strange whistling through the steel beams above and the crash of the water rolling in and out seemed to be getting louder. It was beginning to really worry Fella. He imagined it rolling up and swallowing them. He felt Grebe shiver beside him.

'Go back in the speedcar,' he said. 'You'll get cold.'

There was something else that worried him too. It seemed that the water *was* getting closer and just now he'd thought he felt some moisture touch his face. Maybe thrown up as the water hit the rocks nearby and caught the wind. If they couldn't get in soon they'd have to go back.

'Have you got the paperbook?' said Grebe.

'No—it's in the speedcar.'

'I'll get it,' she said.

'All right.'

As another flash of lightning came, he pulled at the metal door, tears of rage and helplessness welling in his eyes. He was an idiot. This thing couldn't be done. He was risking their lives for nothing. He touched the keypad. No hope of guessing. Then he remembered something.

'Grebe!' He swung the beamlight back towards her. 'The numbers you saw in the paperbook . . . where did you see them?'

'Hang on!'

She was staggering back towards him against the wind, the paperbook clutched to her chest.

'Here . . . try inside the front cover,' she cried. 'D'you think that's the code?'

There was a sudden crashing of water nearby. Grebe screamed and the wind snatched the pages from his fumbling fingers. At last he saw the scratchy pen marks: 6661.

'It's worth a try. Nothing else is going to get us in in time.' He pressed the four numbers, grabbed the metal door handle and pulled.

Nothing.

'No!' Grebe nudged him aside. 'You have to wait before you pull! I said it was old-fashioned.'

She tried the numbers. She paused. Then pulled. The door swung towards them and they stepped inside.

A sudden gust slammed the door behind them, the noise echoing around the great empty space ahead.

'Wow!' said Fella. 'Just *look* at it!'

As Fella flashed the beamlight around the space in front of them, Grebe saw a huge area that felt empty except for some dark shadows of furniture. To either side, through the great windows, the silver-and-black water surged at the edge of her vision. It seemed to be getting angrier, rearing and tossing foam-flecked water onto the glass. She didn't want to look at it. Even though Fella said his mother had done it, and she wanted to believe him, it seemed more and more impossible that you could actually travel in a tunnel *under* that water. But there was nowhere you could look without seeing the water, because ahead of them, through the windows behind a great central staircase, you could see that it really *was* a round house. And it was perched on the very edge of the water.

They headed towards the staircase, with just enough light from the beamlight to show them the high, open space. It seemed to be a living area, because there was an old-fashioned entertainment centre and the blank rectangle of a telescreen. Other shapes, draped in white coverings, looked like sofas and chairs.

'Doesn't look as if anyone uses the place—not at the moment, anyway,' said Fella.

Grebe shivered. It didn't feel as though anyone had been here recently—there was a musty smell and a stale stillness to the air, as though there had been a long time of quiet here.

Just past the staircase, they seemed to be in the centre of the building and Fella stopped at a pillar a few paces wide, running his hands over the smooth metal surface.

'I've been thinking about it. There must be something like an elevator shaft down to the tunnel. Something like this. The only way you could get to a tunnel under the sea is by elevator or steps, and those could only be housed in a shaft—see, perhaps inside this pillar!'

'Oh, please just *find it*, Fella!'

She heard her voice echo over the cold surfaces and, beyond her own tiny voice, the muffled roaring of the water outside. She was just turning back to help Fella search when something snatched her attention. She wasn't sure at first, but then she was.

Way out beyond the rain-spattered glass walls, on the high clifftop down which they had driven, a light was blinking.

'Fella!' She pointed. 'A car!'

Yes, definitely a car. Turning to begin the long descent down the cliff road, just as they had.

'They'll see my mother's speedcar!'

Fella snapped the beamlight off and for long moments they stood and watched the light crawling, suspended in blackness above them.

'It'll take them a while to get down,' he said. 'Twenty minutes or so. We've still got time.'

'But nobody could have known . . . !'

'The Officiate could—if they went snooping after Papa Louis made that TD,' said Fella. 'Come on, keep looking!'

Using the fainter light of Grebe's keycard, they finished examining the side of the central pillar that faced away from the cliff, towards the Outersea. They could find no door, not even a break in the smooth surface. The whistling of the wind had grown into a howl, was wrapping itself around the glass house, so it felt as if there was something alive outside in the darkness trying to get in.

Fella almost had to shout against the noise.

'There's nothing down here. We'll have to try on the next floor. We can just about see by your light. Come on.'

As they made their stumbling way towards the staircase, Grebe glanced out towards the cliff. She couldn't see the light any more. A gust of wind slammed against the glass wall ahead of them. It was almost completely dark in the house now. The silver glint had gone from the water. In fact, they couldn't see the water at all. But, under the howling of the wind, she could still hear the roaring. She reached for Fella's hand as they began to climb the stairs. Suddenly he stopped and turned to look out towards the cliff.

'Fella?'

He didn't answer. There was just enough light to see the

side of his face, which was as still as stone. He was staring straight ahead.

'Can you see that?' he said.

She caught his sudden shudder of fear and looked too, but she couldn't make any sense of what she saw. The darkness beyond the glass was moving. It was as though the darkness itself was alive.

'Have you got your beamlight?' she whispered.

He flapped about with his coat pocket.

She grabbed his arm. 'What is it? What's out there?'

Immediately her words were answered by a great roar and a screeching, groaning sound.

She grabbed his arm as he switched on the beamlight and pointed it straight ahead.

The circle of light was shaking, because he was shaking. And he was shaking because now they could see the thing that was moving behind the great glass walls of the house.

'The water!' cried Fella.

Yes, water. Swirling, surging, pushing angry white ripples against the glass. It was way up above their heads.

'Up the stairs!' he screamed. 'Quickly!'

She was running on legs that wouldn't work properly. They couldn't get up the stairs fast enough and that screeching groan had begun again. It was coming from behind them, from the direction of the front door. As they reached a landing, Fella swung the beamlight back towards the sound and it took Grebe seconds to understand what she was seeing. The sound was being made by metal on metal. Her mother's speedcar was floating up against the glass wall, just about level with this landing, the water pushing it against the steel beams and grinding out the terrible noise. Another gust of wind hit the house and the car was lifted and slammed, this time against the glass.

'Further up!' cried Fella. 'If it breaks the glass the water will get in!'

They ran up another flight of stairs and stopped again on the second landing. Above them was another flight, leading to what must be the top floor.

'Keep going, keep going!' yelled Grebe.

And just as they started up this flight, there was a thunderous bang and a great rush of shattering, smashing noise. And cold air. And roaring, plunging water.

They ran and made it to the last landing. There were no more stairs. They stood gasping. Fella pointed the beamlight back down the stairs, searching for the water. For the moment, they couldn't see it. But they could hear it surging into the ground floor of the house.

Think logically, Grebe, think, she told herself. If the water didn't get any higher, they'd be safe. But there was a terrible fear creeping inside her. A fear of the water. Because, deep down, she believed it was poisoned. Survival time for a human being after contact with contaminated water was . . .

The beamlight flashed towards her.

'Grebe, come here!' said Fella.

He lit the way and she came to where he was standing by a sort of door. Not an ordinary door.

'I think it's the elevator,' he said. 'The way down.'

'But *down* is where the water is. We can't do that!'

'But what if it goes *right* down, right below the house to the tunnel, like my mother says? We have to try. We can't stay here!'

He pressed the button next to the door.

'*Don't!*' screamed Grebe.

'I'm only going to look!'

The door slid open.

'I'm going to see if it says how many levels, then we'll know,' said Fella. He stepped into the elevator.

'It's not safe!' she screamed again.

'It is! The water won't get into the elevator shaft, will it?'

'I don't know! Fella, *please* don't!'

She glanced back at the room behind them. She couldn't see much, but she could hear the water and feel the cold wind rushing up the staircase.

'There's only one level,' said Fella. 'Only one button to push.'

'What does that mean?'

But before he could answer, she cried out in terror. Something had nudged up against her feet, tickled one ankle with wetness. She jumped away from it and heard a squelching sound, then a push of cold water against both ankles.

'The water! Grebe, come on!' Fella leaned out of the elevator, pulled her inside and hit the one and only button.

All she could think of was the wetness on her ankles, the poisoned water that would kill her. It didn't matter what Fella's mother said. Once the water touched your skin it would get into your blood and kill you.

She was sobbing. She felt sick. Fella hugged her close. 'It's all right. Come here. It's all right.'

'But it got me, Fella. It *got* me!'

'It won't hurt you. It's all a lie.'

But she could hear his uncertainty. He didn't know. She opened her eyes and saw that the door of the elevator was closing. There was a jolt. And then she could feel that they were beginning to travel down.

Chapter 26

Grebe collapsed against him and Fella felt the thrumming of the elevator as his back was pressed against the metal wall. The overhead light showed him his own reflection juddering in the polished surface but the face staring back at him was unrecognizable, tight with fear.

He felt Grebe cling tighter as the elevator steadied and, with a gentle bump, stopped. Silently, the doors opened on to darkness that smelt green and damp and like the taste of salt.

He reached down and found her hand. Then he stepped forward.

'No!' She pulled back.

'We have to,' he said.

He gripped her tightly, feeling how she was shaking. He was shaking too.

'We can't go back now,' he said.

Suddenly, the doors began to close. He blocked them with his body, pulling again at her hand.

'Grebe!'

'No!'

'Come on!'

The door at his back was pushing hard against him. There was no time. Still she stood as if paralysed.

'Grebe, *now*! I can't hold it!'

He tugged at her and she shot towards him, squeezing with him through the gap as the doors silently closed behind them.

They stood in the darkness. Then a soft light fell around them. They both flinched, waiting for something else to happen. Nothing did.

How had the light come on? Now he could hear the gentle hum of electric current. An automatic light? Or turned on by someone watching? Fella blinked at the shadows just beyond their circle of light. If anyone was watching they'd speak, wouldn't they? If they were going to be caught . . .

'Hello?' he called.

Only his own shaking voice echoed back at him and, as his eyes adjusted, he saw rocky walls around them. The walls were glistening in places and, way beyond the electric humming, he could hear a drip echo.

Grebe shivered and glanced up at the ceiling. He followed her gaze, looking for audiocams.

'Can't see anything,' he said.

'Look.' She pointed ahead.

In the gloom stood an almost familiar shape.

'Is it . . . it looks like a monorail,' whispered Grebe.

'My mother mentioned a travel pod,' he said. 'Farl told her about it.'

He took a few steps towards the edge of the light and, as he did, it moved with him, washing up onto the blue-painted sides of the pod, then the windows.

'This is it,' he said. 'It's what we've come here to find. The way out.'

He could see through the windows that there was seating for perhaps a dozen people.

Grebe came to stand beside him.

'You were right!' she breathed. He glanced down at her. She looked terrified, amazed, relieved.

'It might not work,' he said.

'Try.'

'It might not have been used for ages.'

He didn't know why he thought this. Somehow, during their short time in the Glass House, he'd sensed there'd been no one there for ages either. He pushed the door button. He flinched as the door hissed open and the interior of the pod lit up. They stepped in.

The air was cold. There was a smell of metal and stale upholstery. Suddenly, he imagined people sitting in the rows of empty seats, turning their heads to stare at the intruders. The checkpoint Guards, Attainment Directors. Farl. He blinked and took a deep breath.

'What if it doesn't work?' said Grebe.

And what if it does? he thought.

He let go of her hand and made his way to the front of the pod. If there were any controls, that's where they'd be.

Yes, there was a touchpad.

'How to activate it?' he muttered.

'Is it automatic?' said Grebe.

He reached forward and touched the part of the pad mark 'Autodrive'.

They both jumped violently as a high-pitched beep sounded. And then a calm female voice. 'Doors closing. Stand clear, please.'

The beeps stopped. The doors closed. A deep, electric whirring noise was building from below the floor.

And then the pod fell silent.

Fella didn't notice it at first, but then he saw that the glistening walls of rock outside were moving. The pod was sliding forwards.

'Fella!' cried Grebe.

She was staring ahead into the tunnel, where strips of light were now yawning into life, showing a track stretching into darkness.

'Might as well sit,' said Fella, surprised by the thin sound of his own voice.

Gently, the pod gathered speed and they sat, holding hands.

For a while, Fella let the feelings wash over him. He was leaving. Getting out, escaping. He couldn't make himself believe it. He was going home. As the lines of light fled by outside, pulling them towards an ever-receding distance, the thrill of it drenched through him. He saw Grebe's eyes shining, felt her fingers laced tightly through his. He wondered if this was what it meant to feel happy—to be full of hope and excitement and to know that someone else was sharing it.

Suddenly, Grebe disentangled her fingers and began to rummage in her pockets. She brought out a wallet, some tissues, and half a packet of fruit sweets.

'That's all I've got,' she said, 'apart from the paperbook, of course. How about you?'

He watched as she opened the wallet. There were a few vouchers and he could see some tokens shining in the zip compartment.

She looked up. 'What?'

'They may not be any use,' he said.

She frowned. 'Course not! I'm stupid!'

'No you're not. It's just . . . we don't know what things are going to be like. We don't know anything. We don't *have* anything.'

Deep in his own pocket, he turned over and over in his hand the only thing he had brought with him. The only thing, in fact, that he had ever possessed. The keycard to the Orphanage.

'We've got our brains,' said Grebe. 'You said to me once that that's the thing no one can take away from you, "You're always free if you can *think*" . . . '

'Did I say that?'

'Something like.'

It sounded like the kind of stuff he'd come out with. Easy to say, hard to do.

'And we've got each other,' she said.

He watched the movement of her short blonde hair as

she tucked the wallet back into her pocket, and a new wave of anxiety hit. What was he leading her into? Grebe, who would follow him anywhere.

She leaned back, her head resting on his shoulder. They watched the lights in the tunnel.

Fella's head suddenly jerked upright and he opened his eyes. His neck was stiff. He must have been sleeping.

Beside him, Grebe was leaning forward, her mouth open, listening. Now he heard it too. A soft, descending note, like a sad sigh. And then they felt it. The pod was slowing down.

Chapter 27

The light ahead was brightening and a platform was
coming into view to one side. Grebe pressed herself
back against the seat.

'What if there are people?'

'Don't know,' said Fella. 'We'll have to run.'

Her heart hammered. Here it came. Ahead, the tunnel
ended in a wall of rock. To the side, the platform.

She looked. And breathed out. 'Empty!'

He leaned forward. 'Yes, I think so.'

The pod whispered to a stop in front of the rock face and
the doors opened.

'Ready to run if we need to, OK?' he said.

'Yes.'

Her legs were wobbly as she followed him to the door.
Other people might appear at any moment and . . . she
stepped out onto the platform behind Fella . . . and how
would they get off this brightly-lit, empty platform?

She saw him look upwards with a slight frown. She
couldn't see any audiocams either.

'There's a door,' he said.

It was a metal door with a keypad. Grebe saw the familiar clench of Fella's jaw and her spirits plunged. Surely they couldn't have come this far only to be stranded here?

'Try the code you used at the Glass House,' she whispered.

But before he touched the pad, Fella pushed at the door and, to Grebe's amazement, it wasn't locked.

Fella looked puzzled.

She shrugged. 'Someone forgot to pull it shut?'

Beyond the door was a flight of brightly-lit steps leading up out of sight. They started to climb, her legs feeling weak and aching. She looked at the walls, the ceiling, examining everything, even the steps themselves. No sign of audiocams or spy-eyes on the smooth, bright surfaces.

'No cams,' she said. It was too strange. She didn't believe it.

'Well, I suppose if this is a tunnel for high-up Downzoners to use, then they wouldn't be spying on themselves, would they?'

She could tell he didn't believe it either.

They climbed on and she began to lag behind. The steps were steep and she couldn't keep up with him. She was finding it hard to breathe. The air tasted strange. He stopped to wait for her.

'Rest a minute,' he said. 'It's a long way up and the air is . . .'

He didn't finish whatever it was he was going to say, but she knew he was thinking the same. The air was different.

He looked at her. 'It *must* be all right,' he said, 'because Farl and my mother travelled to and from the Downzone and the air didn't harm *them*.'

She nodded. Surely, if the air was poisoned, they'd be starting to die by now. Wouldn't they?

'It was all lies,' he said. 'And we don't have to believe the lies any more.'

Suddenly his attention snapped away from her. She listened with him. Nothing. And then a tiny, scraping echo way up above them on the steps.

'Did you hear it?'

She nodded. He crouched down to get a better view up the steps.

'Can't see anything,' he whispered, 'but if there *is* anyone and they see us *here*, they'll know . . .'

He looked suddenly defeated and she couldn't bear it.

'Let's go on,' she said, 'but carefully. We can't go back anyway, no matter what.'

So they went on up, noiselessly, trying not to think about the strange air, willing there to be no one up there above them.

Chapter 28

Grebe's lungs were tight with pain by the time the steps opened out onto a lobby containing another keypadded door.

'We'll rest a moment,' said Fella. Even *he* was breathing faster than normal.

She leant against the wall as he very gently pulled at the door. Again, unlocked.

They looked at each other and she saw the shadow of a smile in his eyes as he listened to the sounds leaking through from the world beyond.

A muffled announcement, distant footsteps, and chatter churned up together, a rumbling sound that she couldn't quite interpret. There was a faint smell of bread.

'I think it's like one of our monorail stations, only bigger,' he said. 'But I can't see anything close to. I think we're tucked away out of the main concourse.'

He waited, listening, a moment more, then said, 'Are you feeling OK?'

She nodded, her stomach fizzing. This was it. They must go now.

He held out his hand and she took it and he pulled the door open just wide enough to get them through.

They were in a dark corner, no one close by. But beyond there were people criss-crossing a huge, bright concourse. There were signboards and advertising screens, shops and coffee stalls. All so familiar, yet she knew it was so, so different.

They walked briskly towards the concourse. There was an early-morning feel. Ahead, she could see that one or two of the coffee shops were just opening.

The first people they were going to pass were clustered around a seating area. They looked like normal people. Some were yawning, some sipping coffee. Others were looking up at information boards. Grebe looked too, at the lists of strange words. The names, presumably, of the places here. And although the names were strange, she could read them. The letters were familiar. She looked around for the Officiate huts. There were none. And no queues of people waiting to be checked.

As they approached the group around the seats, Grebe saw the first really strange thing. She squeezed at Fella's arm. There was a woman holding and *reading* a paperbook. Fella hadn't seen it. She nudged at him and pointed at the woman and, to her horror, as she did so, the woman looked up. They held each other's glance for a moment before the woman looked down to her paperbook again.

Fella tugged at her hand and they walked quickly on.

'Did you see?' she whispered. 'The paperbook!'

But as he led her to another seating area in the middle of the concourse and pulled her down onto an empty bench, she saw other people doing the same thing. An old man with a sandwich in one hand and a paperbook in the other. Reading it! The girl opposite them, hunched over a paperbook. Actually *reading it*!

And they weren't the only ones. There were people dotted all over the concourse doing it.

Fella was scanning the people too, drinking it all in. She knew this expression, this deep watchfulness of his, so well. Orphanage kids were picked on all the time; they had to be good watchers.

'Fella . . . ?' She edged nearer to him. There was something worrying her, but it sounded silly to say it. He'd probably think so, but she had to say it anyway. 'The way that woman looked at me, the one back there with the paperbook—it's almost as if she *knew*!'

He gave a tiny shake of the head, still scanning the scene intently. 'She didn't know,' he murmured, 'she couldn't have. It's just that we're so used to being watched you're expecting everyone to be watching everyone else. They're not. Look.'

She tried to relax and really look. He was right. People seemed to be wrapped up in their own little piece of space. They saw each other—just enough to avoid bumping into each other—but they didn't really *look*. Anyway, no one seemed to be looking at them right now. Except she was sure there had been something in that woman's expression.

Something like recognition, only not quite. Carefully, she looked back the way they had come, searching for the woman. She was still there, but now she was talking into a handheld device. Perhaps a mobile phone like the A-graders on the Island used. She glanced up in their direction and Grebe quickly looked away.

'We're still underground, there's no natural light in here,' said Fella. 'The way out's over there. Ready?'

They set off towards a pair of moving staircases, one carrying people up and one carrying them down, just like in the B-grade malls on the Island where Grebe's mother and her friends shopped.

But probably even their A-grade malls wouldn't have anything like the glass-walled restaurant beside the staircase. As they were carried upwards, they peered down into the dining rooms. Glittering lights shone on people silently chatting across white-clothed breakfast tables with lavish centrepieces. Happy people, richly-dressed, laughing, waving their hands.

'I wonder if *she* went to restaurants like that,' murmured Fella.

Grebe saw the longing in his face. She saw how he kept his head turned towards the restaurant until the staircase had carried them up so high that it was out of sight.

Chapter 29

As they were carried up and up, Fella felt the change growing in the air. Down there, it had seemed thicker, weighed down with smells of strange foods, coffee, and perfumes. Now they were moving into something quite different.

He could smell it now, a fresh, sweet smell that he couldn't name. He filled his lungs, feeling his ribs stretch out against his shirt. This air wasn't poisoned. It couldn't be!

And then, the sun! Slanting through the arched windows of the great hall that opened up ahead, it sought them out, falling on their heads and shoulders, warming and welcoming. The staircase tipped them onto a shining stone floor and they stood drinking in the warmth.

There was hardly anyone around. Just a few people coming up behind them and others scurrying towards the staircase from the great stone exit archway ahead.

'It's beautiful!' whispered Grebe.

Slowly, they walked towards the exit. Through the arch,

Fella could see trees and, as they got nearer, there was a faint hum of traffic.

As they reached the arch, the sun hit them full in the face and it took him long seconds, squinting the view into focus, to realize that they were on a hill. A city was spread out below them. But not a city like theirs. This one had warm colours in its buildings, not the grey concrete that fractured the skyline around the Orphanage. There were delicate spires and golden domes—and everywhere trees.

Grebe swayed on her feet and put a hand out to touch the stone of the archway. Parts of it were crumbling.

'It must be old,' said Fella. He looked out again at the cityscape below. 'Older than anything we know.'

'Shush!' Grebe nudged him as a group of people swept past.

But the people didn't notice them . . . they didn't know, didn't even suspect they were not from this place.

Yes, it looked old. But the people, the trees, the air . . . it all seemed so *healthy*. Where were the heaps of ash, the twisted skeletons of steel, the burnt-out buildings and splintered trees? The'd been shown pictures. They all *knew* the pictures by heart!

He felt Grebe tug at his hand. She was looking up at him anxiously.

'Fella? Come on,' she said.

They waited while a few vehicles passed. They were recognizable as cars, but larger and a different shape to the Island ones. Perhaps they were A-grade cars. He wouldn't know. They crossed the road and Grebe began to steer him towards an open area of grass and trees that sloped downhill. And now they could hear the muffled sounds of a waking city rising to meet them. Familiar noises like traffic rumbling and hooting, yet so *un*familiar because these were unknown people jostling around down there beginning their days in lives he knew nothing about. And suddenly the sense of all these unknown people in this unknown world made him feel small and alone.

'*Can* we go there?' he said, stopping at the gateway to the green space. The grass was washed bright and pure with early sun. It was bound to be reserved for better people than them.

'I think we can,' said Grebe. 'Look, other people are walking there.'

As they walked across the grass, Fella scanned the trees and the lamp-posts. There was no sign of wires snaking up the tree trunks, and the lamps weren't like the ones on the Island. These looked as if they really were just lights. Unless they were a different sort of audiocam, more sophisticated.

Then he saw something that froze him. He gripped Grebe's hand and nodded towards the concrete hut that stood a little way down the slope. From where they were they could see a door in one side of the hut. No sign of any Guards, but they couldn't take the risk.

'Let's get out,' he said.

'No.' She resisted his tug. 'Let's look.'

She set off to the left. He understood that she was trying

to get a view of the broad side of the hut—but by the time she could see whether it *was* an Officiate Guard post or not, it would be too late . . .

He followed, meaning to pull her back, but as he reached her they saw a young couple approaching the hut. Now they could just see a hatch in the side of it. The couple were chatting to whoever was inside. And then . . .

Grebe swung round, smiling. 'It's just a coffee stall! Look!'

He felt like an idiot.

'Yes, all right,' he snapped, 'but it might *not* have been . . . What are you doing *now*?'

She was walking towards the hut.

He hurried after her again. They reached the hut just as the couple were moving away. Grebe fished out her wallet and smiled at the man behind the counter.

'Someone gave me this.' She showed him a low-value voucher of Island currency and Fella's heart clenched. 'But I don't know whether it's worth anything in this city.'

The guy took it and held it up to the light.

'I have to confess I've never seen anything like this,' he said. 'And no, I can't accept it as money, I'm afraid.'

'That's OK,' said Grebe as she took the voucher back.

Her eyes fell on two steaming cups that stood on the counter. She smiled again at the man and he grinned back. He was older than them, but he looked friendly.

'That couple just now said they wanted coffee,' he said, 'then they changed their minds and pretended they'd said tea. So those are going begging if you want them.'

'Oh, thank you!' cried Grebe. 'Do you have anything else "going begging"?'

The man stared at her for a second. Then he disappeared behind the counter. Fella tried to pull Grebe away. The man popped up again.

'Two only very slightly stale buns,' he said. 'Technically not fit for sale, but there's nothing wrong . . . '

'Thank you. Anything else under there?' said Grebe brightly.

The man looked at Fella, then back to Grebe, holding her gaze for a moment before saying, 'Where are you from?'

That was it, then. They'd only been here five minutes and they'd blown it!

'From out of town,' said Fella, 'just looking around. Thanks for these.'

He picked up the coffees and Grebe pocketed the buns and they hurried away from the hut. The guy shouted.

'Oi!'

Fella wanted to run but he stopped himself. There might be armed Guards in the trees.

'Come back!' said the man.

They turned back. The man was leaning forwards onto the counter. The smile had gone and now he looked . . . concerned.

'Look, I'm not being funny, right,' he said, 'and I don't want to get you into trouble. But if you're runaways, well . . . it's usually best to go home and face it out, whatever the problem is. Better than staying here and getting caught up in sleeping rough and drugs and stuff.' He hesitated. ' . . . Unless it's really, *really* bad at home. Don't think I'm prying.'

'No. Thank you,' said Fella, feeling himself redden. 'We can't go home. Thank you, but we'll be fine.'

'Wait!' called the man as they turned away again. 'At least let me give you some more stuff.'

He disappeared behind the counter again. Fella was angry with himself. Why had he said that about not being able to go home? Why hadn't he just lied? Idiot!

'Here!' The guy reappeared, holding up a bag. 'Some out-of-date sandwiches. Don't leave them more than a day, though. And here are some empty water bottles. You can fill up at the public toilets over there.' He pointed towards a path leading into the trees.

Fella didn't know what to say. Why was this stranger helping them?

'Thanks very much,' said Grebe, springing forward to take the bag.

'You're welcome.'

'Nice man,' said Grebe as they headed towards the toilets.

'Yeah,' said Fella. But he couldn't help imagining the man watching them as they disappeared into the trees.

Chapter 30

F ella and Grebe had found a quiet spot underneath a huge tree. They'd decided to take it in turns to rest, but it didn't work out like that. Fella suddenly found himself pulled out of deep sleep by some voices nearby. The voices were loud, prodding, and he woke in panic, realizing that he was supposed to be guarding while Grebe slept.

She was OK, curled into the dusty hollow made by the tree roots, her head on her rolled-up jacket.

But there were those voices again. He looked. The sun had shifted round the tree and now their side was in shade, but the other side . . . he leaned round carefully, because this was where the voices were coming from. And now he knew something else too. The thing that had really woken him up. He couldn't understand a word they were saying.

There was a family sitting in the sun on the other side of the tree. Two grown-ups and three little boys. The boys were squabbling over some food and the woman was telling them off. The father was keeping out of it. Like the people at the terminus that Grebe had first noticed, he was reading a paperbook.

Fella listened hard. Sometimes pleading, sometimes cross and insistent, the words tumbled over each other and he couldn't understand one of them.

What did it mean? Could people here speak more than one language? It had never occurred to him to think about another language . . . but this was because they'd always been taught that there were no other places, no other people left apart from the Islanders.

He leaned back against the tree trunk again and looked out across the sun-swept grass. There were lots of people now—families, couples, older people. Some with dogs, which was puzzling. The dogs were different shapes and sizes and they weren't straining at leashes and snarling—most of them weren't on leashes at all. The dogs and the people seemed to be just playing.

Suddenly, someone was walking straight towards them. He stiffened. Then he saw it was the coffee guy. Fella jumped to his feet.

'You been here all day?' said the coffee guy.

'We've been sleeping,' said Fella.

'Because you've nowhere else to sleep, right?'

Fella hesitated, trying to read the guy's expression. He seemed friendly, as he had before.

The guy held out his hand. 'I'm Jerry.'

Fella took Jerry's hand and said the first name that came into his head. 'Louis. I'm Louis.'

Jerry sat down a little way from Grebe, who was still sleeping.

'So,' he said, 'what do you think of Tompalla so far?'

Fella's thoughts swirled away like tabbacaseed smoke. This wouldn't happen on the Island. People were too suspicious of each other to be friendly to strangers. So Fella didn't know—he couldn't tell. How *could* you tell if a person was good or not? Tompalla. Was that the name of the city?

'I don't know,' he said. 'We haven't been here long enough. The language thing is interesting.'

'Language thing?' said Jerry.

Fella gestured over his shoulder, but the family had gone. 'There was a family there speaking a different language. What would that be?'

Jerry shrugged. 'I wouldn't know—people come here from all over the world, don't they?'

There must have been surprise in Fella's face because he caught a flicker of puzzlement reflected back at him in Jerry's blue eyes.

'Where are you from?' said Jerry.

'Oh . . . the north,' said Fella, his heart pounding. He was used to lying. But here it was a much more dangerous game. He had no idea what would be plausible and what wouldn't.

'Really?' said Jerry. 'Doesn't sound like it.'

What did that mean?

'We travel a lot,' said Fella.

Again that flicker of surprise . . . or was he imagining it?

Suddenly Jerry looked away from him as Grebe uncurled from her sleep and blinked up at him. She scrambled to her feet.

'You'll both be hungry,' said Jerry. 'Come with me.'

'You won't know this yet,' said Jerry, 'but it's lucky you met me first and not one of the evil scumbags that prey on strangers in that park—particularly young strangers.' He glanced at Grebe.

They were sitting at Jerry's kitchen table. Grebe was down one end, watching Jerry's little girl, Emmie, draw pictures. The child had loads of different coloured handpens and she knew how to hold them and draw with them. Fella wished that Grebe wasn't looking so amazed by this.

As they'd walked back to Jerry's place, he'd told them he had the lease on half a dozen coffee huts across Tompalla. His lease was up at the end of the summer, though. 'And then,' he'd said, 'we're off!' And he'd swept a hand skywards in a gesture that Fella hadn't understood.

'Off?'

'Back home to Orrokia. It's where I come from, can't you tell?'

No. Fella couldn't tell anything, and he was still puzzling over things now, while Jerry chatted and cooked.

Grebe glanced up. 'That smells really good, Jerry,' she said.

'Yummy chicken, my favourite!' cried Emmie.

The child beamed up at Grebe. She'd seemed shy with him, thought Fella, but she liked Grebe. He watched them, Emmie chattering, explaining her picture, Grebe listening, smiling . . .

'Hey, Louis,' said Jerry, 'Louis . . . ?'

Grebe looked up sharply at Fella, and coughed. He stared. She frowned. Then he realized. It was time to come clean.

'Oh . . . my name's not Louis,' he said.

'No?'

'No. Louis is . . . it's my father's name,' he said. He felt Grebe's eyes on him. 'My name is . . . I have no name. Papa Louis called me Fella.'

Jerry swung round from the cooker. 'Your own father couldn't think up a name for you?'

'It's complicated,' said Fella, 'but my name is Fella.'

Jerry put the lid on his saucepan and came to sit at the table.

'Look,' he said, 'do you two have parents out there somewhere worrying about you?'

Emmie looked up at her father, then at him. Grebe had gone pale. The gentle rattling of the saucepan lid filled long moments of silence.

At last, Fella heard his own voice say, 'I have no parents. My mother was murdered when I was a baby. And Papa Louis . . . '

But he got no further than that. He heard the scrape of a chair being pushed back and suddenly there was Grebe's familiar smell, her arms around his shoulders as he struggled to hold back the tears.

'Papa Louis died,' said Grebe, 'just the other day.'

Fella felt a light patting sensation on one of his hands and, through tears, saw that Emmie had come to stand by him, her eyes wide and sad.

'My mummy's dead too,' she said.

He wiped his eyes and looked at her. She was only six. He didn't know what to say to her.

'It's sad,' said Emmie, 'and it makes me cry a lot too. I wish she could be alive again. But she doesn't want me to be sad all the time. So if I cry, then afterwards I think of happy things we did with Mummy.'

Jerry held out his arms and Emmie went to sit on his lap.

'I'm sorry about your father, Fella,' he said. 'Do you want to talk about it? Why you're here . . . what your plans are?'

Fella looked at Grebe. She squeezed her lips together and gave a tiny nod.

'Emmie,' said Jerry, 'why don't you take Greta upstairs and you can put your pictures on the wall while Fella and I talk. Supper won't be long.'

Jerry watched sadly as Emmie and Grebe gathered up the pictures and left the room. Then he turned his kind, freckled face on Fella.

'Emmie's mother—my wife,' he said, 'she had a very rare lung disease. Nothing could be done and of course there was no organ insurance available when we were born. She didn't quite make her thirtieth birthday. So—that's why I'm taking Emmie back home. She'll have her grandparents,' he smiled, 'and of course the weather's much better there.'

Fella's head was beginning to ache. His grief, his tiredness and his struggle to understand this new world—all these things had left him feeling empty.

'Do you want to talk?' said Jerry again.

He looked at Jerry and saw that he wanted to help. But how to explain that they were from a different place and that they needed to make a new life here? How *could* they make a life here?

He blinked the last of his tears away and drew a deep breath.

'Well . . . ' he said, 'like I said, it's complicated. But I'll try to explain. My mother was murdered when I was a baby. I don't know who my father is. I was brought up in an Orphanage . . . '

'A what?' said Jerry.

'An Orphanage.'

'I don't know what you mean,' said Jerry, 'can you explain?'

'This is my room,' said Emmie. She seemed both shy and proud as she stood in the middle of the floor, bricks from a half-constructed toy house scattered at her feet. She was watching for Grebe's reaction.

'It's a lovely room, Emmie,' said Grebe. And it was. She had never seen anything like it. It was crammed full of things that told you what sort of little girl Emmie was. A busy little girl, evidently. Beside the toy house was a brightly painted box full of furry toy animals. Next to that a little table strewn with more pictures and . . . Grebe stepped over the miniature bricks and chimneys and bent to look more closely at the table . . . some pages with what looked like wobbly attempts at pen-writing. And on the wall above the table were shelves full of large, brightly coloured paperbooks.

Grebe stared at the paperbooks. So—here they taught their children pen-writing and gave them paperbooks to read. She didn't know why, but she felt as if something had been taken from her, as if she was somehow being kept out. She took down one of the paperbooks and looked at the pictures inside. The smell of the paper, the bright colours of the pictures, and the promise of a story waiting to be told sent a sudden, intoxicating longing through her. Yes, she had been kept out. Children like Emmie were allowed to explore worlds that the Island children would never know.

Emmie was patting at her arm. Reluctantly, Grebe put the paperbook back on its shelf.

'Put my picture there, next to the map,' said Emmie.

For a moment, Grebe didn't answer, because next to the shelves was another astonishing thing. She felt the little girl's watchfulness as she stared at this thing that she had called a map. It was not like any map she had ever seen.

'That's not my best map,' said Emmie, 'I've got loads of better ones. I love them. Do you?'

Grebe nodded, still gazing at the strange shapes floating on a background of blue. This blue must represent what she and Fella knew as Outersea. The strange shapes were coloured brown and green to look like land masses. She stared, trying to make sense of it. Was their Island one of those shapes?

'I *do* love maps, Emmie,' she said. 'Can you show me where you live?'

'Course I can!' said Emmie, climbing onto the table and stabbing a little finger at the top right-hand corner of one of the bigger land masses. It had a long name written across it. Grebe tried to make out the letters on the swirls of brown and green. *Inslannika*.

'We live here,' said Emmie, 'BUT . . . guess what?'

'What?'

'When we go to Orrokia we're gonna get on an airyplane and fly aaaaalllll the way . . . ' Grebe watched as the child's finger traced a path across all the land masses to the far side of the map, 'aaaallll the way over to the other side of the world. Whoooosh. And we land on the runaway here. And Granny and Grandad will come to pick us up and we'll go and live with them till we get our own house but I don't mind living with them because guess what?'

'What?' said Grebe, obediently, her eyes still fixed on the map and her mind racing. She was trying to store that shape in her memory, the shape of this new land mass they were on. Inslannika. All around the top of it were little islands. And Emmie had said they would 'fly' to Orrokia. She was sure she'd heard it correctly.

'Go on, guess *what*?' said Emmie.

Grebe tore her eyes away from the map and made herself smile.

'I can't, Emmie. I can't guess what's in your head, can I?'

'Granny and Grandad have a *swimming pool*!'

'Oooh!' Grebe held the child's excited, blue-eyed gaze for a split second. And then something made them both jump.

A crash. And now there was shouting coming from the kitchen below. Emmie's expression flicked from excitement to anxiety and she ran out onto the landing.

Grebe followed as the little girl ran down the stairs. As they got to the door of the kitchen, Jerry yelled, 'Get back upstairs, Emmie!'

Emmie started to cry. And then Jerry was shouting at Grebe.

'You get away from her! Don't touch my child! If you've contaminated her . . . !'

'*What?*' As Grebe moved away from Emmie, she looked across at Fella and saw blank panic on his face.

'Emmie, upstairs, NOW!' cried Jerry again.

As Emmie ran from the room, Jerry grabbed at what looked like a phone. He seemed to be punching in numbers. Then he said, 'Police, please!'

'Jerry . . . what's the matter?' said Grebe. 'Tell us. *Tell us!*'

'He thinks we're contaminated,' said Fella, 'because we're from the Island.'

'Just keep back and shut up!' said Jerry. 'I don't know whether you're lying or not but I'm not going to take the risk . . . Hello, police?' His fearful gaze bounced between her and Fella as he listened to the voice down the line. 'Yes, I have two intruders here. They say they're from one of the Satellite Islands . . . '

They ran down the lamplit street until Jerry's shouts had died behind them. One man tried to chase them as they pushed past him on the pavement, but he was quite old and they soon lost him. They headed into narrower streets where there were no people and, after taking turn after turn at random, they came out onto a street with a few shops, closed up for the night, and some restaurants bursting with music, chatter, and those strange, spicy food smells they had first smelt at the underground terminus.

Grebe stopped, gasping for breath, in the doorway of one of the shops. She could go no further. Fella stood guard while she gulped at the air.

There was no one on the street. Grebe closed her eyes for a moment and heard the insistent thud of a bassline of music coming from the restaurant a few doors down. Then there was a muffled scream of laughter and a bunch of people cheering. With her eyes closed, she could almost imagine this was back home.

Then, from somewhere in the sky, another sound was growing. Yes! Just like home!

'Fella!' She opened her eyes and saw that he had heard it too.

He dived into the doorway with her.

The low-pitched growling of the engine was coming closer. It wasn't directly overhead. But almost.

They pressed right back against the door. If they were lucky, the awning might help block the drone's heat sensors. And if they kept absolutely silent it wouldn't pick them up. Not with all that racket from the restaurants to confuse it.

Was the drone coming closer? She couldn't quite tell. She held her breath so as to listen harder. It seemed to be behind them, some way beyond the roof of the shop. And now . . . Yes. It was moving away.

They listened to the growl as it faded into a murmur. And then the street sounds washed over it entirely.

They waited until they were sure. Then she felt Fella breathe out beside her.

'If they have drones here, they could still find us!' he whispered.

'Was it a drone? I thought it was, but it didn't sound quite right.'

'Maybe theirs sound different. How would we know?'

They waited long moments more. Across the road, Grebe could see huge tree shapes beyond the street lamps. There seemed to be trees everywhere in this city. And there was the outline of a big building amongst the trees.

'Is that another park sort of place?' she said.

'Looks like.'

'There might be shelter.'

'OK, let's try.'

Carefully, they crossed the street and found an illuminated board that told them this place was a library. An arrow was marked 'You are here'.

'What's it mean, library?'

'Don't know,' said Fella. 'But look, there's trees and bushes . . . maybe somewhere to hide.'

They started out across the grass, leaving the street light behind. Soon they could see hardly anything except the dark bulk of trees and bushes, and they kept close to them. These leafy shadows seemed to have noises of their own—rustling, snapping, and a strange sort of heaving whisper. The breeze moving amongst all those leaves, she supposed. She wasn't sure she liked it.

There was a sudden screech and a dark shape skimmed the edge of her vision. She screamed and flung out a hand for Fella.

'Only a bird, I think,' he said. 'Quite a big one. Come on.' He pulled her towards the bushes. 'Let's see if we can find a place.'

Eventually they found a bush that wasn't too scratchy and they pushed their way into the middle of it. There was enough space for them to huddle with their backs against the trunk. Grebe remembered the one remaining squashed sandwich in her pocket. She handed half to Fella.

'We can't trust anyone, ever again,' he said through a mouthful.

'Well, we can't say we're from the Island again, that's for sure,' she said. 'What was it Jerry called it, "one of the Satellite Islands"? What else did he say when you told him?'

'He just went crazy,' said Fella. 'You know . . . I had that feeling, when he looked at me . . . someone looking at you as if you're nothing, or worse than nothing. Orphanage scum, a noper. I've had it all my life.'

She found his hand. 'Don't. You're not scum!'

'He thought so. He'd have turned us in to the Officiate or whatever they're called here. He was convinced we were contaminated.'

'But why did he think that?' said Grebe.

Fella shrugged. 'No idea. He said, "God forgive me, I've let contamination into my house," and then he started shouting at me, saying things like "how could you do this to a widower and a little girl?" I asked him what he meant and he said that all Islanders were contaminated, that's why we're kept apart. And then I tried to ask him what sort of contamination, and who told him this . . . but he wouldn't listen. I suppose I was getting angry too. And then you and Emmie came down.'

'So the people here are told things about us too.'

'Yes. Lies.'

'But we don't know it's lies,' she said. 'Perhaps we *can* contaminate them.'

'Good!' said Fella.

Silence fell between them. She wriggled her back into the rough trunk and thought about what Jerry had said.

Suppose it *was* true. She thought of Jerry's red face, spitting rage, as he screamed, 'if you've contaminated her . . . !'

Whether it was true or not, Jerry had certainly believed it.

'So . . . what does that mean?' she said. 'That we should go back to the Island?'

She hadn't realized when she opened her mouth that she was going to say this, and she could hardly believe she'd even *had* such a thought. But somewhere in her mind was a terrible fear that she couldn't begin to describe, even to herself.

'We can't.'

'We'd better try and sleep,' she said. His voice had frightened her. And she was so tired and so hungry that she couldn't think any more.

There was just about enough room for them both to lie down. The earth smelt musty and if they moved too much, leaves rustled and branches prodded at them. But at least they were out of sight.

She was just beginning to fall into fretful sleep, when Fella said, 'What did he mean "God forgive me"?'

'What?'

'What Jerry said, "God forgive me". Who is god?' he said.

'Don't know,' she mumbled, ' . . . try and find out in the morning.'

Fella dreamed that a woman was trying to talk to him. A dark-haired woman with deep-brown, familiar eyes. She had something important she wanted to say, but it was like an adscreen or a telefilm with the sound turned off. He couldn't hear her voice. He began to shout at her, angry that, for all her earnest looks and pleading gestures, she couldn't make herself heard.

He woke suddenly, face down, with the sour taste of earth in his mouth. He rolled over, then pushed himself up on stiff arms. It took him a few seconds of bleary consciousness, overlaid with feelings of frustration from the dream, to realize what was wrong.

Grebe had gone.

He sat bolt upright, spiking his head on the branches above. For a moment he could hear only the blood throbbing in his ears. Through the broken weave of branches and leaves he could make out daylight. But no Grebe.

He began to crawl towards the light, his limbs aching. He peered through the leaves.

It was a sunny morning. There were benches scattered around the grass ahead, with people sitting and poring over large sheets of print or reading paperbooks. But he couldn't see Grebe.

He dared not crawl out of the bush on the same side they'd come in. People would see. So he struggled out of the back and emerged between the bush and a tall wall. From there he watched for his moment to wander out onto the grass.

As he walked forward, nobody seemed to notice him. Yet still he felt too tall, too conspicuous. Once these people saw him, they might know, somehow, about the trouble in Jerry's house. And then what would happen? He felt the sweat tickle at his neck.

But no. No one had looked his way yet.

He scanned the open space ahead. The people reading, a man on his knees, digging at a flowerbed and throwing weeds into a wheeled tub, a woman strolling with two small children. They all had the same calmness. They seemed at ease sharing this space with each other, yet not noticing each other. Their calmness fed his own growing sense of panic. They were carrying on as if nothing was wrong. But *everything* was wrong! Where *was* Grebe?

He tried to think rationally. Perhaps she'd needed the toilet again. Perhaps she'd wandered about looking for one and someone had caught her. With a plunging sense of helplessness, he remembered something Jerry had said about evil scumbags that prey on youngsters.

He'd come to a gentle hill in the green and, as he got far

enough to see over the brow of it, he stopped. Ahead was a group of people, perhaps twenty or thirty, sitting on the grass in the morning sun. A woman was standing in front of them, talking, but he couldn't hear what she was saying. He scanned the group and thought he saw a small blonde head. He squinted. He wasn't quite close enough. And anyway, it *couldn't* be, because she wouldn't have gone to sit amongst people.

Even as he watched, people were getting to their feet, talking excitedly to each other, brushing grass from their clothes, going to shake hands with the woman who'd been talking.

And just outside the group, shyly hanging back, was Grebe.

The woman chatted with one or two people, even hugged one. Then she approached Grebe.

Fella's breath stuck in his throat.

Now the woman was shaking Grebe's hand. No!

He scanned again. Would the Officiate close in now? Everything looked normal, peaceful in the sunlight. But how could you really tell?

The woman handed Grebe something, clapped a hand on her back, and walked off across the grass to the big house beyond.

Fella waited until she was clear, then ran across to Grebe. She was looking down at whatever it was the woman had given her, and his sudden arrival made her jump.

'Oh! Hi!' she said.

He was enraged by her bright smile.

'What are you *doing*?' he said.

'That lady, her name's Elsa Rawlings,' said Grebe excitedly. 'She saw me watching and she said would I like to join in. So I just sat down, cos everyone was looking at me. And, Fella, the reason they were here—they were talking about a story written in a paperbook! Anyway, it looks like this story's a very famous one here, because all the people knew it. They were asking things and talking about things that happened in the story, as if the people in it were real people.'

'Why?'

'Don't know. But it was really interesting. Everybody reads paperbooks here. Only they seem to just call them books. Emmie had loads of them. And that library place . . . well, guess what?'

'What?' he snapped.

'It's full of paperbooks! Anyone can go in and read anything that's there! So we can go in. And she's given me this card, so I can borrow paperbooks . . . ' She hesitated, searching his expression. 'But anyway, it'll be a safe place to read *our* paperbook! Nobody will take any notice of us.'

'Haven't you forgotten something?' he said.

'What?'

'We're supposed to be contaminated.'

She dropped her head, her face flushed, and immediately he felt sorry. He stared across to the building called the library and sighed. 'Listen,' he said, 'we were too tired to think properly last night. But—how *can* we be contaminated? There are high-rank Downzoners going backwards and forwards between here and the Island all the time. They couldn't do that if there was a risk of getting sick by mixing with us, could they?'

She looked up at him. She almost seemed nervous of him.

'Why would they lie?' she said.

'To keep our two worlds apart. Ours and theirs.'

'But why?' she said.

Fella stared across at the library, its red bricks soaking up the morning sun. So it was full of paperbooks? He could hardly imagine such a thing, what it could mean.

'It's what we've got to find out,' he said. 'We need to finish reading our own paperbook. And it can't hurt to find out what they write in theirs.'

T he library turned out to have far more in it than paperbooks. It had toilets and a free water dispenser, for a start.

But the thing that impressed Fella, the thing that seemed to thin the air so that his heart beat faster and he had to breathe deeper as he looked around him, was the sheer presence of the paperbooks.

They'd walked up the wide, shallow steps to a double door of coloured glass and stood in front of it, uncertain that they really had the right to go any further, despite the little card clutched damply in Grebe's hand. But then the decision had been taken from them, because suddenly half the door had opened and a woman with a pushchair and a toddler was struggling through.

Fella sprang forward to hold the other half of the door.

'Thanks,' smiled the woman.

But Fella hardly heard her. Now he was inside the building and could see, stretching up ahead of him, a grand staircase with a thick red carpet. There was more coloured glass in a window on the landing. But the thing that hit him in the chest was the glimpse of the rooms either side of the hallway.

These rooms had ceilings at twice, maybe three times, his own height. And the walls were full of shelves and the shelves full of paperbooks.

Fella let go of the door and heard Grebe's indignant yelp as she caught it. Suddenly she was beside him, and if she'd been about to complain of bruising, she too was silenced by what she saw.

And it wasn't only the sights. Suddenly, part of him was right back in the Orphanage and he couldn't understand why until he saw Grebe tilt her nose upwards and breathe in deeply.

Wood polish. It smelt like the polish they used at the Orphanage. A helpless longing drenched through him, knocking his mind and his senses off balance so that, for a moment, he had no idea where he was.

'Can I help you?' said a woman's voice.

They both spun round. They hadn't noticed the reception desk just inside the doorway, nor the woman behind it who was now smiling at them.

'Not been here before?' she said. She looked friendly, greying hair framing a pink-cheeked face. 'I can show you the ropes if you like.'

Fella didn't understand. Did they use ropes somehow to get the paperbooks down from the walls? But it didn't mean that. The way to get the paperbooks down, apparently, was to use a computer.

The woman took them to a screen that looked more or less like the ones at the Attainment Centre. If you wanted to read one of the books, she explained, you had to find its title or number on the computer and then select it on the screen so that one of the attendants would know to go and fetch it for you, using a special ladder that ran around the room on a track.

'Are you familiar with this operating system?' asked the woman, pulling up a chair to sit beside them.

'Um . . . yes . . . ' Fella stared helplessly at the screen.

'I'm not,' said Grebe. 'Can you show us?'

'No problem. If you know the name of the book or its number you can type that in here,' she showed them. 'Or if you don't know that—if you just want to search for books on a particular subject—then you type in the subject. That'll give you all the books we have on that subject, plus their numbers. What would you like to research?'

Fella couldn't think. Then Grebe said, 'The Satellite Islands!'

He shot her a warning look, but she was staring at the screen.

'OK,' said the woman. 'We type in "Satellite Islands" and here we are . . . a list comes up showing all the books on that subject in order of difficulty. So that's the children's books first, going right the way through to the very academic stuff. You can highlight the numbers of the books you want to order like this.'

Grebe smiled up at the woman, 'Oh, thank you!'

'You're welcome,' said the woman. 'Anything else you

want to know, you can ask me or one of the other librarians.'

While Grebe was ordering her paperbooks about the Satellite Islands, Fella found himself a desk in a quiet corner and sat down to look at their own paperbook. He'd forgotten how hard it was to wade through the pen-writing and it didn't help that he'd lost his place, so when Grebe came to ask how it was going, he wasn't in a great mood.

'What?' he said, irritably, as she slumped down beside him.

'Only asking.' She frowned. 'I think I'll have a look around while I wait for my paperbooks. I've asked them to bring them here, to this desk.'

'Yeah, OK.'

She shrugged and wandered off and Fella turned back to the paperbook. He remembered where he'd got to now. His mother was really frightened because of how her friend Alex had been when they'd met in the medi-centre grounds. He'd told her to get off the Island—he'd been drinking and crying and seemed terrified.

And then she'd found out she was going to have a baby. Him.

Fella sighed and smoothed the page in front of him. He wasn't even sure that he wanted to know any more of this story. Stupid woman! Why hadn't she listened to her friend?

Chapter 36

Grebe wandered out into the hallway, not liking how she was feeling. She should be more tolerant, more understanding of what Fella's life had been like and what he was feeling now. But she was too cross to be tolerant. She didn't like the way he snapped at her when he felt like it. None of this was *her* fault . . .

Now she was feeling sorry for herself, and she didn't like feeling like that either.

She should focus on the problems to be solved. Like how not to starve. How not to smell. How long they could live in a bush.

Talking of smell . . .

Somebody, somewhere, was cooking something.

She turned towards the staircase. The rich, meaty smell was coming from that direction. There was an open door to the right of the staircase and beside it an arrow, pointing down a corridor, and a sign marked 'Café'. Immediately her mouth watered. She swallowed hard. She shouldn't go down that corridor. It would only make matters worse.

But she went anyway. She couldn't help it.

As she walked down, the smell built, and, with it, a muffled babble of voices and clinking of china. Just before she
reached a glass door at the end, a sudden loud burst of
laughter sent a wave of loneliness over her. She felt like she
had often felt at the Attainment Centre. Plenty of people
around, but not one of them a friend.

The smell of food was so overpowering now that she was
almost crying with hunger. She put a hand to the glass door.
At a table to one side in the café ahead, she could see a
large group of people from this morning's talk, all gabbling
away. They'd been eating, she saw, and one of them . . .
juices rose in her mouth again . . . one of them had left half
a plate of that delicious-smelling meat dish.

She pushed at the door.

As she did so, some of the group were getting up to
leave. She found an empty chair at the very end of their
table and sat, her eyes fixed on the plate of leftover food.

Now they were all leaving. Some of them were kissing
each other, saying, 'See you next week . . . no, forgot, can't
make it . . . which book are we doing next time? . . . hell,
I'll never read that by then . . . '

By ones and twos the chattering group drifted away and
now there was just one woman left. Grebe kept the plate in
the corner of her vision. It lay just an arm's-stretch away.
Then, to her horror, the woman started to clear the plates,
clattering her way down the table, nearer and nearer. No,
no! She felt so desperate she wanted to scream at the
woman to go away.

The woman was just reaching out her hand towards Grebe's plate when a man bounded back through the door and grabbed her. 'Come *on*! You're doing the waitress out of a job!'

And the woman smiled, 'OK, OK!' She put the plates down again, and left.

The moment the glass door closed, Grebe seized the plate, grabbed the knife and fork resting on it, and began shovelling the food down. It was lukewarm, but she didn't care. She didn't care that she was using someone else's knife and fork or that people might be watching her.

The food was finished too quickly. She could have eaten ten times more. And as she scraped hungrily at the last little pools of gravy, her mind was racing on just how they were going to eat—today, tomorrow, and all the days after that.

Chapter 37

June 10

I've not slept well in recent nights—almost a week. Not because of the baby. It's because of worrying about what happened to Alex. I haven't seen him again. I went looking for him that day and the next, but no one would give out any information about where he was or when his leave began. Worse than that, a couple of the juniors I asked looked nervous at the mention of his name. One denied knowing him, but I think she was lying.

They're so hot on security around the Special Surgical Unit. And because it's way down below ground level it's not easily accessible from the rest of the medi-centre. The first time I managed to get down into the main corridor of the Unit, a senior consultant saw me talking to a junior. He told me to leave immediately. The second time I was caught I got a formal reprimand, so I daren't try going down there again.

I've been turning Alex's words—and the way he

*looked—over and over in my mind. He really meant it.
I can't decide what to do now. Because of the baby, my
instinct is to run back home. But what then? I can't
make a life with Silas. I don't love him any more. Or
rather, I don't respect him any more, for all his
reputation, his position, and his wealth. And if you don't
respect someone, how can you love them?*

*At least if I stay here I'm well camouflaged—no
media attention, no paparazzi clamouring to get the
gossip on why Silas's wife has left him.*

*Thank goodness Farl has gone. Even though he
doesn't work for Silas any more, there was always the
chance that he'd report back to him. And what would
Silas do if he knew about the baby? I doubt he'd
actually come and get me himself. But he'd send
someone to get me.*

F ella stopped reading and looked up into the silence
of the room around him. The walls of paperbooks,
the librarian behind her counter, the elderly man
shuffling across the room with a bundle of papers in his
arms. Normal-looking inhabitants of a new, abnormal
world.

The man called Silas was her husband. His father. And his
father was well-known—or had been fifteen years ago. And
his mother hadn't loved or . . . what was the word? . . .
respected his father any more.

He blinked and rubbed his eyes. He couldn't make it feel
true. Nothing felt real or true any more.

He flicked forwards, hungry to see his own arrival. But a page fell open and the name Farl caught his attention again.

December 15
*Someone watching the house last night and they're still
there now. Have not dared to go into work. My only hope
now is to try to drive to the Glass House that Farl told me
about. Will try to get us clear of the house tonight, and
when we get home, the truth about Silas will be heard, no
matter what the cost. I hate him. I feel sick that I am
married to such a monster.*

He turned the page for more. There was no more. He turned back to find the date of that last entry. December 15. It meant nothing to him. He'd been left at the Orphanage in a wintermonth. That was all he knew. He began to tremble. He couldn't know for sure, but he felt it—that these few words must have been written just before she was killed. For some reason she'd decided to do what Farl had told her and go to the Glass House. Fella saw again the thin face with its piercing eyes. Had he killed her?

He sat, staring at nothing, seeing only Farl's face, until a movement caught his eye and he saw that Grebe was back at the reception counter. The librarian was showing her something on a computer. Grebe was peering at the screen and nodding, her expression a mixture of anxiety and fascination. What was she doing now? Messing around with the computer when he needed her! He willed her to stop it, to come over and . . . help him.

But how could she help? How could anyone help?

Now she glanced over at him with a big smile, thanked the librarian, and made her way back to him across the silent room.

As she approached their desk, she cried, 'The librarian's just shown me the most amazing thing!'

The man on the nearest desk looked up with a frown and Grebe flashed him an apologetic look.

'It's incredible,' she whispered. 'It's called . . . what's the matter?'

Fella found that she was looking straight into him with wide, earnest eyes.

'My father—the man called Silas . . . ' he said.

'Silas,' she said, watching him cautiously. 'What does it say about him?'

He didn't answer.

'Fella?' she said gently.

'He was famous,' said Fella. 'My mother left him. She was trying to find out about part of the medi-centre that he was funding.'

'So he was very rich?'

'Yes. At first she says she didn't love him any more. And then . . . '

'What?'

'She ended up hating him.'

'And he was someone really important?'

'Maybe he still is,' he said. 'There's no way of finding out.'

And now he really needed to find out. Saying she didn't

love him was one thing. But what had happened to make her hate him and feel sick that she was paired with him? What was the truth that she'd wanted to tell? Something bad about his father. The same thing that had frightened this Alex guy? Maybe he didn't want to know. With a shiver, he slapped the paperbook shut and pushed it away from him. It slid to a stop in the middle of the polished desktop.

Grebe looked at him, her mouth slightly skewed to one side. It was what she did sometimes when she was thinking, as if she was chewing the inside of her cheek.

'There is,' she said.

'Is what?'

'A way of finding out about Silas.'

'How?'

She seemed to know a lot, all of a sudden.

'They have a thing here called the Internet,' she said. 'It's what the librarian was showing me. I couldn't ask too much, but I think it's like a sort of . . . I don't know, we don't have anything like it. You type in a subject and get information, so perhaps you can type in—'

'A name?'

'Yes.'

'Show me.'

She nodded to a row of computers behind a glass screen in the corner of the room. 'There's no one using those over there. Come on.'

Chapter 38

'**Y**ou key in the name there,' said Grebe, 'and then click where it says "search".'

She couldn't help liking this—being the one who knew how to do something, for a change.

He keyed in the name Silas. She saw his fingers hesitate. Then he clicked.

A long list came up with the word Silas highlighted in various titles.

Fella breathed out, a long, shaky breath. Grebe took a glimpse at his profile, his jaw clenching, his eyes locked fiercely onto the screen. He was on his own with all these feelings of bewilderment, hope, and fear. All she could do was just sit alongside and watch.

He began his investigation. The first Silas was a twelve-year-old celebrity, it seemed. The second and third were only in their twenties.

'He's got to be at least thirty-five now, maybe older,' said Grebe, 'Try the next one.'

The fourth Silas on the list was called Silas Lindberg and

he was President of a big business called Lindberg International Insurances.

'Doesn't necessarily make him famous, though, does it?' said Fella.

Grebe shuffled closer on her chair.

'You can try and see if there are any pictures of these people,' she said. 'Just click on "images" up there.'

'How would that help?' he said. It didn't matter what the man looked like. You couldn't tell who your father was that way. 'How many people do you know who look like their parents?'

Grebe shrugged. 'None. Just thought it would be interesting.'

They had a look at Mr Lindberg, Fella leaning forward to peer at each of the dozen or so images that appeared on the screen. The man was pale, with gingerish hair. Perhaps he was about fifty, but it was hard to tell. In most of the pictures he was smiling.

And so it went on. Grebe could sense Fella's despair mounting. There was nothing he could grab hold of, no obvious clues, in any of the two or three pages of men that they tried. Most of them were too young, and a couple way too old. There was one guy of the right age, but it said that he'd been happily married for twenty years and had six children.

'And your mother definitely says she's Silas's wife?' said Grebe.

'Yes, of course,' snapped Fella, 'I wouldn't get that wrong, would I?'

'OK, I'm sorry.'

She was beginning to regret telling him about the

Internet. She should have tried first on her own, because she could see what this was doing to Fella. She hadn't pointed it out, but there was a tiny message at the top of the screen saying that there were over 5,000 entries on this list. They simply needed more information. And that meant going back to the paperbook.

'You could print up some details about the ones that are maybes,' she said. 'The businessman, the two doctors, and the builder. They're all about the right age.'

'Suppose so,' he said. 'Yeah, I will.'

And then they must try to get him something to eat. She noticed how his cheeks had sunk, how he looked so tired. There was a faint trace of stubble along his jawline.

They printed up a few pages. Grebe saw, with a pang, how Fella clutched at them, his eyes raking over them as if they might be hiding clues that he'd missed on the screen.

'Come on.' She put a hand on his arm and guided him back towards their desk.

As they approached the desk, Grebe saw its shiny wood surface. She saw the two chairs they'd pushed back in their hurry to get to the computer. Something gripped at her heart and she threw a glance at the desks nearby, thinking she must be mistaken, but she knew she wasn't. It *was* their desk. A sickening panic began to churn at her stomach.

'Fella . . . ?' She hardly dared say it. 'Fella, have you got the paperbook?'

'No. I left it—' He looked. 'What's that?'

He meant the thick brown package that sat where the paperbook had been.

Chapter 39

Fella let out a shout of rage.

He caught a movement from the librarian's counter and heard Grebe call out, 'It's nothing. We're fine.'

And then the package was in his hands. He'd had a desperate, stupid hope that somehow the paperbook might still be there underneath it. It wasn't.

The package was thick and heavy. He slumped onto the chair, clutching it.

Grebe had got down on her knees. Checking the floor. But Fella knew it was useless. He scanned the room, flicking from person to person. Who was missing? Who had taken the paperbook, put this in its place and left? But that was useless too. He hadn't taken much notice of the people in the room. There was a woman in a pale blue dress just heading out of the door now. He had no idea how long she'd been here. She looked normal and harmless enough—but how could you tell? You could *never* tell!

Grebe's head appeared at the edge of the desk. She

hauled herself up into the chair next to him and shook her head.

'It's gone,' she whispered.

'I need to get out of here,' he said.

'But . . . we'll never find . . . '

'No,' he said, 'it's gone.'

A cold realization was sliding into his thoughts. Bad enough that he'd lost the paperbook. Far worse—they'd been followed. Someone knew exactly where they were.

He began to peel back the tape that was sealing the package. Then Grebe nudged him and he looked up to see a thin, elderly man approaching. He stuffed the package out of sight under the desk.

The man was carrying a small stack of paperbooks. He smiled and put them down in front of Grebe.

'For you, miss,' he said. 'Happy reading.'

'Oh,' said Grebe. 'Um . . . did you pick up a book from this desk? We've lost one of ours . . . a brown cover . . . ' She trailed off because the man was already shaking his head.

'We only pick up the library books,' he said. 'They're all marked as ours. Private books we don't touch. Leave a note at the desk. Maybe someone's taken it by mistake. I'm sure they'll bring it back.' He patted the pile of paperbooks cheerfully and left.

'Yeah, I'm sure they will!' said Fella bitterly.

He glanced around the room again. No one seemed to be looking. Slowly, he shifted back in his seat and slid the package up his lap so that it was mostly hidden by the desk. He pulled off the rest of the tape and opened it.

He reached his hand in to draw out one of the bundles of paper that were tightly packed inside. He didn't understand what it was at first, and when he did, it didn't make any sense at all.

He looked up into Grebe's bewildered gaze.

'Money,' he whispered. 'Why would anyone do that?'

Chapter 40

Grebe scurried after Fella as he barged through the coloured glass doors and out into the hot sunshine. He flung himself down the steps and almost bumped into a woman in a pale blue dress, who had stopped to rummage in her handbag. He didn't even notice she was there.

By the time Grebe caught up, he was over by the bushes where they'd spent the night. He was stooping down to crawl back underneath the dense foliage. She looked around. There was no one about, except a man in a smart suit hurrying away from them down one of the garden's many paths. She waited until she thought she wouldn't be kicked in the face by Fella's retreating boots, then followed.

He was right, of course. This did seem to be the only place where they could have a good look at what was in that package. Away from whoever was watching.

He was sitting, leaning against the trunk. She wriggled in beside him.

'They must have been tracking us ever since we left the

Island,' he said. There was a kind of vicious, helpless anger in his voice. 'And that means that wherever we go, whatever we do, it's all completely useless.'

He ripped at the top of the package and shook its contents onto the earth between them. There was enough sunlight filtering through the leaves to see that there were dozens of bundles of money tokens—or what they would call tokens back on the Island. These, like the ones they were used to, had numbers printed on them. Most of the bundles were a pinkish colour, and these were marked 1,000. But there were plenty of blue and yellow ones marked 500 and 200 and some marked 100.

Fella picked up some of the bundles and flapped them in the still, earthy air.

'Who would want that paperbook so much that they'd do this?' he asked. 'Who would know enough about it to *know* that they wanted it in the first place?'

Grebe shifted away from him slightly. 'Perhaps . . . ' she hesitated, ' . . . don't you think that whoever left this actually wishes us well? That is, if it's real money.'

'Someone who wishes us well?' he cried. 'Someone who's stolen my property!'

'Yes, but they could have just stolen it. At least . . . '

'At least they paid for it, you mean?' He glared at her, his face hard with bitterness.

'When did you last eat?' she said.

'Yesterday . . . '

'Well, at least now we can buy food, is all I'm saying. I could go and get you something from the café in the library.'

'Don't be so stupid! We can't stay here. They know where we are!' Fella kicked out his legs, hitting a thick branch and making the whole bush shudder around them. 'We'll never be safe!'

And then she saw something amongst the bundles that wasn't a coloured note. A slip of white paper. She picked it up and saw something printed on it. She moved towards Fella and he snatched the paper from her hand. In a shaking voice, he read:

This should be enough to get you started in life over here. It will be best for you if you forget about the diary and everything in it. Enjoy your lives. Good luck.

He dropped his hand and squeezed the paper into a ball. 'Who?' he said. 'Who would do this?'

They'd been walking all afternoon, trying to get as far away as possible from the library, and now the heat of the day was fading. Grebe wasn't sure, but she thought they might even have been walking round in huge circles.

There were so many surprises, things you'd never see on the Island—winding streets with houses jumbled together, all different shapes and sizes and colours. Trees everywhere, which seemed to give the air its sweet, clean smell. There were grand, old stone buildings but also the more familiar brick and glass shopping malls. There were big, heavy buildings with strange towers, fat at the base and thin at the top, pointing up from the roofs.

There were buildings where the walls were all windows and she could see lots of people—grown-ups—sitting at desks in huge rooms. They were all looking at computers and she couldn't work out what this meant. There didn't seem to be any factory zones. But the one thing that was really strange—they hadn't seen one single Guard Post. Not one single person carrying a gun.

Fella was silent. He had drawn right into himself. She had seen him like this before, but never so bad. There'd been something in the paperbook he hadn't told her about, she was sure. He'd been determined to keep walking, switching direction again and again, fearful that they were still being followed. But she wasn't so sure about that. If whoever had been tracking them had got what they wanted, then they'd leave them alone, wouldn't they? *This should be enough to get you started in life over here. Enjoy your lives. Good luck.* It was what she wanted. To be here. Started in life. With Fella. The note made that feel almost possible.

The person who'd left the money wasn't interested in catching them and sending them back to the Island. Or, at least, that was what she was trying to make herself believe. But really, she didn't know what to think. The very fact that they had been watched frightened her. And, more than any-thing, she wanted to silence the voice inside her that was always telling her to be afraid.

She sighed and looked up as they turned another corner. Up ahead was what looked like a smaller version of a super-market. They'd passed several such places but Fella had refused to stop.

'Fella,' she put out a hand to make him slow down, 'we need to get some food.'

'What?'

He hadn't heard her. Still his face had that locked-down look.

'Give me some money.' She nodded towards the shop doors, where some people were picking up baskets and others were coming out with heavy bags. 'I'll get us some food.'

'Too dangerous,' he said.

'We've got to eat!'

He shrugged. 'Come on then, but we can't hang around.'

She found the part of the shop that had sandwiches and drinks, and quickly piled a whole load into her basket. Mostly cheese sandwiches. Suddenly, came a memory of how they used to share a sandwich lunch at the Attainment Centre. It was the only way they could be outside, together, in relative peace. He liked cheese best. As she stared into the chilled cabinet, the strength of the memory surprised her. The feel and colour of it, the remembered smell of hot tarmac, the thick mesh fencing with the weeds growing through that surrounded their own little corner of the recreation yard. Leaning back, touching shoulders, on their splintered wooden bench. She felt a sudden rush of misery. It wasn't that she missed the place. She missed the way she and Fella used to feel.

She looked around, with a ripple of panic, to see where he was.

He was over by the tills, reading some of the sheets of print that were sold alongside the sort of glossy magazines they had on the Island. As she reached him, he thrust the one he was reading into her basket and stood close behind her as she loaded the stuff onto the conveyor belt. As she watched it move towards the cashier, a slow burn of fear began. What if the note she had in her hand wasn't real money after all? She'd chosen a 200 one. Even if it was real, she had no way of knowing whether it was enough.

All the things had been checked through now. There was no getting out of it. Her hand shook as she held out the note.

'Oh, God, what's this?' said the man at the till, glaring at Grebe.

She waited, not knowing what to say. She sensed Fella tensing behind her.

The man shook his head and thumped at the till.

'Some of you kids've got more money than brains, ain't ya? This is more than my week's wages. It'll take all my change. Haven't you got anything smaller?'

Grebe stared, mute with fear. The man shook his head again and snatched the note from her. He raked around in his till and then slapped a wad of notes and several coins into her shaking hand.

They hurried out of the shop. Shaking, and scurrying to keep up with Fella, she tried to calculate what this meant. If 200 was more than a week's wages, however much money did that package have in it? A lot.

'Fella,' she said, 'all that money!'

But he was rummaging in the supermarket bag. He pulled out the bundle of printed pages and Grebe read, at the top of the first page, *Your World Today* and below that, *Inslannika's finest daily newspaper.*

'Inslannika?' she murmured. She'd seen that word

before. On Emmie's map! 'Fella,' she said, 'I think Inslannika is the name of where we are!'

He still wasn't listening. He was turning the pages of this newspaper thing, searching for something. He seemed to find it, read for a moment, then flapped and folded the papers angrily.

'What is it?'

'I thought it was something about this Silas Lindberg guy,' he said. 'Well, it was. But nothing of any use. Apparently he's given a whole load of money to a children's hospital, whatever that is. I think it's like a medi-centre.'

'Why?'

'Why what?'

'Why did he give the money?'

'How would I know? Maybe he likes children or feels sorry for them or . . . whatever.'

They'd reached a little courtyard place with a fountain in the middle. Grebe looked around, checking for cams. She couldn't see any, and there weren't any people about either. She sat down on the wall of the fountain and unwrapped some sandwiches. She handed one to Fella.

'Cheese,' she said.

'Thanks.'

They ate in silence. She watched him as he watched the water splashing into the pool.

'Fella . . . ?'

'Yeah?'

'Don't get cross. But . . . what else did your mother say about Silas?'

F ella looked at Grebe. Her mouth was squeezed into a half-smile but her eyes were full of anxiety.

'There *is* something else, isn't there?' she said.

He could never hide anything from Grebe for long. Sometimes it was annoying, but sometimes, like now, it was a relief. He huffed out a sigh.

'I think he did something really terrible,' he said, 'but I didn't get a chance to find out what. In the last bit she wrote, she said she'd found out the truth. And then she said . . . ' he could remember the exact words, ' . . . she said, "I hate him. I feel sick that I am married to such a monster".'

Grebe glanced down at the water and said nothing.

'Yeah, sounds bad, doesn't it?' he said.

'D'you have any idea what she could have meant?'

'She was trying to find out about this Special Surgical Unit. It's undergound at the medi-centre . . . '

Suddenly he saw again that long, pink corridor. The two frightened children. Surely that couldn't be it, the Special Surgical Unit?

'What's the matter?' said Grebe.

It could be. How far down had he gone in that elevator? He couldn't remember.

'Fella!' Grebe tugged at his arm. 'What is it?'

'Nothing, I . . . it's just that I think . . . whatever happens in that Unit, it could be something to do with children.'

'Children? What . . . making sick children well, you mean?'

'No. Something bad. I don't know.'

He was trying to remember everything he could about that escape through the medi-centre. But apart from those two children, it was Farl's face that he saw most clearly. That anger. His long, thin face contorted with pain when he'd thrust that tea trolley at him.

'I think it was Farl who took the paperbook, or someone acting on his orders. That's what he was after all along! I think it was Farl who followed us to the Glass House—the lights on the cliff. It was never the Officiate. It was Farl. After *me* because of the paperbook!'

'So . . . is Farl trying to stop anyone knowing this "truth" that your mother was talking about?'

'Yes! Because he used to work for this Silas Lindberg!'

'Or is he trying to find out the truth for himself?'

He looked at her. She was right. It could be either.

'I don't know. My mother was trying to leave the Island when she was killed. She was heading for the Glass House because Farl had told her about it. But . . . I don't know whether he really intended to help her or . . . whether he did just the opposite.'

'You think he killed her?'

'It's possible, isn't it?'

They fell silent for a while, listening to the fizz of the fountain.

He shifted on the wall, feeling the weight of the money pack inside his jacket. Grebe voiced the question.

'But if it was him, why would he give us all that money?'

He could think of no possible reason.

'And . . . ' her voice was thin with anxiety, 'how did he find us?'

He kept his eyes focused on the splashes of water from the fountain. A terrible thought was edging into his mind. His mother had talked about 'tracking chips'. He hadn't quite understood it. But it was obvious that they'd been followed really easily.

'Fella,' she said, 'what are you thinking? How did he find us?'

He turned to her, his glance falling on the pale skin of her neck.

'I don't know,' he said, 'but they can track us somehow.'

'With drones?'

'Maybe.'

'So they'll send us back?'

He tipped his head back and closed his eyes. He could feel a fine, misty spray from the fountain. He knew what he had to do. He'd known it since the paperbook was taken.

'I've got to find my father, Grebe. It's the only way we'll ever feel safe here. If I can find my father and find out the truth.'

'But . . . does he know about you?'

He realized that he didn't know the answer to that question either.

'Anybody's guess.' He shrugged. 'I don't even know if my mother told him she was having a baby!'

He opened his eyes and, seeing her troubled face, smiled.

Her eyes filled with tears.

'What?' he said.

'Nothing. It's just so good to see you smile!'

So he smiled again, even though he didn't feel like it.

'No one's caught us yet,' he said, 'so we'll just keep going. It's all we can do.'

She brushed at her eyes and nodded.

Yes, he had to find his father. But did he really *want* to? It looked as though his mother wouldn't have wanted him to.

They finished their sandwiches and shoved the litter in a bin. Just beside the bin, Fella noticed, was a board like the one outside the library, showing a map with an arrow marked 'You are here'.

'They're keen on this "You are here" business, aren't they?' he said. 'Shame we haven't a clue where we *really* are.'

'We do have a clue,' said Grebe, 'two, to be precise. This Island—or whatever they call it here—is called Inslannika, and the city is . . . Tomp . . . what did you say Jerry called it?'

'Um . . . Tompalla, I think.'

'Well, then. Oh, look!' She pointed to a box below the board. 'You can buy a map, if you have the right token.'

He watched her fish around in her pocket for the change the guy at the supermarket had given her. All day, he'd felt anger clenched up inside him, making his stomach ache, making his mind ache. *It will be best for you if you forget about the diary and everything in it.* How *dare* anybody say what was best for him! He was still angry, but it was a calmer sort of anger. He was beginning to see a way forward. They weren't stupid. They could learn about this place and how to survive in it. And whatever the truth was, it was better to know.

Grebe had found a token and was now pressing it into the slot in the box. There was a clink. A little folded map fell into her hands. She smiled up at him.

'Right,' she said, '"We are here"!'

F ella peered through the window of the Internet café. The list of useful places at the edge of the map had told them about it and he'd managed to follow the map to get them here. He was feeling pleased with himself.

'It looks like one of our computer game cafés, but nicer,' said Grebe.

'Much nicer. No tabbacaseed, no brain-damage music, no idiots.'

There were several youngish men in smart suits staring at computer screens or suddenly tapping away at the keyboards. There was an old man and woman, huddled together uncomfortably on the high stools, grinning and giggling at their screen, and a few others, perhaps a little older than he and Grebe. The idea seemed to be that you could get coffee and food while you looked at the Internet.

They went in and found a girl with long black hair behind the counter.

'Hi, welcome!' she said. She looked him full in the face

and smiled. She seemed so relaxed, so confident. Everyone here did.

They paid for two coffees and an hour on the Internet. Fella hurried over to a free computer at the back of the café, where it was quiet, leaving Grebe to bring the coffee. He'd had an idea and he had to go through with it quickly, without thinking too much about what he might find.

The screen was already set up to search, so he typed Silas. Then he checked the date on the top of *Your World Today* and made a quick calculation.

'Where shall we start?' said Grebe, setting down the coffees and pulling up a stool.

'In the wintermonths just after I was born,' he said.

He felt her breath on his cheek as she leaned to look at the screen. 'Oh! You mean, the time your mother was killed?'

'Exactly. If any of these Silas guys had a wife who died suddenly fifteen and a half years ago . . . '

He keyed in what he reckoned to be the right date, and clicked search.

A list of references came up. A lot of them featured Mr Lindberg.

His glance slid down the screen, scrolling one page . . . another. Beside him, Grebe sat tense, sipping her coffee. It was taking a long time. Maybe he'd got the calculation wrong.

Then his attention snagged on a headline. He leaned forward, his heart pounding.

ELIZA LINDBERG DIES IN CAR CRASH.
BEAUTIFUL YOUNG WIFE OF SILAS LINDBERG . . .

The date was December 20. Five days after the day of the last paperbook entry.

Instinctively, he shot the cursor to the top of the screen and clicked on *image*.

A woman's face filled the screen and he fell back, almost tipping himself off the stool.

He heard Grebe's shocked intake of breath.

It was incredible. Her eyes were the same as his. The thick, dark hair, the high forehead. As his tears blurred the image, she looked even more like him.

'Eliza Lindberg!' whispered Grebe.

He wiped his eyes and stared again.

'Are you all right?' she said.

He nodded, still lost in this face and all the things it meant. A connection. So strange, to look like another person!

'It's *amazing*!' cried Grebe. 'She really *looks* like you— you look like *her*! That's really weird. I can't think of *anyone* who looks like their mum or dad, can you?'

'Just tell me what you see,' he said.

'She . . . she looks kind. She looks honest. Her eyes are like yours. She looks as if she's about to laugh at something. I don't know . . . playful. Like you when you're in a good mood.'

'So I'm not wrong, am I? It's her.'

'It *has* to be,' said Grebe.

His mind was racing. He'd found her. Eliza. Which meant that this Silas Lindberg, this famous businessman, this giver of money to a children's medi-centre . . . this really *was* his father. Should he feel glad? He didn't. He didn't feel anything.

'Don't you want to print her picture?' asked Grebe softly.

'Yeah, OK.'

But he couldn't move to do it. Not yet.

She leaned across and clicked to print the picture for him. The printer gave a quiet whirring noise and with soft, pulsing strokes, the picture of Eliza began to grow from the machine.

He blinked at his mother's emerging hair, forehead . . . Then he clicked back to the news story. It continued:

The 32-year-old, who married Mr Lindberg only three years ago, was involved in a head-on collision whilst holidaying alone in the premier coastal resort of Rimmeri. Mrs Lindberg was killed outright. Her husband, who is said by close friends to be distraught at the death, has had the body flown home in a private jet. The other driver is recovering in hospital.

Although there has been speculation of a rift in the couple's marriage, police are not treating the death as suspicious.

'Rimmeri!' said Grebe. 'I've never heard of that place, have you?'

Fella shook his head. What did this mean? His mother was killed not far from the Orphanage, he knew that, because Papa Louis had told him about the young Guard who'd brought him in. But there was nowhere called Rimmeri . . . and the Orphanage was nowhere near a 'premier coastal resort'.

Then he understood.

'It's a cover-up,' he said. 'They didn't want anyone to know she was on the Island!'

'Shhh!' Grebe twitched her head towards two suited guys who were sitting nearby. But they weren't listening. They were making some sort of jeering joke about the black-haired girl.

He read the lines again, struggling to feel the meaning beneath them. Her own husband had lied about the crash . . . or, at the very least, allowed a lie . . .

'He knew where she was,' he said, 'and he wanted her to go home.'

And the other thing about the report was . . .

'There's no mention of you!' said Grebe.

'No.'

There was another picture at the bottom of the print. He enlarged it and saw this Lindberg man, the man he was now supposed to believe was his father. The face was drawn into a tight mask of sorrow. Fella flinched at the caption: *The distraught magnate mourns his lost love.*

He stared at the man's face and felt nothing. Why should he? He'd gone searching for a father but now he'd found him, he didn't want him. It seemed so obvious now. Papa Louis was his father and he didn't want to think of anybody else in that way.

'What are you going to do?' said Grebe.

His head was beginning to ache. He rubbed his eyes.

'I don't know. I need to find out more about him.'

'I wonder what he'll say . . . '

She trailed off. But Fella knew what she meant. There was so much of this that felt wrong, so much they didn't know about Silas Lindberg. So much the man himself didn't know, it seemed. What *would* he say if he knew he had a son? If they met?

No matter how much he stared at the picture, he couldn't make himself believe this was his father.

Suddenly he caught a movement behind them and looked round to see the black-haired girl with a tray of mugs.

'Not rushing you, but we'll be closing up in ten minutes,' she said. 'There's still some coffee left in the machine— needs finishing up, if you'd like a freebee.'

'Oh. Right.' Fella glanced at the window. It was dark outside and their hour was running out. There were only them and the two suited guys left in the café.

'No thanks,' he said, 'we're nearly finished.'

He wanted to ask her whether there was anywhere nearby to sleep but he didn't want to draw attention.

Then Grebe said, 'Is there anywhere round here we could stay the night?'

'Nothing nearby,' said the girl. 'What're you looking for? Hostel? Guest house? Hotel?'

'Anything,' said Grebe.

The girl swept a glance up and down them. 'Your best bet's to get the choob back to town,' she said. 'Head for Maple Vale. A lot of young people stay there.'

'Oh,' said Grebe, 'OK, thanks.'

She turned back to him with a sad shrug. They had no idea what the choob was or where to find it.

Carefully, he folded the picture of Eliza and tucked it in beside the money package inside his jacket.

'Looks like another night in a park,' he muttered.

Chapter 44

Grebe linked her arm through Fella's as they strolled along the dark street. They were walking past houses, terraced like the C-grade areas, except these houses didn't have high walls in front of them. You could see straight in through some of the brightly-lit windows. It felt wrong, but comforting too, to see these little glimpses of other people's lives. A bit like spying on people as they sat snuggled on a sofa, or sharing a meal, or . . . there was one woman carefully brushing a little girl's long, blonde hair.

She saw that Fella was looking too.

'They seem to like children here, don't they?' she said.

'We haven't seen enough to tell,' said Fella. 'I wonder what their Attainment Centres are like.'

'Must be better than ours. Emmie had loads of paperbooks and she was learning to pen-write. And she was only six. D'you think all children here are like her?'

'Who knows? There's so much to find out,' he said. 'But we will. We can survive here if we can learn to fit in. We'll go back to the Internet café tomorrow, shall we?'

'Yeah.'

And where would that lead? Would they try and meet Mr Lindberg? She felt uneasy about this, and she sensed that Fella did too. But she didn't want to ask him. It was too soon.

They came to the end of the row of houses and Fella stopped under a streetlamp to look at their map. She still couldn't feel safe stopping near these lamps and she glanced upwards nervously. Just as she did, a scream slashed the evening air.

Fella looked up, his eyes fierce, listening for the direction of the sound. It came again, sharper, more desperate.

Fella thrust the map at her and spun towards the sound. He hesitated a second, then ran towards a scrubby piece of land where dark, angular shapes pierced the skyline. As she ran after him and her eyes grew accustomed to the semi-dark, she saw that it was a children's playground with the outline of a hut to one side. It looked horribly like a Guards' hut.

The screams were coming faster and louder and she thought she heard a shout too. Or was it Fella shouting as he leapt over the playground's fence and hurled himself at the door of the hut?

There was a sound of splintering wood and Fella disappeared through the door. It was all happening so fast that Grebe couldn't understand it, didn't know what to do to make it stop. Fella was a good fighter. All the kids at the

Orphanage knew it and they'd look to him for protection. But here the rules were different. He shouldn't get involved. Desperately, she yelled after him.

More shouts, and two men, youngish, ran from the hut, stumbling over the shattered door. One was wiping at his mouth. They came straight at her and she had no time to move. The bigger one pushed her, hard, in the chest and she fell, cracking her head against the fence.

She blinked. There was something running into her eye. She wiped at it, squinting and blinking to pick out the two blurred figures heading away down the street, hunched together in a staggering run.

'Grebe!' She heard a scuffing of gravel and Fella was down beside her. 'What did they do?'

'Only pushed me.'

'You're bleeding!'

'It's opened up the cut again.'

She heard a stifled sob. A female voice. She was vaguely aware of someone leaning against the fence above her. As Fella helped her to her feet, she saw it was the dark-haired girl from the Internet café.

'Are you OK?' She put a hand to the girl's arm and found that they were both shaking.

Now the girl gave a great, shuddering sob and Grebe stood, looking on, feeling helpless. Then she put an arm around the girl and tried to comfort her.

'Are you all right?' she said. 'They didn't . . . ?'

'No,' cried the girl, 'thanks to him.'

'What's your name?' asked Fella.

'Josie.'

'Do you live near here?'

'Not far.'

Grebe looked at Fella. She could see what he was thinking. They shouldn't risk getting involved, but . . .

'We'll walk you home,' he said.

Chapter 45

I t was a couple of streets away. A white terraced house with tall windows. As Josie opened the little front gate, it whined on its hinges.

'We'll wait here till you're safely in,' said Fella.

He was still feeling shaken-up himself. It was only after it was all over that he'd thought about what could have happened. They were bigger than him. They might have had guns, knives—anything. But then, it was clear what those men had been intending. Ripping at her blouse as he'd pulled them off. Scum. He was pretty sure he'd broken a nose, and he wasn't sorry.

'No,' said Josie, in a wobbly voice, 'you needed somewhere to stay. Stay here. My landlady won't mind.'

'Oh . . . no. We can't,' said Grebe.

'It's no trouble. Beatrice has loads of room—her kids have all left home. What's happened to my keys . . . ?'

But before she could find them, the big black front door opened. A large woman was filling the doorway.

'Oh, Beatrice!' cried Josie. She flung herself at the

woman and was wrapped in a hug that stifled her sobs.

The next thing that happened took everyone by surprise. A large, honey-coloured dog hurtled past the woman, barking loudly, and threw itself at Grebe. Grebe screamed.

The woman looked over Josie's head. 'Don't let him frighten you!' she bellowed. 'He only wants to play!'

The dog had its paws on Grebe's chest and they were both disappearing into the hedge. Between barks, it was trying to lick her face.

'What the hell . . . ?' yelled the woman again. 'Hero, will you shut up, we can't hear ourselves think! In you come! Come on!'

Fella wasn't sure if she meant them or the dog. Either way, they must leave now.

Grebe sprang back out of the hedge as the dog released her and bounded back up the path and into the house. Now the woman was heading towards them. She grabbed hold of Fella with surprising force.

'Come in, dear boy. And your friend. Come in, come in. Tell me what's happened. Oh God, you're bleeding, girl! Come in!'

They were taken into a kitchen at the back of the house and the woman called Beatrice poured them all small glasses of tea-coloured drink while Josie told her story. The men had jumped her from behind and dragged her into the hut. Fella had rescued her. If it hadn't been for him . . . she broke down sobbing again.

'Right,' said Beatrice, 'you three put together all you can remember while I call the police.'

Fella looked at Grebe. They both remembered that word. 'Police' was what Jerry had said. So it meant Officiate, or something like.

'We can't remember anything,' said Fella.

'You must remember *something*. You thumped one of them, didn't you?' said Beatrice.

'We've really got to go now.' He stood up.

But Beatrice was blocking the doorway. Josie looked up, a puzzled expression in her swollen eyes, then she said, 'It's all right. I know who it was. And they'll be on the security cameras.'

Fella's stomach was already churning. Now he felt really sick.

'Will they?' said Beatrice. 'Are you sure?'

'Yes,' said Josie. 'It was a couple of guys . . . ' Her face twisted and she scrubbed a hand across her forehead. ' . . . they've been hanging around the café the last few weeks. City types. I thought they were just joking around. I thought I'd handled it. They must have waited and followed me . . . '

'So they were in the café tonight?' said Beatrice.

Josie nodded.

'And they'll definitely be on the security cameras?'

'Yes. The cameras are on all the time.'

'It's still your word against theirs. We'll still need these two as witnesses.'

Beatrice looked at Fella. She seemed to have the same knack of looking straight into you that Grebe had. It wasn't an unkind face, but it was firm. Large, bright eyes with arched eyebrows that made the face look startled. The face also looked as if it had been boiled, but perhaps that was because she was angry and worried about Josie.

'Well?' she said. She was still blocking the door.

'We have to go,' he said again.

'That's disappointing,' said Beatrice, 'because perhaps next time these bastards will actually succeed in raping someone.'

Josie was looking at him too. And Grebe. He felt sweat begin to trickle.

'We can't . . . '

'We can't help you,' said Grebe suddenly. The blood had dried on her forehead. She looked hopelessly pale.

'We can't,' she said. 'We can't afford to get arrested.'

'Now we're getting somewhere,' said Beatrice. 'Why should the police arrest you? What have you done?'

'We've run away from home,' said Grebe, 'because my parents were trying to force me to get married.'

Fella stared at her. This was no lie. But it was a terrible risk.

Beatrice let out a wail that ripped across the tension in the room, '*Marry?* Look at you, scrap of a thing! How old are you?'

'Almost sixteen.'

'*Marry?* At *sixteen*? Good God, that's preposterous!'

Fella didn't know what she meant, but it sounded about right. Grebe pressed home her advantage.

'So if we're caught and sent home, that's it. We might as well be dead.'

Again, no lie.

Fella stared at Grebe's fragile, stubborn little face and a wave of feeling hit him. Feeling that he couldn't name.

'I see,' said Beatrice. 'Then you have three options. You leave now and give no statement to the police. Or you give a statement under false names, which is perjury. Or you give a statement under your real names and hope that you won't be called to court or, if you are, your families won't get wind of it. I'm going to call the police now. I should think you'll have about ten minutes in which to scarper if you want to.'

Beatrice left the doorway and went to the other end of the room to make her call. If they were going to run, this was their chance. Fella threw an urgent look at Grebe and caught the look of confusion on Josie's face. Then Josie turned to pat Grebe on the hand. 'You know,' she said, 'by law, your parents can't force you to marry against your will.'

Anger and frustration were fighting it out inside him. It would help if they understood the things that were being said. Law, statements, perjury. Behind him, he could hear Beatrice talking to these police people. Were they like the Officiate? Did they perhaps have links to the Officiate?

Now Grebe was saying something to him. 'We'll be on the security cameras too.'

She was right. If they ran, they'd look guilty. It could make things a whole lot worse.

The dog called Hero padded over to him and slumped against his leg. Beatrice had finished her call and was filling a bowl with water. Now she began dabbing at Grebe's cut forehead. Mid-dab, she looked up at him, as if she had felt him watching. A twist of grey hair escaped from the multi-coloured scarf wound round her head. And as she turned back to smile at Grebe, a dimple snuggled down into each plump cheek.

'You could just tell the truth,' she said. 'Josie's right. You'd have the protection of the law.'

Nobody spoke. As Beatrice produced a strip of dressing for Grebe, new beads of red began to glisten along the line of the cut. Josie took another sip of her drink, both hands gripping the glass. The dog sighed and slumped heavily onto Fella's feet.

And then the doorbell rang.

There was a man and a woman, both dressed in green uniforms with hats and fluorescent strips. Fella scrutinized this clothing as closely as he dared. It didn't seem to be concealing any weapons. They seated themselves at the kitchen table and began asking their questions, of Josie first. He heard how brave he had been, how he'd smashed one of the guys in the face and the other had run off.

Then they turned to him. The police woman first. She had a little black box, about the size of a tabbacaseed carton, fixed on her right shoulder. Once or twice a crackly voice had come out of it and she'd answered it. He'd tried to keep his face neutral, not to look surprised by anything he saw or heard. Inside he was churning with panic. He wasn't even sure he could control his bladder or bowels. Or his voice.

'Now,' said the police woman, 'am I to take it that you'll give us a statement about what happened?'

Fella nodded, numb with fear. They would surely see it.

Suddenly, a voice came from the box on the police woman's shoulder.

'Excuse me,' she said. And she got up to leave the room, talking into her shoulder as she went.

Fella looked across at Grebe's pale face. Too late to run now.

The police woman came back.

'Right,' she said, 'they'll be ready for an identity parade as soon as we can get you there.'

'Identity . . . ?' said Grebe.

'Get where?' said Fella.

'The police station,' she said. 'It won't take long.'

Fella watched the streetlamps stripe by as the police car carried them through the quiet streets, back past the children's playground, the terraced houses, and the Internet café.

How had this happened? Was it a trick? Had they been watched, followed, and trapped? Would this car fail to stop at the police station or anywhere else? Would it carry them all the way back to the Island? He couldn't see Grebe, who sat silently on the other side of Josie. Where was Beatrice? She'd said she'd follow on in her own car, but that may have been a lie. If she'd already done her job in trapping them and calling the Officiate.

The car did stop. Outside a wide, tall building that was all windows. But windows that you couldn't see into. As Fella looked up, just before the police man took his elbow and guided him in through the automatic doors, all he could see was a cliff of black glass rearing up into the paler black of the night.

They were taken down long, plain corridors. Terror was

pulsing in his head as they turned a corner and saw a metal arch, a sort of gateway, ahead. He felt Grebe's hand slip into his. Was this the gateway to a pod station? A gateway back to the Island?

He heard heavy footsteps behind them, someone puffing, and, judging from the pitch of the puffs, it was a woman. He turned to see Beatrice.

'Blasted warren of a place!' she cried. 'God knows if I'll ever find the car again! And if I get a parking ticket I'll bite someone!' She swept a glance round the group. 'Cheer up! All be over soon!'

'We just need to get you all through security screening,' said the police woman. 'I need you to place all your belongings in this tray, being careful to include all metal objects—watches, jewellery, mobile phones, coins—then walk through the arch.'

'Darned rigmarole!' muttered Beatrice as she twiddled with her earrings.

Fella's heartbeat was punching his breath away. This machine would surely detect his terror. Yet he could not run. There was nowhere left to run to.

Josie and Beatrice went through the arch and stood, as directed, with their arms held out while a new police woman patted up and down their bodies. Another woman sat at a monitor, watching the things in the trays as they passed through a covered conveyor belt.

'OK, mate,' called the police man.

This meant him. He put the envelope of money in the tray and stepped forward. Through the arch. Held out his arms. Tried to stop himself trembling as the strange hands patted his body. The woman finished and stood back.

'All clear. Thank you, you can collect your things,' she said.

He stuffed the envelope back into his jacket and turned back to see the blank terror on Grebe's face as she waited to come through. He tried to give her an encouraging look. She walked forwards until she was level with the metal sides of the arch. Then she took another step.

And suddenly the air was pulsing with a high-pitched siren.

Grebe froze, looking around her with huge, helpless eyes. Then she put her hands to her ears, closed her eyes and hugged her head down onto her chest.

The police woman stepped forward.

'Leave her alone!' yelled Fella. 'She hasn't done anything!'

The siren died and a tense silence flooded into its place.

Then Beatrice's voice: 'Blimey! You can tell these two have never been near a police station in their lives. Don't panic, boy! They're not going to shoot her.'

The police woman had reached Grebe. 'Any jewellery you've forgotten?' she asked. 'Any body piercing?'

But Grebe wasn't hearing her. She was still hugged-up, eyes squeezed shut, unable to move.

Gently, the police woman touched her. 'Hey there! It's OK.'

She repeated her question and at last Grebe looked up and shook her head.

'No?' said the police woman. 'OK, then go back and we'll try it again. It may be something wrong with the machine.'

'All right. Walk back now,' said the woman at the monitor.

On unsteady legs, Grebe walked back through the arch. The second she stepped through, the siren's pulsing scream came again.

The monitor woman shook her head, and shouted above the noise, 'There's definitely something there.'

As the siren died a second time, the police woman signalled to Grebe to hold her arms up. She began her search. Fella could see Grebe's outstretched arms trembling, her breath coming in gulps as she tried not to cry.

Suddenly the woman at the monitor looked up again. 'Oh sorry!' she cried. 'My mistake. False alarm. She's all clear.'

The woman handed Grebe her belongings back and Fella saw her lean forward to whisper something. As she did so, she was patting at her own neck. Grebe hesitated a second, then turned away from the woman.

'Come on then, let's get this identity parade out of the way and we can all go home,' said the police man. He smiled at Grebe. 'All right?'

Grebe made no answer. She wouldn't even look at Fella as he took her hand. She just wiped her eyes and stared at the floor as they were led down yet another corridor.

'It's only a chip.'

The woman had patted her neck as she said it.

'The identity chip for your organ insurance. Easy to forget it's there, love.'

That's what she'd said. It had been a microchip that had set the sirens wailing.

Now, lying in the dark in the bedroom that belonged to Beatrice's son, Grebe put a hand to her neck, as the woman had.

Where was this chip? It seemed, from the woman's gesture, that it was in her neck. Organ insurance. The words made no sense to her.

She drew a deep breath and flopped onto her back. As she did so, there was a click at the door and a stripe of light darted across the floor. She recognized Fella's outline.

'You awake?' he whispered.

'Yeah.'

He came to sit on the bed.

She hadn't told him about this chip thing. There hadn't

been time. They'd looked at the identity parade and picked out the men who'd attacked Josie. Then Beatrice had brought them back here for the night.

'What happened?' he asked.

His voice sounded so anxious and gentle that it made tears prick at her eyes.

She waited, trying to calm her breathing.

'I mean at the security gate,' he added, 'when . . . '

'I know what you meant!'

'Sorry.'

She found that she didn't want to say it. It was shameful, somehow, to have this thing that had been put in her neck and she never knew. But she must say it. She counted to three and said it.

'That woman told me I had a chip. Here . . . ' She reached out and found his hand and guided it down to her neck. 'I didn't know what she meant. But I suppose it's made of metal. You didn't set the alarm off. So you haven't got one. Why have I got one and you haven't?'

His fingers found the tears on her cheek and stroked them away. He pulled her towards him.

'Shussh, it's all right.'

He was ruffling her hair and rocking her gently. But she could feel the tension in his fingers, in his chest. She could feel him thinking.

She pulled away and looked at him. She couldn't see his face properly, just his profile as he stared out into the dark-ened room.

'Fella? Say something. Do you know what it means?'

As Fella opened the little attic window, the sounds of the city below drifted up to greet him.

Still, sometimes, he would wake up, as he had this morning, not knowing where he was. Sometimes, even as he remembered, he had to come and look out of this window, to convince himself that this new life was real.

Some of the city's noises were muffled, some sharp, like the occasional hoot of a vehicle that pierced the canopy of sound. Something like his feelings. Some muffled, some sharp. In these last few weeks he'd been happy in a muffled sort of way. Beatrice had let them rent these rooms at the top of the house, above Josie's. There was even talk of them sharing a job in Beatrice's café bookshop. It looked as though they wouldn't have to talk to the police again about the guys who'd attacked Josie because they'd got something called DNA evidence. They'd gleaned bits of information, from what Beatrice had said, about how punishments worked here, but not much had made sense. If you were accused of something, you could have someone to help you tell your side of the story and a gathering of people would listen and decide who was telling the truth. On the Island, they didn't have these things called Law and Justice and, of course, they couldn't ask too many questions about how things worked in Inslannika. It was frustrating.

He leaned on the windowsill, the dried shards of old paint tickling his arms. Perhaps it was better not to know too much. He knew they'd been lucky, and he'd sort of decided to try and get on with his life. Forget about the paperbook. And forget about Silas Lindberg.

But every now and then the unease pierced through. Were they still being watched? How had they been followed in the first place? He thought he knew, and, if he was right, they could be picked up and taken back at any time. He and Grebe hadn't talked about the chip since the night they'd come back from the police station.

Suddenly, he heard her step on the little landing outside his bedroom door. Then a knock. Not her usual gentle tapping.

'Come in.' As he turned, he saw that there was something very wrong.

'Josie's ill,' she said.

The words hung heavily between them as his thoughts darted around the possibilities. 'Could just be . . . '

'What if it's us?'

'What sort of ill?'

'Being sick. And a fever. She's too bad to get to a doctor, so one's coming here, Beatrice says.'

'Is Beatrice OK?'

'So far.' She stared, pale-faced and questioning. 'What if it's true?'

He leaned back against the wall. They'd assumed it *wasn't* true. All the stuff they'd read in the books borrowed from the library down the street . . . all the stuff on the Internet. They'd learned a lot in the past few weeks. Just as they'd been taught that the 'Downzone' was a wasteland, so the Inslannikans had been taught that the Satellite Islands were contaminated. Worse than that, they believed that the Island populations carried diseases that could kill people on the mainland if contact was made. Everyone here believed what Jerry had believed, it seemed.

'It *can't* be true,' he said. 'People like my mother and Farl and that Alex Wingford . . . all the senior people in the medi-centre . . . they went to our Island and they didn't get ill. People are going there all the time on secondment.'

But he couldn't quite convince himself. Because this panic in Grebe's voice . . . it had pulled something up from his recent memory. His mother had written about the 'inoculations' she'd had before going to the Island. He hadn't known what that word meant at the time, but, only just the other day, he'd found out. An inoculation was meant to protect you from disease.

But they'd lived in this house with Beatrice and Josie for . . . what? Nearly four weeks now. Surely, if something was going to happen, it would have happened earlier than this?

Nevertheless, the panic churned. If they *had* made Josie sick, how bad would that sickness be?

There was a heavy thud of footfall on the stairs, the sound of Beatrice puffing. A gusty sigh as she reached the landing and then, 'Anyone at home?'

They looked at each other, silently agreeing not to answer. But Grebe hadn't quite closed the bedroom door. They waited. Maybe Beatrice wouldn't glance through.

The door moved open a little further. Beatrice's head appeared.

'Ah, there you are,' she said. 'Sorry, haven't caught you at a bad time, have I?'

Fella flashed a smile. 'No. We didn't hear you.' Stupid thing to say. No one could ever *not* hear Beatrice.

'You all right?' said Beatrice. 'Look a bit odd.'

'Yes . . . no, we're OK,' said Grebe. 'We were just talking about Josie. How is she?'

'Pretty bad, poor old thing. Doctor can't get here until eleven and I don't want to leave her. I've made a list. Will you go to the chemist for me?'

'Of course,' said Grebe. She hesitated. 'Beatrice . . . '

'Yes?'

'What's wrong with her, do you think?'

'It's very odd,' frowned Beatrice. 'Her temperature's all over the place and she seems delirious at times. Could just be a bad bout of food poisoning, but we'll see what the quack says. Anyway, sooner the better with this.' She held out a piece of paper. 'Oh, and here's some money. Should suffice.'

'OK. Back as quick as I can!' Grebe took the list and the money and scuttled out of the room.

Fella felt Beatrice watching him as he turned away and pretended to tidy the papers on the little desk next to the window.

'You feeling all right?' she asked.

'Yes, fine, thank you.'

'What's up?'

'Nothing.'

'Right. Well, if you want to use the computer in Milo's room today you're very welcome, you know that, don't you?'

Milo was Beatrice's youngest son, away at some place called University. Fella had already used his computer on a couple of occasions and now, with a pang of horror, he realized that he could have contaminated the keyboard, the chair, everything he'd touched . . . But no. He *had* to believe it wasn't true.

'Thanks, but I'll probably go to the library.'

He didn't dare turn to look at her.

'Fella, whatever it is, don't bottle it up,' she said quietly.

He had not heard this saying before, but he sensed what she meant. He couldn't think of anything to say. He heard her give a puff of exasperation.

And then she left, and he gazed out of the window for a long time.

Chapter 50

Fella stared at the screen. So much for trying to forget about Silas Lindberg. Something had happened, it seemed, to make him a big story. At least, as far as *Your World Today* was concerned.

The headline was pulsing out at him. His breath caught as he tried to make sense of what he saw.

Silas Lindberg to be questioned over dying child.

If he clicked on the headline he could find out what this meant. He snatched his hands away from the keyboard.

He had made up his mind not to try and find out more about this man. Forget him. He wasn't *really* his father, he'd told himself.

So why had he come to the library? Why had he keyed in the name?

Stupid, stupid!

He wished Grebe was here. Or Papa Louis. In his mind's voice, he asked Papa Louis what to do. And then shuddered with a wave of pure misery as he remembered the old man's voice, his eyes, his smile.

'Excuse me.'

The voice sent a shockwave through his nerves. There was a youngish woman standing over him. How long had she been watching him? Instinctively, he scanned the space behind her. No, there was no one else closing in. He blinked, realizing that his eyes and cheeks were wet with tears.

'You seem upset,' said the woman. 'Is there anything I can do to help?'

She was one of the librarians, he remembered. She smiled. So kind. Why was everyone here so kind? It almost made it worse.

'No . . . thank you.' He sniffed, feeling foolish now. His nose was running. He fumbled for a hanky but couldn't find one. The woman leaned down and offered a little packet of tissues.

'Take them,' she said, 'I have plenty more.'

She glanced at the screen. 'You're interested in this case?'

'Umm . . . ' he mumbled, 'not really.'

He scrabbled at the plastic wrapping of the tissues and at last managed to get one out and blow his nose. He couldn't think clearly any more. He wished the librarian would go away. He blinked at the screen. The headline was still there.

Silas Lindberg to be questioned over dying child.

'That story doesn't ring true to me,' said the woman. 'Silas Lindberg is a good man.'

As he looked up, she blushed. 'I'm sorry. That wasn't very professional of me. We're here for information, not to give out opinions. Hey, don't listen to me. You get on with your studies. You at university here?'

'Umm . . . sort of.'

'Feeling better now?'

'Yes.'

'Good.' She patted him on the shoulder and walked away.

He squeezed the damp tissue in his hand. So. Silas Lindberg was a good man? Or not? What *was* the story?

And whose were these words now whispering in his mind? His own, or . . . ? No, they were his mother's words. She'd said something in the paperbook, about choosing: *You can choose to know, or you can choose not to know.*

Chapter 51

Grebe watched miserably as the man behind the counter packed the medicines into a bag for her. He looked up and held out his hand for the money. This was the bit she hadn't wanted to do. If her disease had got onto the notes . . . if she made this man sick too. All the people who could have touched the money she'd touched . . .

Suddenly, she remembered little Emmie.

'Love to give you these free, but can't, I'm afraid,' smiled the man.

She gave him the money with a trembling hand and saw him frown.

'Something wrong?' he asked.

'No. Just worried about my friend.'

'Well, these, the tablets in the white packet, should help bring the temperature down. Two every four hours. But you said the doctor's coming?'

She nodded.

'Well, then,' he said, 'she'll get the treatment she needs, don't worry.'

Grebe glanced up at his face. He seemed a nice sort of man. She hesitated. 'Are you . . . do you know anything about diseases?'

'Well, I'm a pharmacist,' he said, 'so—quite a bit. Why do you ask?'

'It's just . . . nothing really. I'm doing a project. If someone was going to one of the Satellite Islands, and they needed inoculations, what would you give them? I mean, what diseases might they catch?'

She gave him a faint smile, but already his expression had changed.

'Who's set you this project?' he said.

'Umm . . . no one . . . it's just . . . '

'You need to go back to your tutor, or whoever has set you this project. Whoever it is should know that we can't answer questions like that.'

He handed her the bag, his face closed. 'You'd better hurry along with these.'

She'd almost reached the door when she heard the man talking to another customer. She dared to glance back. He'd forgotten about her. Whatever mistake she'd made, whatever line she'd crossed, it wasn't so serious that it would get her into trouble. But she must shut up about diseases. People here were frightened by the whole idea of disease.

She hurried back to the house, trying hard to get little Emmie's face out of her mind.

Chapter 52

Beatrice looked completely different when she was being serious. Almost as if she had two faces: the rosy, smiley one and this tight, anxious face, stripped of colour and somehow older.

Grebe couldn't stop herself trembling as she stood in the doorway, watching Beatrice dab at Josie's forehead with a damp cloth. Josie was hardly recognizable either, her black hair, lank and damp, clinging around her neck and shoulders as she lay, horribly still now. The smell of vomit clung to the room.

'I don't like the look of this at all,' said Beatrice. She glanced at her watch. 'Doctor's late. If he doesn't come soon I'm calling an ambulance, get her into hospital.'

Suddenly, Beatrice looked across at her as if she'd made a noise. Perhaps she had. She hadn't meant to. But she couldn't hide her fear any more.

'You go, Greta,' said Beatrice, almost sternly. 'There's nothing more you can do.'

'I'm sorry, I'm sorry!' she cried.

'Don't be silly, it's . . . '

'*I'm sorry, I'm sorry, I'm sorry . . . !*'

'Oh, Greta, darling, it's not *your* fault . . . '

'*It is!* Will she die? She's going to die, isn't she?'

Beatrice's stare deepened and suddenly Grebe felt that she *knew*. Beatrice knew that it was all their fault!

The buzz of the doorbell cut across the silence. Grebe still stood, staring back at Beatrice. Now Beatrice was saying something.

'Greta! The doctor! Go, please!'

Grebe fled down the stairs and along the hallway and hauled open the front door. A woman stood there. Quite young. Pretty.

'I'm Doctor Phillips,' said the woman, 'come to see the sick girl.'

The doctor followed the direction of Grebe's waved hand, climbing briskly up towards Josie's room.

'You're her friend?' she asked as she reached the door.

'Yes, I live here too.'

'Then would you wait out here, please?'

Josie's bedroom door was shut in her face. Grebe sat down on the dusty old carpet and huddled into the corner opposite the door to wait.

Chapter 53

As Fella left the library, slow splats of rain were dotting the warm paving of the courtyard ahead. He stood breathing in the fresh dampness. He turned his face upwards and let the drops pat his face.

He had made his decision and he knew it was the right one.

And now he had something else to get on with. He drew in another deep draught of the sweet air and headed off towards the shopping area.

He found the place he'd had in mind and examined the contents of its window carefully. Then he went in and stood in the middle of the shop, looking round at the brightly-lit cabinets and their glittering displays. He had no idea what to choose but he sensed that the right thing would be here somewhere.

Suddenly, he saw his own reflection in a mirror. He walked towards it, looking for his mother's face in his own, and finding it easily. It was so strange, this feeling of looking like, belonging to, another person. He smiled at his own face and felt her smiling back. It was going to be all right.

There were necklaces and earrings in the cabinet beside the mirror. This too was strange—the feeling that he could buy Grebe a birthday present. A bit late, but never mind. He'd never been able to before.

He hurried home with the neatly-wrapped present in his pocket. As he turned into their street, he glanced towards the house. He stopped to look up at the attic windows and, for the first time since Papa Louis had died, he felt he had a hold on something. He couldn't even describe what that something was. But it was as though a piece of him, a tiny seed of future, had been planted and was beginning to grow. He'd be a fool to risk that by going in search of a man who'd never been part of his life.

There was someone sitting on the park wall opposite the house. A tiny, fragile silhouette with an odd upsweep of fringe. She was staring out into the soft rain, waiting, it seemed. Perhaps waiting for him. A sudden dread gripped him and he began to run.

He was quite close when she heard him and turned. She drew her feet up onto the top of the wall and twisted round, her face shining.

'It's all right!' she cried. 'Josie's not going to die. Beatrice was right, it was food poisoning and some of her friends got it too because they ate prawns or something like that, anyway, I don't know and I don't care. It's not us! The doctor's given her something and she'll be fine in a few days! She's not going to die!'

She made to jump down and, instinctively, he reached up to help her. As she slithered down into his arms, her shirt rucked up on the rough wall and he found his hands on the warm, soft skin of her back. As she swayed back against the wall, he pulled her towards him. He could feel the energy pulsing through her, the energy of relief and hope. He stroked his fingers across her back and found the dip where her spine lay.

'Did you scratch yourself on the wall?'

'No.'

She was staring deep into him. She seemed to have stopped breathing. He pulled her closer and she reached up and locked her arms around his neck.

The blood was thundering around his body as if it wanted to burst free. He found he was shaking.

'We don't have to believe the lies any more,' he said. 'This is what we'll do. We'll forget about the past. I don't need to know about a father. I had a father and he's dead, but he'll always be with me. He would have wanted us to be here, Grebe. There's so much we can *do* here!'

She couldn't quite reach his mouth with hers. Maybe she pulled herself up, maybe he lifted her. All he could remember later was that they seemed to be sharing the same dizziness, swirling free in the sweet, wet air, while the rest of the world stood still.

Chapter 54

231

'**G**reta! Are you still on the planet?'

A stuffed toy dog flew across the bedroom as she turned to look at Josie. It bounced feebly off her head and Josie laughed, then bent to rummage in the bags they'd brought back from their shopping trip.

'You're supposed to be hanging up your new clothes, not throwing dogs at people!' said Grebe. Her glance fell on the bag at her feet. It contained the first dress she'd ever bought for herself.

'Only way to get your attention,' said Josie. 'The way you're staring out of that window, you'd think your brain's just flown out of it. I *said*, will you and Fella be around for my birthday party next month? I'd be really grateful if you could help with the food. Oh, and Beatrice has threatened to make a cake.'

'Of course,' she said. She hoped it wouldn't involve any actual cooking. She'd never cooked a thing in her life. She and Fella had been living on salads and cooked chicken from the supermarket. And fruit. She'd never seen so many different fruits.

'I won't be a teenager any more!' Josie pulled a sad face. 'Hey, c'mon, why so moochy?'

'Moochy?'

'Have you and Fella had a quarrel?'

Grebe felt her face begin to burn. 'No!'

Josie pulled another face, as if to say she didn't believe her.

'How long have you two known each other, anyway?'

The question knocked Grebe off balance. It had hit the heart of the problem, perhaps. Not a problem, exactly. More a confusion. There hadn't been another kiss since that first one. Ten days ago now. Just the thought of it plunged a burning sensation into the pit of her stomach and she could feel the warmth spreading and tingling through her. She loved this feeling. But it confused her. It was as though there was something between them that neither of them dared touch, like one of those sleeping dragons that children here had in their picturebooks. Was it because they'd known each other since they were five years old, and now things seemed . . . not wrong, but not completely right, either.

Suddenly, she could see his five-year-old face again. They were on benches opposite each other in the assembling room of the Infant Attainment Centre. It was cold, a wintermonth. The nurse was coming down the row of children, handing out the pills. Another nurse followed her to make sure the pills were swallowed. It had been then that she'd first really noticed Fella. She just happened to see what he did. He'd pretended to scratch the side of his mouth and she'd seen the little white pill slip into his closed fist. By the time the second nurse reached him he was ready to give an obedient swallowing movement and turn a dull stare up at her, just like all the other dull children. But Fella had never been like the other children. She'd known that, on that very first day, as the nurse moved on and his gaze had settled on her. And that's when she'd decided. If this boy Fella wasn't going to take his pill every day, then neither would she. Even back then, the two of them had been outsiders together.

She looked across at Josie. 'Since we were little. Five.'

'So how long have you been together?' asked Josie.

She frowned. 'Since we were five. Eleven years.'

'No!' Josie seemed to find this amusing. 'I didn't mean *that*!'

Grebe searched Josie's face for what, exactly, she did mean.

'I meant boyfriend and girlfriend,' cried Josie. 'Going out together, sleeping together, IN LOVE!'

Grebe's face burned. She couldn't think of anything to say, so she stood up to go, but Josie lurched towards her, hand outstretched.

'Oh . . . I'm sorry, Greta! I didn't mean to embarrass you. You know, when you said your parents were trying to force you to marry someone else, I just assumed you and Fella were young runaway lovers. I wasn't judging you.'

Grebe was at the door. 'I've got to go!' she said.

'No. Greta, I am sorry, really,' said Josie. 'It hadn't occurred to me that it might just be a friendship. You two seem so . . . *close,* that's all.'

'We *are* close. But we're not Paired!'

'Paired?'

'We're not . . . it's just not the same for us as it is here!'

There was no way of explaining it, what Pairing meant. The Officiate chose who you could marry and the Officiate decided who should be selected to go to the medi-centre and start a baby. They didn't seem to have that here. Someone like Josie would probably be free to choose.

Now Josie looked confused.

'I'll see you later,' said Grebe.

'Wait!' cried Josie. 'This is important.'

Grebe turned back and saw that Josie was looking anxious now. Any trace of teasing had gone.

'If it's the case . . . ' Josie hesitated, ' . . . if it's the case that you're, well, inexperienced in these matters and you need some sisterly advice, you know you can talk to me, don't you?'

Grebe stared. She had no idea what Josie was talking about.

'I'm sorry, I didn't mean to intrude,' said Josie. 'As long as you're safe and happy.'

'Yeah, I'm happy,' said Grebe. And she closed the door on Josie's anxious smile.

She ran down the stairs, not knowing where she was going, beyond the fact that she had to get out of the house.

Out in the warm, sweet air she walked fast, without thinking about where she was going, until her mind had begun to calm. She put a hand to her neck and pulled up the little silver disc on its chain. It was his birthday present to her. It had a little figure on it, of a man. Fella had said that, according to the Inslannikans, this man was something to do with keeping travellers safe on their journey. She had decided, when he carefully fastened the chain for her, that she would never, ever, take it off.

But she must focus on the other things Fella had said, that afternoon, as they'd sat huddled on the sofa with the rain pattering at the panes of the attic window. He'd talked about what he wanted to do with his life and how he thought he might do it. He was interested in this idea called the Law.

'What happens to us, on the Island, if the Officiate doesn't like something we've done or thinks we've done?' he'd said, his voice charged with anger. 'We're dragged off the street and interrogated . . . I've seen it happen, shoving people into their cars . . . and then what? What happens to these people? Have we ever asked? No. There's no one to ask. And even if there was, we daren't. The Island State thinks it *owns* the people. And that's wrong. A State shouldn't act like it *owns* people! But it's not like that here. People expect to be treated as if they *matter*, as if their lives are worth something.'

She'd huddled closer, breathing in the smell of his skin. Her own skin tingled as she remembered his smell again.

'So there's this thing called the Law,' he'd gone on. 'It's there to make sure people have what they call a fair hearing, with people arguing for them. I'd like to do that.'

'Arguing? Do you think you'd be any good at that?' she'd said.

'Very funny!'

And he'd drawn her closer and they'd sat, thinking and dreaming, until darkness fell.

Now she stopped in her tracks, a sudden sense of purpose gripping her. *She* could do something useful too. She remembered that Josie had told her about a book that listed where you could go to learn things. Evening classes. That was it. She was too young to go to university like Josie and Beatrice's son Milo did, and anyway she didn't know anything, she didn't have the certificates Josie had. But maybe she could get them, one day, somehow.

She walked on, quickly now, to where she knew there was a little book and magazine store. She skipped through the open door, ready to ask for help in finding this book. But there was a little queue of people already at the counter and no assistants in sight, so she went to look for herself.

She still couldn't get used to the sight of rows and rows of paperbooks. She'd bought some already, started her own collection, with advice from Josie. But now she made herself concentrate on the magazine section, because that was where she'd find this book that was called a *Guide to* . . . what was it? She scanned the racks, hoping it would be obvious.

Suddenly, her glance was snared by a face on a magazine. A woman's face, framed by a thick sweep of black hair. Familiar eyes. She recognized this woman and, as she realized why, panic seized her and she grabbed the magazine. In a split second she saw two things: that this woman *did* look very much like Fella's mother, Eliza, and that the name Lindberg was there too, written in bold yellow letters on the cover:

Lindberg investigation: Why has Carys Winton refused the case?

She examined the woman's face. It might be Eliza, but she couldn't be sure. She flicked through, trying to find the story. Here it was, right in the middle, a large picture of Silas Lindberg and, on the facing page, other pictures and a story about a girl called Molly Robson who was dying.

Now she was sure. There *was* a small picture of Eliza, with the caption *Eliza Lindberg: who killed her?* And the other woman, the one who looked so like Eliza, was pictured above a caption that said, *Top lawyer Carys Winton turns down the chance to destroy former brother-in-law Silas Lindberg.*

Grebe unscrambled the meaning . . . yes, it *did* mean that this woman Carys was Eliza's sister. She flicked over the page. There was a whole load of stuff about her and Silas Lindberg and the Robson family.

She took the magazine to the cash desk, impatiently jiggling the money in her pocket while the old lady in front of her slowly took out her purse.

'Hello there. Thank you,' smiled the man at the desk as the old lady moved away.

Who killed her? . . . What was this going to do to Fella?

She paid for the magazine and, almost tearing it from the man's hand, ran from the shop.

It was a couple of streets away that she managed to find somewhere reasonably private to sit. A children's playground, which made her think of what had happened to Josie and how that had led to their new life, their new home. 'We'll forget about the past,' Fella had said. But what if the past wouldn't let you forget?

She sat a moment on the bench, watching a woman push two little girls on a swing. Then she opened the magazine.

Chapter 55

Part of her didn't want to know the story. Even as she looked at the words, trembling hands gripping the glossy pages, she wanted to hurl the magazine away from her. But you couldn't hide from the truth, she knew. She took a steadying breath and read:

Burglars deal a callous blow to dying Molly

As they woke up this morning and surveyed the wreckage of their home, Molly Robson's parents must have been wondering just how much more tragedy they have to endure. The burglary at their modest house is the latest blow to the parents whose 16 year old is waiting in desperation for a heart transplant.

And, in a move that the Robsons say is 'beyond belief', Silas Lindberg, Inslannika's wealthiest tycoon and owner of Lindberg International Insurances, has stepped in with an offer to pay for the complete refurbishment of the wrecked home. 'This is a generous gesture,' says a Lindberg spokesperson, 'and is made because Mr Lindberg feels genuinely sorry for what the Robsons have suffered at the hands of this callous thief.'

However, the Robsons see things very differently. 'Lindberg thinks he can buy us off,' said a distraught Mr Robson, 'but he couldn't be more wrong. He knows very well that we bought full organ insurance with Lindberg International Insurances when Molly was born. But now that she needs a new heart, he's denying all knowledge of the contract. Now all our insurance documents have been taken in this burglary and he insults us with his charity. We don't want new furniture, we don't want anything except for our little girl to be well again, and Lindberg is denying us that.'

Yet another blow came to Molly's parents when top prosecution lawyer Carys Winton, sister of Lindberg's dead wife Eliza, refused to take their case. A spokesperson for Ms Winton has been at pains to point out that her former family connection with Lindberg would prejudice proceedings. However, it remains surprising that Winton has turned her back on what could be a prime opportunity to destroy her former brother-in-law. Tensions have long

existed between them
over the tragic death of
her sister—a source close
to Ms Winton has even

gone so far as to allege
that the lawyer believes
Lindberg guilty of
murdering Eliza.

Grebe stared out across the playground and pulled her thoughts to where they didn't want to be. Had Silas Lindberg really killed Fella's mother? Why would he? Why did her sister think he had?

She glanced down at the man's picture and tried to read his face. If you stared at a face long enough, could you read the truth? If only you could. This face was closed. Harsh. Pale hair, possibly greying. She didn't even know how she'd describe his eyes except that they were so unlike Fella's dark, deep eyes . . . But she had seen this sort of expression before. In the Officiate. It was the look of someone who knew they couldn't be challenged.

And this woman Carys. Her expression *was* like Fella's. She had the keen, sharp gaze of someone who was seeking something. But there was kindness there too. And she looked so like her sister, his mother.

She knew she had to tell Fella about Carys. But telling him about Carys meant telling him about Silas Lindberg, and it wasn't sounding like good news. She didn't understand all the organ insurance stuff, but it was clear that this girl's parents thought he was swindling them. There was a picture of them too, their faces full of bewilderment and misery as they stood amongst the debris in their home.

Fella had closed the door on his father. He'd said so.

But did he mean it?

She glanced up as the two little girls began giggling and shrieking. They were on a roundabout now, their mother pushing it slowly. What did it mean, 'heart replacement'? How could anyone replace something like that? She didn't know much about a heart, except that it made the blood go around your body. Where would you get a replacement heart *from*? There was so much that they did differently here, so much they didn't understand.

But what mattered now was how she was going to tell Fella.

Chapter 56

Fella was standing in the tangled back garden with Beatrice. They'd been hacking through weeds to get to an old shed, which, said Beatrice, contained some furniture that would be useful for their flat.

But when Fella had tried to open the door, most of the shed had fallen down. So now they were looking at a jumble of splintered wood and Fella was finding it hard not to laugh.

'It's not funny!' cried Beatrice. 'This was once a shed of the highest quality.'

'Obviously,' said Fella.

'Oh, shut up! It can be mended.' She caught his eye. 'Everything can be mended.'

They fell into a rhythm together, sorting and stacking the broken wood. Hero was lying on the grass nearby, watching them intently, his nose snuggled between his outstretched front paws. Watching from the garden wall, with an indignant glare, was a large ginger cat. Odd how people here seemed to like having animals around. He liked it too. The whole thing began to feel good, the rhythm of the work, being with Beatrice, the sun on his back and the smell of the crushed vegetation. It began to make him feel something like normal again.

In these last few days he'd felt anything but normal. He didn't know what he thought or felt about anything any more. If you wanted to find your father, you should *know* that's what you wanted. But he didn't know what to feel about a 'real' father. How could he? And he didn't know what to feel about Grebe because . . . but you'd *know.* You'd know if you loved someone in that way. Why had he kissed her? Because he'd wanted to. Because he knew *she* wanted him to. Did he want to do it again? Yes. But the way he felt about Grebe was more complicated than that. He was afraid, because if he messed things up, he'd lose his best friend. Maybe better not to start at all.

As he worked, his hands became blackened by the soil. It worked its way under his fingernails without him even noticing and when at last he stood to stretch, the sight of the crumbly black stuff on his hands shocked him. For a heartbeat, he believed again what he had been taught all his life. That the soil would kill him. Just as Grebe had believed the Outersea water would poison her, just as they'd believed they were disease-carriers.

So much control that you could have over people through fear.

'What's the matter?' said Beatrice.

He looked up to see her watching him in that deep-seeing way she had. Sometimes she reminded him of Grebe.

'It won't kill you, you know,' she said.

'I know!' He rubbed his hands on the back of his trousers.

'I meant the hard work. What did you think I meant?'

'The hard work, I suppose.' He looked away.

'Did you have a garden back home?' said Beatrice.

'No.'

'So what *did* you have?'

'What?'

'What was it like,' said Beatrice, 'your home.'

'Oh, you know, just . . . normal.'

'Codswallop!'

Fella had no idea what the word meant, but there was no mistaking Beatrice's tone of disbelief.

'All right, then,' she said, 'how long have you and Greta been in this country?'

He shrugged. 'Since the summer began.'

'Strange way of putting it. But I think that's the truth, isn't it? And not everything you two tell me is.'

'Probably most of the things Greta tells you are the truth,' he said. 'She hates lying.'

Beatrice hurled a piece of wood to the ground and puffed out a sigh.

'Tell me, Fella,' she said. 'Whatever it is, tell me.'

He turned away.

'I've had five children of my own,' she said. 'So there's not much that frightens me. Perhaps I can help.'

'You have helped, Beatrice. More than we ever thought anybody would. But I can't tell you all the truth about me.

Some of it's just too hard to explain. And some of it I don't know myself. But we're not bad people.'

'You're not contaminated?'

'What do you mean?'

'What do you think I mean?'

He didn't know. It couldn't be that Beatrice *knew* where they'd come from. She couldn't possibly know that!

'Please . . . we're not bad people.'

'Oh, I know *that,* dear boy. If you were, you'd never have got through my front door.'

At that moment Hero yawned, came trotting towards him, then sat on his foot and leaned his warm body against his leg. Fella reached down and twiddled the dog's soft ears.

'I found out who my real father is.' It was easier, somehow, to tell it to the dog. 'He seems to be very well-known. But I don't know if I want to meet him. I thought I'd made up my mind not to. I'm not sure he's a good person.'

'Want to tell me who?'

Fella shook his head. 'Can't. As far as I know, he doesn't know I exist . . . '

'So . . . who brought you up?'

'Papa Louis. In the Orphanage . . . '

Beatrice clamped a hand on his arm and squeezed hard, made him look at her.

'Fella, be careful. The word "Orphanage" is no longer used in this country.'

An icy tickle shot down his spine. He looked into Beatrice's bright eyes. It was happening again. Everything he thought was safe was fracturing around him. He swallowed. 'Then I won't use that word again.'

'*Tell me*, Fella.'

He pulled his arm away, a lump forming in his throat.

'One of the Islands?' she asked softly.

He couldn't speak, couldn't look at her.

'Oh, God, and I was hoping I was wrong!' she said.

'We'll go!' he cried. 'We'll find somewhere else to live. But please, *please* don't tell . . . '

'Fella . . . '

'You know we're not contaminated, don't you? It's a lie! So we can't harm you!'

'Fella, stop! There's no question of you going anywhere, and certainly no question of me telling anyone!'

He looked up at her at last, wanting to see that she meant it. He saw the fear on her face.

'I'm sorry, Fella,' she sighed, 'I don't think I'd really pre-pared myself for how to react if my hunch was correct.'

'*How* did you know?'

'It was clear that you were runaways from somewhere— you said as much yourselves, with Greta's story about a forced marriage.'

'It wasn't a story, it was true.'

'But then, I puzzled over where, exactly, you *were* from. So many little things that you didn't seem to know, and big things too. And then, when Josie was ill, Greta was so convinced that she would die and that it was all her fault. So, once all the drama was over and Josie was recovering, I began to think . . . what had caused such deep-rooted fear, such ingrained belief? And from there it was a short step to thinking the unthinkable. That it was possible for two youngsters to escape from one of the Islands without being traced and taken back. That it was possible for *our own* fears and beliefs about the Islanders and their diseases to be based on nothing but lies . . . '

She looked at him sadly, and he held her gaze. Another question he'd forced out of his mind, but now it was screaming at him. What would happen if they were sent back? He knew.

'And you're really not going to send us back?'

Now she looked angry. 'Do you think I would? You must know as well as I do what would happen to you.'

'They'd kill us. But how do *you* know that?'

She looked confused. 'I *don't* know that! But I do know it would be prison . . . '

Fella snorted in disgust. 'No. It *wouldn't* be prison. We know too much, don't we?'

Beatrice looked at the ground. Neither of them said anything. The dog whined and slumped at Fella's feet.

'So,' said Beatrice at last, 'are you saying that your father is from Inslannika? Then why were you brought up on an Island?'

'My mother and my father both came from here,' he began, his voice shaking. 'My father had some sort of . . . business interest on the Island. My mother went out on what she called secondment, to work as a nurse. She was still there when I was born. I don't know whether she told my father about me. Anyway, he never came to find me.

I was only a baby when she was . . . ' He hesitated. If he used the correct word, he'd have to explain about the paperbook. 'She was killed in a car crash,' he said.

'Which island?' asked Beatrice softly.

Fella shrugged. 'I don't know what you'd call it here. We call it the Island State.'

He watched as she stabbed at the ground with a piece of wood. He saw the holes form in the soft earth. Then the picture blurred with tears. He was like the Glass House, a broken shell filling up with an uncontrollable flood. He blinked and stared at her downturned head, fearful, full of rage, willing her to look at him. Perhaps she didn't want to look at him. Not just Orphanage scum, but Island scum too.

'We're not contaminated,' he said at last, desperate to fill the silence. 'It's a lie. We're told lies and you're told lies! If only you *knew* . . . ' He stalled, grasping for the thoughts that were beginning to grow. 'But you *do* know some things! You know that if we're caught we'll be sent back. What else do you know?'

For once, Beatrice didn't seem to have an answer.

'Well?'

She took a breath, but no answer came.

'If you know,' he said, 'if all of you here *know* what it's like for us, then why don't you do something! You do *nothing*!'

The next thing she said shocked him.

'What would you like us to do?'

'I don't know! Make it right! Make it so that we don't have crushed lives, so that we have choices like you do here, so that we don't have to be afraid all the time!'

'That's a concept that we call justice,' said Beatrice.

'Funny,' he said bitterly, '"Justice" isn't in our word file.'

'What makes you think we *do* know what it's like for you?' she said.

'You must! Because there's a link, isn't there? I've read books about it! You use the things we produce. One Island for "white goods", another for wheat and food animals, another for fuels. How many more? Useful places, these Islands, aren't they?'

Again, she didn't answer. She rubbed a hand over her face, leaving a faint trace of earth. The hand was shaking, he noticed. And, despite the growing heat of the sun, her cheeks had lost their colour. Then she said, 'When you say "what she called secondment"—what do you mean? You couldn't have had a conversation with your mother if you were only a baby.'

'I can't tell you how I know that. It's complicated,' he said.

'Will people come after you?'

'Maybe. They . . . '

'They what?'

She sounded frightened. For him, or for herself? He shrugged away from her concerned gaze. No, he couldn't tell Beatrice about the paperbook, about how they'd been tracked and . . . he just didn't *know* if they were still being watched, if people would 'come after' them.

'Well, they haven't come yet, have they?' he said.

Beatrice frowned. 'But how on earth did you get here?'

'One day I'll tell you, not now . . . ' He could hardly

believe it himself, let alone explain it to Beatrice. That journey in the speedcar, the Glass House . . . It seemed like another life.

'Will you try to find your father?'

'No. Beatrice . . . please. What do you know about the Islands? Have you ever been to one?'

She shook her head. 'Years ago, before I was married, I applied to go over to one of them—perhaps it was yours, perhaps one of the others. I was a teacher, you see, I thought I could help in some way. But the authorities here were very selective about the sort of people who could be seconded. The whole thing was very secretive. Before they would let you do the extra training you had to sign documents to say you would never disclose anything about where you had been. It wasn't the sort of thing I felt I could do.'

'And you left it at that?'

'Yes.'

'You weren't curious at all?'

'I just got on with my life.'

Suddenly she seemed smaller, her loud, cheerful energy gone. She looked as though she was going to cry. She turned away. 'You're safe here, you know that. As long as you're under my roof . . . '

And then she stomped off into the house, leaving him standing amongst the fallen planks.

Chapter 57

F ella lay in the silence, staring at the sloping ceiling above his bed. He knew he was supposed to feel grateful to Beatrice, but right now he couldn't. All he could feel was a sense of betrayal. And fear, because yet again something he'd thought was solid was shifting, cheating him, somehow, and there was nothing he could do about it. The rules kept changing.

He heard Grebe climbing the stairs, her soft call wondering if anyone was home. He had loved the feeling of having a home, his own room, his own little kitchen and bathroom. To Grebe it must seem a bit shabby, though she never said so, but he loved it, loved the fact that she was here too. But now things were not as they had seemed. How many Inslannikans knew more than they were told in the books? How many asked or cared?

A gentle tapping on the door. He didn't want to talk, but he didn't want to be alone either. He called out to her and her head appeared.

'Hi. Had a good day?' she said.

'I've been helping Beatrice with some things.'

'Oh.'

There was a silence. He knew he must tell her. She'd gone to sit at his table and was staring out of the window.

'Grebe . . . '

His voice seemed to make her jump.

'Yes?'

'Beatrice knows about us—where we're from.'

She blinked, taking it in. 'How?'

'She'd half-guessed already. Because of when Josie was ill and you thought it was all our fault . . . '

'You did too!'

'Then she pushed me into talking . . . '

That's how he saw it, now. Grebe shouldn't have made such a fuss. He should have been more wary of Beatrice's questions. There was so much stuff that should have been left unsaid.

'So . . . ' She looked stricken with fear. 'What's going to happen? Will she send us back?'

'No. We're quite safe here, she says. Good of her. Because she knows very well what would happen to us. She knows more about the Satellite Islands than she's prepared to admit. They're all in it together.'

'What do you mean?'

'The Officiate who control us, and the people who control *them*. Nice, kind, decent people from Inslannika who couldn't care less where things come from!'

'Fella, stop it! I don't understand . . . '

'I wanted her to say that she had no idea about the Islands and what goes on there!' he cried. 'But she did know some things. She knew that we'd been lied to about the contamination over here. And she knew what would happen to us if we were sent back, so she knows that we're not free like they are here. So what else does she know? She must know what things are really like for us, mustn't she? People don't get executed for trying to escape from *here*!'

'Don't! Don't attack Beatrice!'

'Why not? People like her can do whatever they want while our lives are crushed to pieces. They know about it and they do nothing. Why shouldn't I attack her?'

'She's been good to us!'

'So what? It hasn't cost her anything, has it? And we're supposed to be grateful! In its way, this place is as bad as the Island . . . '

'It isn't!'

'It *is*! And if you can't see that, you're even more stupid than the Attainment Directors said you were!'

Instantly, he regretted saying this. He looked across at her speechless stare. Then she was moving towards him, fast, her face full of fury. He thought she was going to hit him.

'You arrogant little shit!' she cried. 'You think you're better than me, don't you? Just because you come from a clever family . . . '

She stopped dead, her face colouring suddenly. But the look of confusion lasted no more than a second. Her face hardened again and she said, quiet and close, 'Don't ever speak to me like that again!'

And then the door slammed behind her and he was left in silence again.

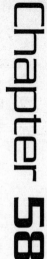

Chapter 58

F ella hesitated outside Grebe's closed bedroom door. He wanted to make her understand, but there was still a pulse of anger running through him. So he should leave it, or there'd be another quarrel.

He thumped down the stairs, meaning to head off to the park to clear his head. As he reached the first floor landing he was stopped by a voice calling out.

'Hi. Are you Fella?'

He glanced through the open door of Milo's bedroom. A tall guy with curly brown hair appeared, his hand held out.

'I'm Milo,' he grinned.

Fella nodded. 'Oh, right.'

'Hey, I think you left something on the computer desk. Come in.'

Milo lurched back into the room. Reluctantly, Fella followed. He didn't feel like meeting Beatrice's son. Not now, not like this.

'Sorry,' he mumbled, 'Beatrice said it would be OK . . . '

'Oh, yes, yes, that's fine,' said Milo, 'I don't need the

computer when I'm not here, do I?' He was moving towering piles of papers and books from the desk. 'God, I've only been back five minutes and already I've made the place look like a recycling depot! Ah, look. Here!'

He swept up a fistful of printed sheets and held them out, smiling. Was the guy *always* smiling, thought Fella.

'Oh, yeah.' Fella flicked through the pages and gave a snort of bitter laughter. 'I was looking at stuff about how the Satellite Islands were set up.'

'Gosh,' said Milo, 'that's pretty academic stuff.'

Fella had been about to leave, but now he hesitated, frowning. 'What do you mean?'

'Well, when you say "set up",' said Milo, 'are you referring to the theory of Professor Rodez?'

'Um . . . what theory's that?'

'Ah well,' said Milo, 'we covered this in the first term at uni. Professor Olrick Rodez. Great name, hey? He's been largely discredited as a crackpot, and he's dead now, of course, but about fifty years ago he published this theory that at one time there had been a deliberate government programme to take people from here and resettle them on the Islands.'

Fella stared.

'Why? I mean . . . why would a government do that?'

'Well, his theory was that there was so much crime, so much overcrowding, so many unemployable people at that time, that the government formed this policy to strip out the troublemakers and the dead wood and put them to work doing something useful. Dump them on the Islands with the basic infrastructure in place, get them working productively, lie to them about why they can't ever come back. So that those who remained could have a better life, basically . . . '

Before he could stop himself, Fella let out a cry of indignation.

'I know,' said Milo, 'it's very far-fetched, which is why his ideas are never given any credence, although as history students we have to be aware of them. There are no government records from the time that would back up his theory.'

'And I wonder why?' cried Fella. 'Has it occurred to anyone that the records could have been *destroyed*?'

But if Milo heard the anger in his voice he didn't react. The guy just shrugged and grinned again.

'Perhaps they were. Perhaps it *might* just have been possible to do what Rodez suggests was done. Who knows?'

'Yeah,' said Fella bitterly, 'who knows?'

He watched as Milo stacked books onto shelves. This guy was supposed to be really clever, according to Josie.

'Come on then, how do *you* think the Satellite Islands were set up?' he asked, not bothering this time to hide his contempt.

'Me?' said Milo. He hesitated, blew out his cheeks. 'I don't buy the Rodez theory. I think the Island societies just evolved like anywhere else. But I think they must always have been pretty grim places because they've always had harsh regimes in power. And I don't think the people could afford to travel over here, even if we could let them. Which we can never do, of course.'

'Because of their diseases?'

'Of course.'

'Why don't you go and see for yourself, instead of . . . ' Fella caught Milo's look of surprise and hesitated. ' . . . haven't you ever been curious about the Islands?'

Milo shrugged. 'Oh, I suppose if it were possible to get inoculations, then it might be interesting. But . . . no, not really. There are so many wonderful places in the world to explore, aren't there?'

Fella felt like punching Milo's bright smile right off his face. He had to get out of here.

'Yeah, well,' he muttered, 'see you.'

'Let's get together sometime,' said Milo, 'maybe see a film or something—you and Greta, isn't it?'

But Fella was already hurrying down the stairs and across to the park opposite the house. He found a bench and slumped in the hot sunshine, eyes closed, listening to the sounds of some children playing nearby as the anger pulsed through him. It was just too hard to make sense of it all. He wanted to push it away, forget about the Island, but he couldn't. He wanted a new life. But how could they live here in Inslannika, knowing what they knew? Knowing that there were as many lies here as there were back there?

Suddenly, he sensed he was no longer alone and opened his eyes. There was Grebe. She sat beside him. He tensed, not wanting to talk.

'I'm sorry,' she said.

He huffed out a sigh. 'No, I'm sorry too. It was me. I was just really wound up . . . '

He turned to see one of her deep gazes resting on him.

'What?' he said.

'I have to talk to you about something.'

He sensed danger.

'Bad?'

'Maybe—and maybe good too. Something I found out. Quite by accident. I was going to tell you . . . '

'What?'

'Well . . . ' she began carefully, 'you think you have no family. But you have. You have an aunt called Carys, your mother's sister.'

His thoughts took off like a flock of startled birds.

'My *mother's*?'

'Yes.'

'Alive?'

'Yes.'

'Where?'

'I don't know where she lives. She's a lawyer. I found this . . . '

He saw the magazine clutched to her chest. She hesitated, looking down at it.

Why hadn't he thought to look for his mother's family? An aunt! He held out his hand but she wasn't going to give it up just yet. There was something wrong.

'What?' he said.

'It isn't all good news,' she said. 'There's some bad stuff. I'm sorry.'

She gave him the magazine, opened at the middle. He saw the picture of Silas Lindberg and a woman . . .

'Go on,' she said, softly, 'read it.'

Grebe wanted to go with Fella. She understood when he said he had to go alone, but she had a bad feeling about it. There was a terrible, clamped-down energy about him. He'd said nothing about the possibility that his father had murdered his mother.

'If I can talk to my aunt I can find out more.'

He'd tried to sound reasonable about it. 'You've been so wrapped up in my problems, it's not fair on you. It's best you stay here. You've got all your studying you want to do. And I won't be gone long. I just have to find her.'

He meant it. He wasn't going to share the thoughts and feelings that were tearing at him.

And he wasn't planning to tell Carys he was coming. She could sort of understand it. It would be so difficult to explain his existence over the phone. But once she saw him there could be no doubt that he was Eliza's son. And that worried her. It would be a shock for Carys. What if she was angry, or didn't want to know him? Just because you were related to someone, it didn't mean that they would want you and love you. Grebe knew that very well.

She watched as he packed his things. He'd bought a bag that you could carry on your back. He wasn't taking much. So he would be back soon. She willed him to come back soon, and safe.

She turned away to go through the papers on the desk. There was a ticket so that he could travel on the train to and from the place where Carys lived. They'd found the place, and how to get there, on the Internet. It meant going to a railway station that was about half an hour's walk away from here. But Carys didn't live close to a railway station, so they'd bought a map and Fella had studied it, trying to work out how to read the lines and colours and shapes. The map was a beautiful thing—much more detailed than the one on Emmie's wall—its squiggly lines and swathes of green covered the area where Carys lived. Grebe picked it up and looked at the picture on the front. These rearing humps of land with rocks and trees scattered about them were mountains, apparently.

She happened to glance across at him as he looked up from his packing. He gave a shallow, fleeting smile, and looked away again. Things still weren't right between them and she mourned over this with an unshakeable, aching sadness. Perhaps they both needed some time alone to think.

Her hand fell on one of the two mobile phones they'd bought. He would take one with him so that they could keep in touch. She'd insisted on that, because they still couldn't be sure they were safe in Inslannika. And there was a wallet full of money.

'Are you ready for these?' she asked. 'Tickets, map, phone, money.'

'Yes.' He zipped up the bag.

'And you're sure you don't want to tell Beatrice?'

'Grebe, I'm tired of having to explain myself! I need to get things clear in my head. Just a few days!'

'I know.' She turned away. She took a long, deep breath, as silently as she could. If he could hold his feelings in, so could she.

He was behind her now, picking up the things from the table and stuffing them into his pockets.

'Hey,' he said.

She turned to him and he reached out, cupping her face with his hands.

'Only a few days,' he said.

And he kissed her softly on the mouth. She opened her eyes in time to see him slip through the door.

Chapter 60

Beatrice had come breezing in almost as soon as Fella had gone, and brought her here to the café bookshop to work with Milo. Beatrice knew. Grebe didn't know how she knew, but she did. Perhaps she'd seen Fella leave. It didn't matter. She'd asked no questions and, in her cheerful way, had set about making sure that Grebe was busy, so that she couldn't fret every single second.

There was some comfort in work. And there were the books. Before Fella left, she had been racing through them hungrily. Josie had given her a list of suggestions as to which stories she might like. She reached into her pocket to get the little notebook of titles.

And tucked into it was the note from him, written in pen-writing.

I will be back soon. Take care of yourself. I'm sorry.

He must have been practising, because the writing looked really good. Large and confident.

'Fancy a break?'

She looked up to see Milo coming towards her with a tray of coffee and biscuits.

'Yeah, thanks,' she said.

'It's gone quiet.' He nodded towards the sofas where people sat to read and drink coffee. There was only an elderly lady in a hat and her small, squashed-face dog. She was reading and the dog was eating cake.

'So . . . how are you getting on?' said Milo, brightly.

'Oh, I've put all three boxes of new stock on the shelf, and . . . '

'No, I mean in choosing books for *you*. What sort of books do you like?'

She blushed. Did he know that she wouldn't have read any books at all before she came here? She couldn't imagine that Beatrice would hide things from her children, so she might have told Milo the truth. On the other hand, Beatrice wasn't the sort of person to betray a secret. Either way, she knew she would seem very ignorant to Milo.

'Well, I just love good stories,' she said. 'Josie's given me a list of her favourites. I like the ones with people in them who . . . I don't know, who stay true to themselves, who don't give in, no matter how many bad things happen.'

She felt Milo looking at her and blushed again. Perhaps she had said too much. She'd never talked about why she liked the books she did, not even to Fella.

'I think that's great,' said Milo, waving at the shelves in

front of them. 'That's what all this lot is here for. To suggest possibilities, to share thoughts and dreams. The thing I really love is when you suddenly realize that some other person out there has thought or felt exactly the same as you. It makes you feel like you're not alone.'

'But *you're* not alone!' she said. 'You've got Beatrice and your brothers and sisters . . . '

'No, I didn't mean in that way. I meant . . . well, we're all part of the same family, in a way, aren't we?'

Grebe looked up at him. The foolish, friendly grin that he hid behind wasn't the whole story with Milo, she thought. He was looking more serious now, almost sorry for her. Perhaps he *did* know.

She looked away. 'I suppose we are,' she said, although she didn't feel it was true. What would Milo know about other people, in another place, living very different lives?

'I need to look for these,' she gestured to her list, ' . . . while there's no one here.'

'Yeah, OK,' he said. She thought she heard a sad note in his voice. He looked over to the sofas. 'Our lady and her dog have gone home, I see. Do you mind watching the shop while it's quiet? I need to dash out and get some change for the tills.'

'Yes, of course.'

'I won't be long.' He smiled.

'OK.'

She turned back to the shelves as the shop doorbell jangled. She heard the click of the closing door. She stared up at the wall of books and sighed, wondering if it would ever be possible to change things, to show people over here what went on on the Island and how wrong it was. She thought about Beatrice. Perhaps Fella was right, perhaps she was guilty of closing her eyes to things, not asking questions. Fella had always been keen on questions.

The doorbell jangled again and she turned.

She didn't recognize him for a second. The tall man in a pale suit. And when she did, she didn't understand. And then she *did* understand . . .

It was Dr Farl. And there could only be one reason he was here.

She moved away towards the back of the shop.

He reached out, a hand spread wide as if to calm and explain. Those fierce, hard eyes. But he was smiling. It was a trick.

'You must trust me,' he said, 'I mean you no harm.'

The door to the yard was behind her. Slowly, she backed towards it, watching his eyes.

'Greta, please. I need you to listen to me.'

She turned and ran, behind the wall of books, to the back door. There were two heavy bolts, one at the bottom. She drew it back easily and reached up for the top one. Something flicked into the corner of her vision and she pulled as hard as she could on the bolt. It wouldn't shift. It pinched the skin on her fingers with a searing pain.

Now he was moving towards her down between the back shelf and the back wall of the shop. She pulled at the bolt again. It was still stuck, and there was no more time. The stockroom was just to her right and, leading up from it, the stairs. She ran to the stockroom door, through it, and slammed it. There was a lock, but the key wasn't there. No time. She ran through the stockroom, tripping over one of the boxes she'd just emptied. She recovered herself and got to the bottom of the stairs. Already he was through the door behind her.

Her legs felt as though they weren't part of her. She couldn't make them move fast enough and she stumbled, smashing her knee into the staircase. She threw out an arm to pull herself up. Up, up. The only way was up.

Farl's voice. Too close. 'Greta, don't run from me!'

Up, up.

'It's all right! I've come to help you!'

If she kept on going, she'd be trapped on the top floor. The only hope was to get out onto the old metal fire escape that ran up the outside of the building. She could get down that way and out of the back yard gate. If she could open one of the windows leading onto the fire escape.

The first window was at the top of this flight. If she could make her legs move faster, ignore the tearing pain in her chest. She reached the window, grabbed at the bottom of the frame and tugged upwards. It started to shift.

'Greta, please! Let me explain!'

She turned. He was there, just a few steps below her. He held out a hand again. She tugged again at the window frame and it shot upwards with a bang of wood on wood. She climbed out and saw the three flights of metal steps leading down. Now her legs were really shaking. She could hardly move them. She stumbled again but managed to pull herself up on the handrail. She reached the little landing space. Only two flights to go.

But as she turned, she saw him.

He was just behind her. He stopped dead.

'Leave me alone! Leave me!' she screamed. 'I'll jump rather than go back! I mean it!'

There was a movement in the yard way below her. Her gaze was split by the fleeting impression of the top of Milo's curly head. As it flitted back to Farl, he lurched towards her.

She ducked out of his way, throwing her weight onto the handrail beside her. She felt the rail move, heard a scream from the yard.

And then a sickening sense of weightlessness. Plunging. And panic. Someone was screaming, 'No! Oh, God, no!'

The train flashed through the residential areas and quickly left the city behind. Fella had never travelled so fast. He watched, exhilarated, as the landscape flew open around him. The backdrop was every imaginable and unimaginable shade of green. Great clouds of trees. Grasslands that streaked alongside the train and then leaped and plunged to fold into hills and valleys.

Every now and then, colour would flash across the green. Red soil, or yellows, blues, and purples amongst the grass. These might be flowers, like the ones in Beatrice's garden. Suddenly there was the glinting, milky-blue water of a great river.

This river, when it first appeared alongside the train, was plunging over rocks, as if frantic to get away from something. Later it became lazy and swollen. Later still, it led Fella's eye to a horizon that clenched his heart and made him wriggle in the plush seat to press even closer to the window.

The horizon was gleaming liquid blue.

The Outersea.

The train slowed slightly here, swinging in a long curve. And at first he didn't understand what was going to happen. The train seemed to be heading straight towards the water. But then, at the last moment it settled on its path, with steep, rocky cliffs on one side and, on the other, just below his window, the gently lapping, sun-stroked waves of the Outersea.

Fella stared out across the water. He tried to capture his feelings. But there were so many feelings and no names that would do. Rage that he'd lost the childhood he might have had in this land? Rage didn't quite say it. Joy that such a beautiful place existed and he'd found it? No—joy didn't go anywhere near. He stared out of the window and heard his mind's voice ask, where *are* you, Papa Louis? Eliza?

Where *were* they?

His heart was full of things and he couldn't share them with the people who had loved him most. Much more than sorrow. Lonely. That was the word.

After the Outersea came the mountains. The train swung back inland and the land around him was swelling upwards so that he had to lean close to the glass and tip his head back to see the tops of the steep, rocky hills.

From time to time, he looked at the map. He was pleased with himself because he'd quickly understood the contour lines, the symbols, and the different colours of shading. He loved imagining his way into a map, building a picture of the real thing from the clues on the page. It was what he and Grebe would have to do for a long time, maybe for ever— build the real thing from clues given.

Carys lived in a village—a word he hadn't known—somewhere in one of the deep valleys. It was near to the town called Vennro, where she had her law offices. As the train approached Vennro, the land opened out again to show high, jagged peaks snagging the distant clouds. Along the skyline, some of the peaks were draped in white. He'd read about this. Snow. The stuff was unknown on the Island. Or, at least, maybe they had snow in the A-grade vacation areas, he wouldn't know.

At the railway station he knew he would have to find the bus that would take him as near as he could get to Carys's house. Then he'd have to walk.

The nearer he got, the more nervous he felt. Grebe had wanted him to make contact with Carys somehow before he went. She hadn't said so, but he'd known what she was thinking. Now, he wondered if she'd been right. It would be a shock for this woman to discover that her dead sister had a son. Maybe she wouldn't want to know him.

The on-train information was sounding. Two beeps to get everyone's attention, and then 'Ladies, gentlemen, and children, we are now approaching Vennro. Vennro will be the next stop.'

The calm tones of the announcement only made his nerves worse. What was he doing? What was he hoping to find? The train was slowing. 'Ladies, gentlemen, and children . . . ' They were entering the covered area of a large station and now he could see his own reflection as he turned to the window to read the city sign. Vennro.

The glass showed him large, anxious eyes but, as he

looked deep into his own shadow-face, he lost some of his fear. It will be all right. Don't give up. Do what you have to do, he told himself. And his reflection seemed to understand.

He stood up, walked the few paces down the carriage and got off the train.

In the crowded concourse, the advertising screen was almost the first thing that caught his eye. Looking for the way to the buses, he'd glanced upwards. There, above the exit, above the swarm of people, was an enormous picture of a large white building. And emblazoned across it were the words *Vennro, home of Lindberg International Insurances.*

He stared up at the screen in shock and wonder as the crowd flowed around him. That building . . . the centre of his father's business! He hadn't expected this, nor the whole mess of feelings that came with it. The words taunted him. This famous man, with his great wealth and successful business, was his own flesh and blood. The Lindberg name was his name, and that beautiful building with its towering walls of white and glass, gleaming in the sunshine and surrounded by trees, was part of a world he'd never known. Did Silas Lindberg live in Vennro, then? If Silas and Eliza had lived here together, then maybe this is where he would have grown up. But that didn't matter to anyone but him. It was as though a life that might have been his own was going on without him. And, suddenly, every feeling of loneliness he'd ever had flooded through him in a great tide of helplessness. He was nothing. Nobody knew he existed. He shouldn't have come.

He found he couldn't move. Didn't want to. Didn't know where to go.

Someone knocked against him and took hold of his elbow. He turned to see the face of an elderly man. 'Sorry, lad. Wasn't looking where I was going,' he said. And with a crinkled smile and a squeeze of his elbow, the old man turned away. Fella watched him shuffle into the crowd, a strange feeling dragging through him. As though that squeeze, that smile, was pulling him back to himself, some-how. He started after the old man. But he was gone. No point in going after him, anyway. It wasn't Papa Louis. But for a fleeting moment he'd felt that Papa Louis *was* there.

He stood a few seconds more. Then he headed for the exit. Outside, he stood in the fading afternoon sun, examin-ing his new surroundings. Already he could feel that this place was different to Tompalla. It felt more frantic, full of noise and smart people hurrying, and the buildings around him all looked new.

And then he saw the Lindberg building again. The real thing this time. It was perched on a wooded hill some dis-tance beyond the sleek office towers. Could he find his way across the city to get there? Yes. He had to.

He stared up at the building one last time to fix its direc-tion in his mind, then started off, walking briskly, into the streets beyond the station.

T he steep climb was pushing the breath out of him in gasps and making his legs ache. He could see the building ahead of him now, at the end of a grand driveway, and he stopped. Not for the first time, he asked himself the question Grebe would have asked if she was here. What, exactly, was he planning to do? But it was pointless to think about it. He had no plan. He was drawn to this place. He had to see it. That was all.

The road was levelling out, leading to a gateway of solid pillars holding black iron gates within the white wall. Again the Lindberg name, in the same lettering he'd seen on the adscreen, was slashed across the white. He walked towards the gates and the very thing he hadn't been expecting happened. A gap appeared in the centre and, very slowly, they swung open.

He looked upwards, as he had been doing all his life. Gates like this wouldn't open so casually unless there was some way of tracking who came through. And, yes, there it was, the first cam he'd seen in Inslannika, a little white box discreetly fixed on the wall.

As he cleared the gates, they began to close behind him.

He was a hundred yards or so up the drive when an engine noise made him turn and he saw the gates open again to let through a large bus-type vehicle full of people. He stood aside as it passed, then followed as it continued slowly up the drive.

He was heading towards a great fountain that stood in front of the grand entrance to the building. As he drew closer, he saw that around the wall of the fountain was inscribed a legend. *Giving life a second chance,* it said, and he thought again about the girl who was waiting for her replacement heart. It was Grebe who had voiced his immediate question—how can you replace a heart? He looked up at the building. From close to, it was even more impressive. It looked like the sort of place where anything was possible. Perhaps here they really could give life a second chance. The thought made him angry. On the Island, people could die suddenly and the medi-centres never gave a reason, let alone treatment. No second chance for them.

The bus had stopped beside the fountain and people were climbing out. He couldn't guess what sort of group this might be. They were all young, in their twenties, perhaps, mostly couples. A couple of bored-looking girls maybe not much older than him. Some of them looked up as a woman in a dark suit and high heels came clipping down the steps of the entrance to meet them. She was saying something he couldn't quite hear and gesturing to the great white building.

Then the group began to straggle along behind her and

he understood. She was going to show them round! He didn't even think about it. Keeping close to the fountain, he crossed the few yards of driveway and tagged onto the end of the group.

A rising panic was snatching at his breath as he mounted the steps. He must make himself calm, or he'd attract attention. Just ahead of him were the two bored girls. He followed them, not too close, but close enough to make it look as though he might belong. And, willing his pounding heart to slow, he stepped into the building.

Inside was a huge hallway, cool and quiet, under a glass dome. Rather like the Glass House, he thought, as he looked up into the mass of glass supported in its steel frame. Ahead, the suited woman had stopped and turned to face them, with a dramatic gesture to the wall above her. A large part of it was covered by a picture of Silas Lindberg.

Fella made himself examine the face of this man.

What would he say if he knew who was standing in his hallway?

'Welcome to Lindberg International Insurances, my name is Helena,' said the woman. 'Today we hope to give you just a taste of the important work we do here. Giving life a second chance. As we progress on our tour, you may see a camera crew. Please ignore them, they are here to make a documentary about our work and will be filming in various locations.

'Our story begins twenty-five years ago when our Company President—Silas Lindberg, you see him here—put up a substantial sum of money to develop research into transplant medicine—what we now know as organ replacement. To date, we can proudly boast that we have saved the lives of over two thousand individuals who would have died were it not for this generous foundation and the talents it has fostered.

'Ladies and gentlemen, please follow me to our lecture theatre, where our president himself will address you. I believe our film crew will be at the back of the auditorium. Please watch out for cables.'

Fella followed as the group pressed through some thick metal doors. Inside, the darkened room was full of plush red seats facing a white screen and a little platform. As the people shuffled along the rows of seats, Fella saw a movement to the side of the screen. A door was opening and a man was walking through.

His heart clenched. He sank into the seat beneath him, his eyes still fixed on the man. Silas Lindberg. His father. He was taller, broader than he'd imagined. He touched a hand to his cuff and smiled. 'Good afternoon and welcome, ladies and gentlemen.'

A surprisingly light and friendly tone to the voice. Immediately, the audience hushed.

Fella watched his father's flowing, confident movements. And the more he watched and listened, the more uneasy he felt. In flesh and blood, this man was nothing like his pictures had suggested. None of them had shown his warm smile or the way he drew his audience into listening to him. People were eager to laugh at his jokes, eager to have his gaze fall on them, especially the women. Even the two younger girls, sitting just a few seats away from him, squirmed and grinned when he looked their way. They were charmed. Fella was charmed. He found himself wanting this man to look at him too. He wanted one of those smiles for himself.

Silas Lindberg was now throwing his arms wide. 'Ladies and gentlemen, some of the younger ones amongst you may have your organs insured here with us because of the responsible foresight of your parents. Over the next few years you may want to start thinking about how you might protect your own families. The purpose of the tour is to show you what we have to offer and to help you think about these vital life choices.

'As some of you may know, Lindberg International has always been at the cutting edge of cloning technology. It had long been known that, in theory, you could take genetic material from an embryo and use it to grow organs for transplant should they ever be needed by that person. The problem was timing—how to grow an organ to be ready at the precise time when it was needed. So the solution was to grow organs, as insurance, at the same rate as any potential recipient would themselves grow. A great idea in theory, but one of the key stumbling blocks was *storage*. And I'm proud to say that this is where we were way ahead of the field. It was here at Lindberg International that the big break-through was made some twenty years ago. We perfected the growth *and storage* of organs created from the genetic material of the potential recipient.'

Smiling, Lindberg paused to receive a murmur of appreciation from the audience, then continued.

'It is in this building that the replacement organs are grown and stored in our special tanks. And, of course, ladies and gentlemen, we store them in the profound hope that they will never be needed. But if they are, here's how we swing into action. The microchip that will have been implanted, just here, in the recipient's neck, shortly after birth, will now be read.'

Fella stiffened in his seat and watched and listened carefully.

'On this chip is information, coded in much the same way as the bar code on your food. The stored organs have the same bar code as the recipient, and the code is filed on our computers, with state-of-the-art back-up facilities, of course. As a final fail-safe, an identical chip, carrying that same, unique bar code, will be found on the tank itself.

'Our tanks are stored across six floors in the heart of this building. Wrapped round them are the research labs and the operating suites. Around the perimeter of the building are the recovery wards, with every comfort provided. We now propose to take you on a short tour of these facilities, but first, I'd be happy to answer any questions you may have.'

There was a ripple of shuffling and coughing and a few muffled giggling noises. But no questions. Silas Lindberg scanned the audience with an encouraging smile.

'No? Well, I'm delighted to have explained myself with such eloquence! In that case, ladies and gentlemen, since workload will deprive me of the pleasure of your further company this afternoon, I shall now leave you in the capable hands of your guide, Helena.'

He was just about to leave when there was a flurry of

cries—surprise and disapproval—from somewhere in the middle of the auditorium. Someone had stood up. And now there was a thin, blonde woman, face tight with anguished determination, striding down the steps, heading straight for the little platform on which Lindberg stood. As she reached him she unrolled a poster, a picture of a girl, and held it up to the audience.

'*I have a question!*' she cried. 'Why are you letting my daughter die, Mr Lindberg? Can you tell these people that? Can you?'

Fella had a fleeting sense of his father's face thunderous with anger.

But that wasn't what shocked him most.

As security guards ripped the poster from the woman and dragged her, still screaming, from the room, Fella could only think of one thing.

The girl on the poster looked exactly like Grebe.

Silas Lindberg waited until the woman had been removed and her screams silenced behind the thick metal doors of the lecture theatre. Fella watched him wait. The anger seemed to have gone, but so too had some of the easy charm. He fingered his cufflinks and turned a sad smile on his audience.

'Ladies and gentlemen, you will understand that I cannot comment on the outburst you have just witnessed. I do hope you will not allow it to spoil the rest of your visit. Thank you, and good afternoon.'

'Excuse me!'

The voice came from the back of the auditorium this time. Fella craned his neck round. In the darkness, he could just make out the form of a woman with a mass of hair.

'Would you tell us,' said the woman, 'exactly how you keep the stored organs alive?'

Fella looked back towards his father. His eyes had narrowed, trying to see the questioner.

'Well,' he said, 'it's an extremely complex business, but in brief, it's to do with the fluid in which the organs are kept—you'll see the tanks for yourselves in a moment. There's a special mixture . . . '

'What's in this mixture?' said the woman.

'Ah, now, I'm afraid that's a Lindberg International secret. You'll understand that we wouldn't want our competitors to copy—'

'So this is really just a straight commercial enterprise, isn't it, Mr Lindberg? There's nothing altruistic about it.'

Now Silas had shifted towards the front of the stage. A slow smile was spreading across his face. 'Ladies and gentlemen, I won't delay you any further. This lady is from the television company making our documentary and she knows very well that she can come and talk to me at any time about matters that are unclear.'

'But people are interested, Mr Lindberg,' persisted the woman. 'Molly Robson's mother has just been thrown out of here. *She's* interested in knowing—'

'Thank you and goodbye.' He turned crisply and left by the little side door.

The audience sat in silence for a second, and then the murmurings began.

'She's right,' muttered a man in front of Fella. 'That woman they threw out, she's the mother of the girl that's waiting for a new heart. Doesn't say much for their approach to customer service, does it?'

His companion pulled a face. 'And they say they've paid all that money!'

The guide was talking now, raising her voice above the

rumble, directing people to the exit and the next stage of the tour.

'We'll now take a look at the storage tanks, ladies and gentlemen.'

Fella followed the chattering crowd towards the door. Glancing to the back of the auditorium, he saw the woman who'd questioned his father. A man was helping her load what looked like a camera onto her shoulder. As he shuffled with the others out of the lecture theatre and along a corridor, his feelings were swirling. For a few seconds, he'd thought it *was* Grebe's face on that poster. It had shaken what he thought he was beginning to feel about his father. That, and his expression when he was questioned.

Growing replacement organs so that people didn't die unnecessarily was a good thing, a great thing. An incredible achievement that they couldn't begin to imagine back on the Island. But suppose it really had been Grebe instead of this other girl, and his father had cheated her, somehow . . . how would he feel then?

'Whole thing could be a con,' said a man in front of him.

'Don't be ridiculous,' answered a woman's voice. 'He'd never get away with it. And what about the two thousand people saved?'

The people ahead were now moving through another set of thick metal doors at the far end of the corridor and, as they did so, were falling silent. As Fella stepped through the doors he saw a vast dome, the ceiling rearing higher than any entertainment dome he'd ever seen on the Island. There was a walkway running out of sight around the perimeter of the dome and, in the centre, towering up to the ceiling, was a stack of what looked like glass boxes supported on a framework of metal shelves.

'Ladies and gentlemen, the tanks.'

And in each of these glass boxes, something was suspended in liquid.

It took him a while of staring at these strange, muddy-red shapes to comprehend their meaning.

'This is the liver section,' said Helena the guide. 'As Mr Lindberg said, the organs are suspended in a special fluid that contains the preservative chemicals that keep the organs healthy.'

The whole group stood silent, necks craned upwards. It didn't seem real.

The guide was running through some statistics: how many thousands, how much money. Fella barely heard her, and when the group started moving around him he was still staring at the thing in the tank nearest him. How was it made? His father had talked about cloning and genetic material. The words were unfamiliar, but the meaning was clear. This thing floating in front of him was an exact copy of someone's liver. A piece of a person!

The rest of the group was moving out of sight now. He mustn't draw attention to himself by getting left behind. He jogged to catch up and found them peering through a window on the wall opposite the tanks.

The window overlooked a room below, where four people in white were bent over a table. The lights above the table threw a harsh light on the person lying on it. The person was draped in a green cloth and there was a wide gash in the middle of the body, showing a mess of yellowed and blood-ied stuff inside.

'This is the final stage of the replacement operation,' said Helena. 'In layman's terms, tidying up. They'll then close up—nice neat stitches or staples—and the patient will begin the process of recovery. Follow me and I'll show you where this lucky patient will be relaxing in a few days' time.'

She was making it sound like an A-grade holiday. When they got to the recovery suite, Fella could see why. He'd always been in awe of Grebe's B-grade house. But he'd never seen anything as sumptuous as the bedroom they were shown. As well as the automatic bed that could put you in any position you wanted to be in, there were thick carpets, enormous sofas, and a telescreen covering half a wall. There were call buttons for nurses, doctors, and even the chef. Outside were gardens full of flowers, and special outdoor beds with sunshades. You could have meals brought to you whenever and wherever you liked, said Helena.

Fella wondered how much all this would cost. Only A-graders, or whatever the Inslannikans called them, would be able to come here.

Next, Helena led them out onto a bright lawn where tables had been set up. 'Ladies and gentlemen,' she said, 'we'd now like to offer you a light lunch, and during this time you will have the opportunity to browse through some of our litera-ture. If you have any questions, please feel free to ask me.'

Fella grabbed a jug of juice and sloshed himself a huge

glassful. His throat was dry and his head aching. Nearby, a young couple were looking at one of the brochures.

'Could we afford to do this?' said the woman. 'I mean, when we have kids.'

Helena drifted towards them with a smile. 'The question some people ask themselves is, can we afford *not* to do this?' she said. 'Some people feel that organ donation from a stranger, with all its risk of disease and rejection, is not acceptable. And, of course, there might not be an organ available when you need it.'

The couple looked at her with worried frowns, then back at the brochure.

'A premium service has certain costs, of course,' continued Helena, 'but I'm sure your children will be worth it. Perhaps you'd like to look at some further information . . . ' and she steered the couple away.

Fella wasn't feeling hungry, but he took a few tiny sausages anyway. As he turned away from the table, he almost knocked into someone.

'Sorry!' she said.

In the daylight, the bright frizz of coppery hair was startling. So was her wide smile. It was the woman from the film crew, the one who had dared question his father.

She leaned across him and began piling food onto her plate. 'You enjoy the tour today?' she said.

He hesitated.

'It was interesting . . . ' he said.

She glanced at him, a strange mix of questioning and playful.

'Interesting?'

'Yes.' Her glance had given another stir to his mixed feelings about the whole place. Had she sensed his unease? She was looking at him again.

'Well, I suppose . . . it's a great thing to do, isn't it?' he said. 'Helping people who are so sick they need something replaced?'

'Sure is. Last year my sister's eldest boy had a liver replacement that saved his life. Because it was effectively his own liver, grown as a spare, there was no danger of rejection like there used to be in the old days. My name's Frankie, by the way,' she smiled, 'I'm the camerawoman and this is my technician, Baz.'

'Oh, hi. I'm Fella,' he said.

'Hi, Fella.' A bearded guy next to Frankie grinned and waved the large piece of chicken he had just grabbed.

'So . . . ' said Fella, 'if you think it's good, why were you giving him a hard time?'

'Who, Lindberg?' Frankie helped herself to a glass of wine and took a gulp. 'Well, you've got to ask questions about this Molly Robson business.'

'The girl who needs a new heart?'

'Yes. Who's telling the truth? Could something have gone wrong with the heart they grew for her? Maybe some fault in the storage procedure. Or maybe they've just *lost* it.'

'But he's saying she never had insurance in the first place . . . ' said Fella.

'Excuse me!' It was Helena, who'd suddenly appeared behind Frankie. 'Could we ask that the buffet be enjoyed by the guests alone? I've arranged a separate luncheon for film crew in the White Garden.'

Frankie threw a grimace at Fella, then leaned into him and said, 'If you're interested in all this stuff, we're doing a live broadcast from here tomorrow evening after the five o'clock tour. Catch it if you can.'

'Yeah, I will!'

'Film crew *this way*, please!' persisted Helena.

Fella watched as Frankie and Baz were led away across the lawn. Suddenly, he didn't want to be here any more. Frankie's words played in his mind: *Who's telling the truth?* He turned his back on the great white building and walked, fast, back down the drive.

When at last he was past the Lindberg gates, he stopped and dug out the mobile phone that he and Grebe had bought. Carefully, he dialled her number and put the thing to his ear.

He couldn't hear anything. He looked at it and saw some writing on the little screen, *No signal*. He tried several more times, each time feeling more angry and miserable. He needed to speak to her.

He tried one last time. But the thing wasn't going to work. He stuffed it back into his bag and headed off down the hill.

The path up to Carys's house was uneven. Or was it just his steps that were uneven, his feet not falling where they were placed, so unsure was he that he was doing the right thing? But he'd been waiting, staring at this strange little house, with plants twisting up the walls and flowers clustered around the door, for too long already.

The building was old, the wooden door crooked in its frame. As he raised his hand to knock, a slight breeze brought the scent of the flowers, the names of which he did not know.

He knocked and waited.

The moments passed and the shrill twittering of birds around him seemed to deepen the silence breathing through the door.

There was no one home. Of all the things he had imagined might happen, he had not imagined this.

He knocked again and waited again.

He turned, went back down the path and had his hand

on the latch of the gate when he heard a creak behind him. He swung round—too quickly. And there she was.

His heart stumbled and knocked breath from him. She was so like Eliza. Probably about the same age as Eliza was when she died, he realized.

'Did you just knock on my door?' she said. A beautiful voice, sonorous and strong.

'Yes.'

'And you've been waiting around here for a while, haven't you?'

He nodded. There was something odd about the way the woman was staring at him. She was nervous too, it seemed.

'You're Carys Winton?'

'Yes.'

There was no way to do this gently.

'You're my aunt,' he said into the woman's piercing gaze.

'I beg your pardon?'

There was a tremor in her voice. Was she angry? Perhaps. But, if so, not just angry. There was something else. Fear or disbelief, perhaps.

She was still staring, this strange mix on her face, when a sharp wail snatched her attention.

'My baby,' she said, 'he's crying.' She looked confused. 'You'd better come through.'

He followed her along a passageway to a door at the back of the house. It led onto a garden and there, on the bright grass, was a playpen.

At least, in the Orphanage they'd have called it a

playpen. It was a bit like the one by Papa Louis's desk, the one where newly-arrived infants used to play under his careful eye until he was sure they were settled.

As they approached, this little boy closed his fists around the bars of the pen and hauled himself up, staring at Fella with huge brown eyes.

The woman put a hand down to ruffle the dark curls on the child's head. Then she turned back to Fella.

'What did you just say?' she said.

'You're my aunt. My mother was Eliza. Your sister. Eliza Lindberg.'

He couldn't read her face. It had re-aligned into a steady, serious gaze that seemed to contain no trace of reaction to what he'd just said.

'I need to know why you think this,' she said.

Fella didn't know what to say. He held the baby's gaze, as if this speechless infant would have an answer of some sort. As the baby thrust out his arms to be lifted and the woman bent down to him, he swallowed the iron lump in his throat. Her stooping, lifting, wrapping the baby into her shoulder . . . it reminded him of Papa Louis. It reminded him that he had no family now.

'When she died . . . ' he fought to steady his voice, 'the news reports about her death—they were all wrong. She didn't die in the place called Rimmeri. Did you know that?'

The woman didn't answer. Instead she said, 'May I ask why you think this?'

'She died in the place where I was born,' he said. 'She died on the Satellite Island that we call the Island State.'

He waited. Would she flinch away? Would she run, with her baby, from the risk of infection? No. She didn't move.

'I was a couple of months old,' he continued. 'I was taken to an Orphanage. I don't know whether Silas Lindberg—my father—I don't know if he ever knew about me. He can't have done, or he wouldn't have . . . '

Something like a muted snort of disgust came from the woman. She looked away.

'She wrote in a paperbook that she didn't love him any more,' he said. 'He'd done something to make her hate him. Do you think that's why he killed her? I *know* you think he killed her!'

The woman turned away and gently placed the baby back in his playpen. When she turned to face him again she had tears in her eyes.

'They call you Fella, don't they?' she said.

He couldn't have been more shocked if she'd hit him.

'You *know*?'

'I'm sorry. I was hoping not to have to deal with this just yet.' She beckoned to chairs and a table shaded by a tree. 'Sit.'

'"Deal with this"?' he cried. 'With me, you mean! You *knew* about me!' he cried. 'All these years . . . !'

'No, not all these years. I've only known about you for a few weeks.'

Fella stared. She met his gaze, but he sensed a deep uneasiness in her.

'How? How did you find out about me?'

'I can't discuss that now, I'm sorry. It's been a shock for me too.' She placed a hand on his shoulder and gestured him to sit. She sat next to him and leaned forward, hesitantly, to put a hand on his knee. 'But I'm glad you found me, really I am. For her sake and for mine.'

They stared at each other for long moments while bird-song and the wordless chatter of the baby flooded the silence. There was deep sorrow and something like relief in her face.

He looked away, and as he did so, caught sight of something. It was on the edge of a chair that was tucked under the table, just the corner showing. He grabbed it and turned on her.

'The paperbook! How did you get this?'

She seemed as shocked as he was. She swept her hands through her hair and groaned.

'You stole it!' he cried. '*You* left the money?'

'Arranged for it to be left,' she said. '*Yes!* And arranged for you to be watched to make sure you were safe. *Yes!* I know it must seem hard-hearted.'

'Why not just *tell* me I had an aunt?'

Carys hesitated and shook her head. 'This is very difficult . . . '

'I'm not *stupid*!'

She leaned back, palms spread as if in surrender.

'All right! All right, I'll explain. But, Fella, what I have to say must not be repeated to anyone. And it will cause you pain.'

The earnestness in her face frightened him.

'Tell me,' he said.

She sighed. 'Well, you're right, I *do* believe your father

murdered your mother. I always did. But I was only nineteen when she died. Our parents were both dead too. I had no family to help me, no power—no proof. So I threw myself into qualifying as a lawyer, and then into my work, but . . . Eliza's death was always there. And in recent years I've been watching Silas . . . ' She hesitated. 'Anyway, I'm preparing a private prosecution against your father for the murder of your mother.'

'What makes you so sure he killed her?'

She looked at him with wide, sorrowful eyes. Eyes like his own. 'How much of this diary have you read?'

'Not much! They don't teach us to read pen-writing. And you stole it before I could finish it!'

'I didn't *steal* it . . . '

'And you're supposed to be a lawyer . . . ?'

'Yes, all right, I arranged for it to be taken. The point is, in order to investigate Eliza's death, I needed to know exactly what she had discovered on the Island. The diary was the obvious place to begin.'

'But how did you know about it in the first place?'

'Through you. Several weeks ago I initiated investigations on the Island. I'd always known that she'd gone there—she told me what her plans were, to look at what Silas was doing over there. One of the first things I discovered was that she'd had a child. I realized . . . I *hoped* . . . that there was a chance the baby might have survived. I sent someone to search the Orphanages . . . '

'Farl!'

'Yes, Dr Farl. Not long into the investigation we discovered, quite by chance, that the Officiate had picked out some audiocam footage of Louis Morelli handing over a book to one of his boys. This was significant, because I knew that Eliza was in the habit of writing a diary—she'd done it since she was a teenager—and books are unknown among the Islanders. The camera had recorded, but there was something wrong with the microphone, which meant there was no sound to the footage. But the images were enough—as soon as Dr Farl saw them, he realized that there was a very strong possibility that you were Eliza's son. We had to keep the Officiate away from you, so Dr Farl took over their investigation. However . . . by the time he got to the Orphanage, you'd gone on the run. And when we discovered where you were heading . . . my God! You know, that Glass House had been abandoned for years. It was completely derelict and unsafe! It's a miracle you got out.'

'You're saying that Farl intended to bring me *here*?'

'Yes. He'd emailed the footage across to me here and I saw . . . ' Her voice faltered, 'I saw so much of my sister in you. I *knew*. So we planned to get you out of there. Never mind about the wretched diary—it was *you* I wanted.'

'But why send Farl? My mother didn't trust him, did you know that?'

'I do now—she says so in there.' She gestured to the paperbook. 'I chose Dr Farl because he now works with Silas.'

Fella stared at her in disbelief. '*What?* He works with Silas? My father? The same Silas who you think killed my mother?'

'Yes. He has knowledge that . . . ' She hesitated. 'He could be crucial to my investigation. Now I think we should stop this discussion.'

'But you shouldn't trust Farl!'

Her eyes hardened. 'I'll be the judge of that.'

'But how do you *know* it was my father who killed her?' he cried. 'It could have been Farl! He was obsessed with her, she says so in here!'

'Fella, it's pointless to continue with this. You must just let me complete my investigation—'

'But how can you be *sure* it was my father?'

She sighed. 'I know he was having her watched. He must have organized an ambush of her car.'

'*Must have?* Don't treat me like an idiot! On the Island you can haul people off and get them shot on a *must have*—or less! But you don't do things like that here, do you? Here you have the Law. Here you need proof! Truth and justice! You can't have a trial based on a "must have"!' He saw a tension in her face and, at the same moment, a realization came. 'So it's not the murder itself that you can prove, is it? There's something else!'

And now she looked at him in a different way. He'd surprised her, he could see that. And for the first time since Papa Louis died, he felt that an adult was looking at him as an equal human being.

'All right, Fella, you're quite correct. There's something far worse than my sister's murder involved. But I simply can't prejudice the case by discussing it, even with you . . . '

'But . . . '

'Fella, the law is like a game. You have to play by the rules or you lose. You're right. Truth, proof, and justice. It's the only way. And that's final.'

Her face was set. This time he knew she meant it. He sat, a mess of thoughts swirling, trying to piece together all the bits of meaning to make something he could understand.

Then a sudden feeling of nausea gripped him. *He was having her watched*. He looked up at Carys, needing to know at least this.

'You know for certain that my father was having her watched?'

'Yes,' she said, holding his gaze with her beautiful dark eyes. Of course, she knew that he could see the significance of this.

'So my father knew about me. If he killed her, then he meant to kill me too.'

'We can't say for sure. All Louis Morelli's notes say is that you were brought to the Orphanage by a single Guard. It looks as though it was he who saved your life by getting you away from the scene of the crash.'

'But we can't be sure that my father meant me to be saved.'

'No.'

Her eyes were swimming with unease and, he realized, sorrow for him.

Fella's thoughts went numb. For a long time he gazed at the baby, who was playing happily with a wooden car.

'What's his name?' he asked at last.

'Louis. A strange coincidence. It's always been one of my

favourite names.' She leaned forward and touched his hand. 'Believe me, I would have come to you. I was biding my time. I didn't want you involved in any way until I'd got Lindberg behind bars. Because I knew how painful all this would be.'

He kept his eyes fixed on the baby called Louis. 'So he's related to me, in a way.'

'More than in a way. He's your cousin.'

Fella went over to the baby. He picked him up and smiled into the child's surprised, exploring gaze.

'You must be tired,' said Carys. 'Stay with us tonight. In fact, we're ready for our supper. Would you like some?'

Fella hesitated, 'Is it just you? You and Louis?'

'Yes. My husband's away on business.'

He smiled. 'I do feel hungry, actually. Thanks.'

She got up and walked across the lawn to the house.

Carefully, Fella put Louis back into the playpen. He wriggled and gave a whimper of disappointment.

Fella watched until he was sure Carys was well inside the house. He scanned the garden. There was a low fence between the lawn and the road. He could easily clear it.

He picked up the paperbook. He could feel the little boy's fierce gaze on him as he turned and ran.

Fella hurried down the aisle of the Tompalla train, searching for a quiet seat away from other people. At last he found one and threw himself into it, scrabbling to open his bag and get to the paperbook.

His hands trembled as he opened it. What *was* it, this thing, this 'something far worse than murder', that his father had done? If Carys had found her proof here, then so would he. *No one* had the right to stop him finding the truth.

He riffled through the pages, searching for something that would leap out at him. Nothing did. And then he noticed that, towards the end of the book, someone—it must be Carys—had marked sections of the writing with little crosses.

28 October
I should have got myself off this Island long before this. Now I am terrified by the prospect of giving birth here. I've even thought about trying to contact Silas, which shows how desperate I've become. It may already be

*too late. Not feeling good tonight, the baby very
restless.*

29 October

*They've brought me into the medi-centre maternity unit
because I thought the baby was coming. False alarm.*

*There's a poor woman here having a terrible time
with her new baby. She won't even look at it and the
poor little thing won't stop crying. The woman's name is
Hannah. I tried to make friends with her, but when I told
her I was a nurse, she said I was her enemy. When I
asked her why, she just said that we'd forced her to
have a baby that wasn't hers. Possibly post-natal mental
trauma.*

30 October

*Overheard two bluecoat doctors talking about Hannah.
One of them said, 'We get this sometimes with the
embedded ones. There's a procedure for dealing with it. A
course of tranquillizers and hormones and most of them
accept the child eventually.'*

*What do they mean by 'embedded'? To me, it means
hidden within something. Are they implanting women
here with someone else's embryo? Does this explain the
strange attitude I've seen in some parents? Too many, it
seems to me, don't really love their children, or even like
them, at all. Easy to do under this Island's controlled
reproduction regime. But why implant with someone
else's child?*

2 November

*My beautiful boy born yesterday. I could look at him for
ever. I didn't think any sort of love could be as powerful
as this.*

Fella took a deep breath to quell his own emotion. He
had never known his real birth date. He glanced at the
pages describing the first days of his life. But he must leave
them for later. He thought about Grebe and her parents. It
was true, what Grebe had always said. They didn't love her.
So was Grebe someone else's child? He flicked forward,
looking for Carys's marks.

30 November

*The embedded children are born to a mother that is not
their own, and then chipped so that their whereabouts
can be monitored. Put this together with the Organ
Insurance Programme at Lindberg International and
there is one terrifying conclusion that can be drawn. I
cannot make myself believe that Silas is really involved
with this. But it would be so simple. Frozen, cloned
embryos sent over here. Children grown as 'spares'.*

This was the last entry that Carys had marked. Fella
blinked, his eyes trying to find focus as they withdrew
from the page. That word 'cloned' again, which meant
making a copy. But embryos. He didn't understand the
word, but it seemed that these embryos were used to
make babies. He turned the page and, with a searing

anguish, he saw the last few entries. That familiar word, December.

December 14

I think I'm being followed. I need to get off this Island as soon as possible. My only hope is to contact Farl. I tried his number, but it said service discontinued. I tried again and again—same thing. It must mean that there's no phone contact between here and home. You can't buy equipment for email here—the concept is unknown. It's a risk, but I'll have to see if I can get any sort of email access at work.

December 15

Someone watching the house last night and they're still there now. Have not dared to go into work. My only hope now is to try to drive to the Glass House that Farl told me about. Will try to get us clear of the house tonight, and when we get home, the truth about Silas will be heard, no matter what the cost. I hate him. I feel sick that I am married to such a monster.

Fella felt a surge of misery. He squeezed his eyes closed to stop the tears and when he looked up again he saw that the train was filling up. There was someone—a large man—overflowing the seat beside him, and two people opposite.

What did she *mean*? That you could do this 'cloning' and make an exact copy of one of these embryo things? And if an embryo was used to make a baby, then that would mean two babies exactly the same. But grown by two different mothers. So that if one of those babies ever got sick and needed, for instance, a new heart . . .

'Are you all right?'

It was the man opposite. Youngish, with a kind face.

'What?' said Fella.

'I said, are you all right?' smiled the man. 'You were staring straight at me, and then you went very pale.'

'Sorry, I didn't see you . . . I mean, I wasn't staring . . . ' And before he knew he was going to do it, the question came.

'Could you make two embryos exactly the same?'

The man smiled again. 'Well, I couldn't personally, unless I were to father identical twins. But, yes, it's possible to make a copy of an embryo.'

'And then grow them both into babies inside two mothers?'

'Well, yes, quite possible. Illegal, but possible. As I say, the legal way is to do it naturally and have identical twins.'

'Twins?'

'Yeah, well, twins are naturally-occurring clones, aren't they, if they're identical? Two people who look exactly the same.'

Fella felt as if everything was being sucked out of him in a cold rush of fear. Grebe and Molly Robson. Grebe's chip. Copies of Inslannikan babies being grown on the Island. So that if the Inslannikan person ever got sick . . .

He tore at his bag, elbowing the man beside him, desperate to get to the mobile phone. When he got it, his hands were shaking so much he couldn't press the keys.

'Hey,' the man opposite leaned forward, 'you're *not* all right, are you?'

Somehow he found the stored number. As he listened to the ringing, he saw again the faces of those two children in the Special Surgical Unit. Terrified, as though they were waiting for some sort of punishment for something they hadn't done. The more the phone rang, the more difficult he found it to breathe.

At last it answered.

'Grebe? It's me—'

'Fella . . . ' It was a male voice.

'Who's this? I wanted Grebe!'

'Fella, it's Milo. I've got some bad news.'

'What?' The squeeze was tightening on his breath.

'She's in hospital. She had an accident. The doctors think she'll be OK—'

'What happened?'

'She fell from the fire escape at the—'

'Will she be all right?'

'They think so. But she needs an operation . . . '

Milo was still talking, but Fella wasn't hearing him.

'Milo! Don't let them operate on her. Get Beatrice there. Promise you won't let them touch her! Milo! Promise!'

He waited, his whole being pleading.

'What d'you mean?' said Milo. 'Mate, I can't tell the doctors what to do. If they say she needs an operation—'

'Don't let them touch her!'

'But it's scheduled for later on this evening. They can't give us an exact time, because—'

'Which hospital?'

'Tompalla Central.'

'They mustn't touch her. Do you understand?'

'But, Fella—'

'Stop them! Promise!'

'All right, I'll try.'

'I'll be there. Just stop them!'

He looked at the man next to him, who was now staring.

'What time does this train get to Tompalla tonight?'

'Nine fifteen. Just over an hour,' said the man.

'You have to help me!' he said.

The man opposite reached across to him. 'Perhaps I can help,' he said, 'I'm a nurse. Try to keep calm.'

The man covered Fella's hand with his own and now Fella realized that his breath was coming too fast.

'I need to get to Tompalla Central Hospital,' he said, 'I MUST—'

'It's all right. We'll get you there,' said the nurse. 'Let's try to slow that breathing.'

'NO, NO . . . !'

His whole body was shaking now, chest tight and blood thundering. The man next to him moved to make way for the nurse. He felt the firm but gentle hands touch him, ease him back into his seat.

He could no longer speak but it felt as though his whole body was screaming.

I have to get there, I have to get there.

Chapter 66

F   ella watched the woman's thick fingers tapping the
    keyboard.

'Greta Jenson. She must be here!' he said.

'When was she brought in?'

'I don't know.'

'Are you a relative?'

'Yes.'

'An accident, you said?'

'Yes.'

'A sixteen-year-old girl?'

'Yes, yes! I said so!'

'Calm down,' said the nurse beside him.

'I know what you do with people here!' he cried. 'Just let
me see her.'

The woman at the keyboard pulled a despairing face at
the nurse.

'I think it's Bessinger Ward, but they might have moved
her by now,' she said.

Fella scuttled along beside the nurse, willing him to walk

faster down the long, pale corridors. Just like the medi-centre corridors. The memory of those two children slammed back into his mind.

'Here we are,' said the nurse.

And suddenly he saw Beatrice.

She leaped up. 'Fella! You're not to worry. They're very confident that—'

'Where is she?'

'They took her down over an hour ago. She'll be back—'

'Took her where?'

'To the operating theatre.'

'NO!'

'Fella . . . '

'I told you not to let them take her! I *told you*!'

Suddenly another nurse was next to him. 'This is a hospital,' she said, 'you can't behave like this here.'

'Listen.' Beatrice put a hand to his arm. 'We spoke to the man she was running away from.'

She was running away from someone? Fella couldn't speak. Somebody supported him as he fell onto a chair.

'It seems there was a misunderstanding,' said Beatrice, 'Dr Farl has explained—'

'Farl?'

'He's the one she was running away from. He's a surgeon. He's doing the operation.'

Chapter 67

Now there was another woman, in a different coloured uniform.

'Would you step into the office, please,' she said.

Beatrice gently took hold of Fella's arm.

'Just the boy,' said the woman firmly. Then, to Fella, 'Come with me.'

Pain was clamping his skull. He let himself be led to a door, which the woman opened for him to walk through.

'Thank you, Sister.'

Fella looked up at the sound of the remembered voice.

There was Farl. He'd got them trapped at last. But Fella didn't run. There was no point, without Grebe.

The Sister closed the door behind him and Farl gestured for him to sit. He didn't move.

'Greta will be back on the ward as soon as she's come round from the anaesthetic,' said Farl.

'I don't believe you!' he said. 'You're working for Lindberg! You've killed her! You've taken her heart!'

'Fella, she's alive,' said Farl.

He looked deep into the man. He didn't understand the expression he saw there.

'She's injured,' he said, 'but she'll recover. I understand why you think what you think. But please believe me when I say I've just saved her life.'

Fella hesitated, watching.

'What do you mean?'

'I've removed the microchip that would have identified her as Molly Robson's clone.'

Fella stared.

'You understand what I mean, don't you?' said Farl.

Fella hesitated again. Heat was pulsing through him and he felt weak. He couldn't think.

'Do you understand?' repeated Farl.

Fella nodded. 'Grebe was an embedded—'

'She was an embedded child,' said Farl. 'As such, she had a chip which could identify her.'

Again, Fella tried to read the man's expression. The face was set hard, but underneath . . . perhaps he was afraid.

'You *knew* about it all!' he cried.

The weakness had left him now. All he felt was a sickening rage. And something was changing in Farl. He saw the man's hands trembling.

'You work for my father! You *knew* about it all the time!'

'Fella, I didn't!'

The mask was sliding. Farl hesitated, seemingly lost in painful thought for a moment. At last he met Fella's gaze. 'I understand if you don't believe me, but that's the truth. I left your father's employment some time before your mother went to the Island. And at that time I knew nothing about the Special Surgical Unit.'

'You did! You tried to warn her off!'

'Only because I'd seen what Silas was like if people crossed him. She'd gone behind his back to try and find out what he was up to. Men like Silas don't take kindly to that. I was afraid for her. But, Fella, you must believe that at that time I knew nothing about his organ insurance programme and how . . . how it operates.'

'So why are you working for him now?'

'I began working for him again a few months ago at the request of your aunt, Carys Winton, in order to try and establish evidence against him.'

'And have you?'

'Your friend Greta is evidence,' said Farl. 'And there's plenty more at Lindberg International. I've established the exact chemical make-up of the fluid that's used in those tanks.'

'Which is?'

'Coloured water.'

Silence hung between them while Fella struggled for words. At last he looked up into Farl's stricken face. 'And the real organs are in living people on the Island!' he cried. 'People with chips so they can be identified and their organs taken. And *nobody* made the connection?'

'That's the point, Fella! There *was* no connection between Lindberg International and the Special Surgical Unit on the Island. Eliza was the only one who knew that Silas had set that unit up. And she *didn't tell me* about it! If she had, I'd have got her out of there, I swear to you I would! But as it was . . . I *tried*, but . . . ' He hesitated, glancing away, 'she wouldn't come home just for me.'

He heard the tremble in the man's voice, sensed the pain in him. It made him angry, but the anger only added to his own misery.

A tense silence stretched out until Farl sighed and said, 'Fella, you should go back with your friend Beatrice now, get some rest. I'll talk to you in the morning.'

'I'm not leaving her!'

'You can see Greta in a short while,' he said gently. 'She had a head injury, but it won't cause complications, and she also broke a leg. It should heal well.'

'And the chip really has been removed?'

Farl nodded, his hawk-eyes meeting Fella's stare.

'So there are people like you . . . trained like you . . . who do these operations. They kill people to get the organs,' said Fella.

Farl nodded again. 'He has a team of corrupt surgeons working on the Island. Those working over here simply think that the organs come from the tanks.'

Fella felt the tears burning, but he blinked them back.

'I want to see her,' he said.

Chapter 68

The side door of the lecture theatre opened. There he was. Silas Lindberg. Fella locked on to the easy smile, the gesture of welcome. His heart was hammering, but he had his plan. He would stay calm, he would stay hidden in the group.

Lindberg cleared his throat. Clasped his hands before throwing his arms wide. It was a well-rehearsed welcome routine. Welcome to the rich fools who don't know what the man in front of them really is.

As Fella listened to the speech once more, he stared at the man. Stared in wonder, because he still didn't want to believe that this seemingly generous, humorous, benign person could be such a monster. And most of all he didn't want to believe this was his father.

Lindberg smiled, then fixed his face in a more serious expression. 'Ladies and gentlemen, we all value our children's health above anything . . . '

And Fella saw a baby brought to an Orphanage. He saw Grebe, pale as the sheet on which she lay, blink up at him in confusion. The bandages on her head and neck. If they hadn't got off the Island she'd be dead now, her heart cut out of her.

The people around him were nodding and smiling. It was almost more than he could bear. He pushed down the revulsion that was welling like vomit.

He had to stay calm.

Lindberg was taking his leave now. Just as he was going to turn, he stepped back towards someone in the front row. A woman with a toddler. Fella leaned forward in time to see him brush a hand against the toddler's cheek and smile. Then he stepped through the side door.

Fella stood a moment with the other people who had risen to follow the guide out of the lecture theatre. Then he slipped out of the end of the row and down to the door through which Lindberg had just gone. He paused, looking back into the darkened auditorium. The last few people were gathered round the exit, their backs to him. He pushed at the door.

It opened onto a corridor. At the far end, he caught a movement. Someone disappearing from sight.

This had never been part of his plan, and he knew he should go back.

But the man should know. He wanted him to *know*.

Silently and quickly, he moved along towards where a shaft of light now spilled into the corridor.

Chapter 69

Fella had been standing in the doorway for a few seconds before something made Lindberg spin round. He stared, as Carys had stared, and Fella knew why. He saw the likeness to Eliza. But if the man was startled, he quickly hid it and found a smile.

'Can I help you? The tour is moving towards the tank area, I believe,' he said.

'I know,' said Fella. 'It was you I wanted to see.'

'Me?' He feigned surprise. Annoyance was growing under the smile.

'You're my father.'

The man stared again, then made a snort of ridicule. 'I don't think so, young man!'

'My mother was Eliza Lindberg. Your wife,' said Fella. 'She was killed in a car crash. In Rimmeri, so the papers said. You were distraught. Only the papers didn't get it right, did they?'

Something changed in Lindberg's face. A narrowing of the eyes, perhaps, or a tensing of the jaw. It was something so small it was almost invisible. But Fella knew. This man was guilty.

'And you knew my mother had a baby—me—didn't you? When you had her killed, you meant to kill your own son too.'

'My dear young man, you are *very* wrong—'

'Don't patronize me, you bastard!'

'I think you'll find that it is *you* who are patronizing *me* if you expect me to believe this deluded nonsense. Now, if you don't mind, I'm weary of this conversation.'

He was leaning forward to press a button and that could only mean one thing. There was no time left.

'What about Molly Robson?' said Fella. He could feel the heat pulsing through him, the heat of fear. Lindberg paused. He took his hand away from the button. 'You couldn't find her clone, could you? And now you never will.'

Lindberg stared. Fella could sense that he was working out how to play this game.

'This is quite ridiculous, young man,' he said. 'But since you have these false assumptions about me, let's sit down and talk about them.'

He gestured to the chair in front of his desk. He smiled. And that smile told Fella that if he sat in that chair he'd lose the game.

'No,' he said. 'You tried to kill me once—d'you think I'm going to let you have another go? Because what I know is enough to get me killed. It was enough to get my mother killed.'

Suddenly, Lindberg lunged across the desk and he felt

the man's strong grip on his forearm, saw the hatred in his eyes. Fella wrenched his arm upwards, but the grip bit harder into him. So he punched, hard, and heard his father's yell of pain. He pulled free and turned and ran back down the corridor, onto the bright stage of the lecture theatre and up the steps of the darkened auditorium, expecting any second to be tackled to the ground. He stumbled in the darkness. He couldn't see the exit door. And then a crack of light showed him. As he swung the door open he heard a noise on the stage below. He threw himself out into the corridor that led to the tanks and ran for the heavy double doors, hoping that they hadn't been locked behind the tour group. He hit the doors, grabbed the handles and pulled. Still open.

He plunged through the doors and skidded to a halt, the great wall of tanks ahead of him, the last of the tour group disappearing out of sight along the walkway.

To his left was a small scaffolding platform, with cameras and lights set up. On it stood Frankie and Baz, staring at him.

'Holy Moly, where's the fire?' said Frankie.

'Is this the live broadcast?' he yelled, his voice horribly loud in the silence.

'Will be, in about twenty seconds,' said Frankie.

'Get this boy out of here . . . ' A woman strode into view. Neat suit, microphone clipped to it, a bunch of papers, which she was now flapping at Fella. 'I'm about to start the broadcast! Get *out*!'

'Frankie,' he cried, 'I've found out the truth about what goes on here . . . ' He was losing his breath now, his legs shaking.

'For God's sake!' said the suited woman.

'*Murder,* that's what goes on here . . . '

He looked at Frankie, pleading into her startled face.

Then Baz turned to Frankie. 'Start rolling,' he said.

Frankie darted into position behind the camera and he heard her voice, loud and firm. 'Tell us what you mean, Fella.'

'I mean that people are killed to get the organs. These are fakes!'

'Get the lunatic out! We're on air in fifteen seconds!' shrieked the woman.

A slamming of doors echoed behind them and Fella spun round to see two security guards.

'Keep going, Fella,' called Frankie, 'on air in thirteen seconds.'

Fella lurched forward to drag one of the weights from the camera platform. As he swung it free, he saw the security guards draw their guns. He staggered, with the weight, to stand in front of the tanks. He heard Baz's clear, calm voice begin to count . . .

'Ten, nine, eight . . . '

Fella turned to face the security guards. 'You're not going to shoot! What if you hit the tanks? They have living organs in them . . . '

'Four, three, two . . . '

Suddenly, he saw his father behind the guards.

'Don't they?'

'ON AIR!'

And he lifted the weight with both hands and hurled it with all his strength at the wall of tanks behind him.

rebe screamed and struggled upright in her hospital bed, staring at the telescreen in front of her.

She watched as Fella hurled something at the glass tanks behind him. There was the sound of smashing glass and now liquid was pouring from the tanks. She didn't understand.

A woman appeared in the foreground. 'We're bringing you these dramatic scenes live from Lindberg International, where an intruder . . . '

'Lindberg International?' said Milo, sitting on the bed beside her. 'What the hell's he doing . . . ?'

The woman ducked out of sight and the camera swung in to show Fella picking up the thing he had thrown and hurling it again. Now you could see that the tanks all had something in them. As the glass and water showered down on him, Fella bent again to pick up something that had fallen out of one of the tanks. He held it up to the camera and yelled, 'It's a fake! A plastic heart! A fake!'

'Oh my God, my God!' breathed Milo.

Suddenly, two big men in dark uniforms hurled themselves at Fella and there was a flailing mass of arms, legs, helmets, and batons. But still you could hear him screaming.

'They'll shoot him!' cried Grebe.

'They won't.' Milo grabbed her hand and squeezed it. 'They daren't do that. Not here.'

Now Fella was on the ground, face down, both guards on top of him. One, with a knee jammed into Fella's back, had grabbed hold of his hair.

Grebe trembled with a sickening feeling. She could feel the pain as if it was her own. She gulped down the sobs as Milo put an arm around her.

Fella was arching his back, pushing his head up so that he could twist it round to face the camera. He shouted at it. No, not at the camera. To someone out of sight just behind it.

And no matter how hard the guard tried to push his head back into the floor, he kept on shouting, his face red and stretched tight with rage.

'MURDERER! MURDERER!'

Grebe sat in the reception lounge with all the other visitors. She was getting used to the smell of the place. In a way, it reminded her of the Orphanage. She had sometimes wondered, in the hours she had sat here waiting for him, what effect this would have on Fella.

A tutor came and beckoned to the middle-aged couple sitting opposite her. They jumped up, smiling, and headed for the double doors that led to the living quarters. Grebe caught the tutor's eye. He gave a sympathetic smile. She supposed he felt sorry for her, waiting every day, sitting alone to the end of the visiting hour.

Gradually, in ones and twos and little family groups, the other visitors were called to go through and see their boys. Sometimes, over the past three weeks, she had wondered about these other families and why their boys were here. This Academy was supposed to give them a fresh start, to help heal whatever wounds had been inflicted on their lives. She wondered whether any of those wounds could be as bad as Fella's.

Alone in the room now, Grebe shifted on her seat and glanced again at the clock.

Suddenly, the double doors opened.

She looked up, hoping. She always hoped.

But the tutor didn't call her. Instead, he came to sit beside her.

'My name's William.' He smiled.

She looked at him, sensing bad news.

'I'm Greta.'

'And you're here to see . . . ?'

'Fella.'

'You're a relative, or . . . ?'

'I'm . . . I'm his friend.'

William nodded. She could see the kindness in him. He didn't want to hurt her feelings.

'I'm afraid Fella doesn't want to see anyone.'

Grebe felt her eyes fill with tears.

'I'm sorry,' said William. 'But we can't override the wishes of our students except in very special circumstances.'

'But these *are* special circumstances!' she cried. 'His father has just been accused of mass murder.'

'I know . . . '

The memory of Fella's face when he was smashing those tanks had been with her night and day since it happened. It had frightened her so much. She looked at William. She didn't know how to explain it.

'He can't bear to be Lindberg's son,' she said at last. 'He'll die in his heart, in his mind. But I've got to try and help him understand . . . he isn't just Lindberg's son. He's Eliza's too.

But the most important thing is, he's his *own* person . . . ' Her thoughts stumbled again. ' . . . When things get really bad, you have to find strength in *yourself,* don't you? And sometimes you need people to help you with that—people who love you. And if Fella's got to stay here for two years, he'll need the strength inside himself. He *must* get it back!'

'I know.' William placed a hand on her shoulder. 'We're all trying. And we will need you too. You've just got to keep coming back.'

She rubbed away her tears.

'I will,' she said. 'Of course I will.'

Chapter 72

Grebe had known he would look different, but still it was a shock.

The first thing she noticed about the hunched figure with his back to her was that his body, so familiar to her, had shrunk. In one glance she saw the outline of his shoulder blades beneath his shirt, his knuckled spine, the harsh angle of his knees.

But it was the stillness that really frightened her. Fella, who had always been so full of energy, was sitting at the head of his bed, face to the wall. Absolutely motionless.

She scanned the room. It was painted a cheerful pale orange. It had its own bathroom and a big window full of late afternoon sunshine.

She sat on the bed. Beside him, but not too close.

'Fella, it's me.'

He didn't even seem to be breathing. She waited in his silence.

After a while she said, 'Everybody sends their love. Beatrice and Josie and Milo. And your aunt Carys and little Louis.'

She blinked at the wetness in her eyes.

'We're allowed to bring things, if there's anything you want. Food. Or books . . . '

They'd only allowed her fifteen minutes this first time, and she wanted to say something that would make a difference to him, leave him with something. But she was afraid. She wanted to touch him, but she felt it would be wrong. Intruding, somehow.

She looked at what she could see of his face. Jaw and sunken cheek. A dull, staring eye. She drew a deep breath.

'Molly Robson has had her heart replacement,' she said. 'All the publicity . . . they found a donor, a girl who died in an accident. So Molly will live.'

She watched. Maybe he blinked. Maybe she heard a breath.

'I'll come back tomorrow,' she said.

Chapter 73

Towards the end of the third week, Fella was sitting in a different place. They'd put an armchair by the window. His head moved as she came into the room. Just a fraction, in her direction.

She put down the new books she had brought, adding them to the pile that was growing on the floor. She checked the position of the pile, as she did each day. And today it seemed that the top book had been shifted out of line a little.

She looked up at the side of his face.

'You know the course I've just started,' she said, 'the one about literature? Well, you can do the same course here. And loads of others. And they have a swimming pool. One of the tutors showed me. It's real A-grade stuff . . . '

She halted, angry with herself for saying anything that might bring back memories of the Island. But then, the Island was part of both of them. She didn't know how to do it, but she knew that, as time went on, they would have to look at the bad things. Look at them, and then let them go.

He was staring out through the window into the distance. Perhaps Carys was right. She'd said there were things going on in Fella's head that only a mind doctor could fix. She had tried to imagine what was happening in Fella's mind. Just the imagining had terrified her. It was worse for him than it was for her, she thought. It was *his* father. She shuddered, despite the warm sun shining on them both.

'Little Louis is beginning to walk,' she said.

She couldn't think what else to put into the silence. She'd been prattling on every day about Beatrice and their flat, Milo and Josie and Carys and Louis. Just ordinary stuff. She had no idea whether it was helping.

She went to sit on the floor beside his chair and reached up to put her hand on his knee and sit in silence with him.

After a while, as if waking her from a dream, she heard the familiar bell that signalled the end of the visiting hour.

She looked up at Fella's averted face. Suddenly, she thought of something she had read.

'Strong minds can break strong chains, Fella,' she said. 'You've done it once. You can do it again. You've just got to trust . . . '

At that moment, his head turned. He looked down at her. Sad, confused, as if he was trying to understand or remember something that was just beyond his grasp.

The bell sounded again.

He was staring with faded eyes. But at last came a tiny

glint of the Fella she knew. Coming towards her down a long tunnel.

'Time to go,' said William from the doorway.

She stood and kissed the soft curls on his head.

'Trust yourself, Fella,' she whispered.

Chapter 74

I t was what Papa Louis had said. Now he remembered.
'Trust the goodness inside you, Fella. Goodness is more powerful than evil. It *always* is.'

And slowly, as the days and weeks went on, he became less afraid. He might have a monster's blood in his veins, but he had Papa Louis in his heart and in his mind.

One day, as he sat with Grebe, he asked her, 'Do you think people will hate me?'

She was shocked. 'No!'

'Because of what Lindberg did . . . '

'No!' She grabbed his hands, her nails digging into his palms. 'No, Fella. You must never think that. People admire you for what *you* did.'

He looked at her, wanting to believe it.

'Just think,' she said, 'of all the lives you've saved.'

'Islanders' lives,' he said. 'Do they care about that here?'

'Yes! All sorts of things are happening, questions being asked . . . '

Questions. We have a duty to be curious. Who was it who'd told him that? Papa Louis, of course.

'And you saved my life too,' she said, 'bringing me here.'

'We did that together.'

'Yes. We did.'

She gave him one of her looks and he felt a stumbling sensation in his chest. How awful things must have been for her. Growing up with no one to love her. Knowing now that she had only existed as someone else's insurance. He admired her strength. He admired the way she was making plans for her life.

'I've written an essay,' she said one day, as she added some more books to the stacks she had brought him. Sunlight blazed across her hair as she smiled up at him. 'It was bloody hard work, as Beatrice would say, but I'm quite pleased with it.'

He hadn't told her he had begun to read the books she'd brought. He wanted to surprise her one day, he told himself. But it wasn't just that. It was as though something was going on between him and the books that he wanted to keep private. Whole worlds were opening up from those pages. And he loved the feelings that it gave him. He knew that she checked the piles. He was careful to leave no clues.

He watched her as she scanned the books. She glanced up at him. Did she know? Probably. He found he didn't mind after all.

'I'm getting a new room tomorrow,' he said.

'Thanks for telling me.' She grinned.

'A bigger room, with a proper desk and shelves. And a computer.'

'That's great! You'll be able to do *so many* things!'

'Yes.' He smiled.

There were so many things he wanted to do.

Chapter 75

F ella took a thick black pen and wrote *Law* and *Philosophy* on the lid of the box. Then he packed the last of his books into it. Books that Carys had brought. He loved the conversations with Carys—the way she made him justify his opinions and thoughts. He loved the way she argued back and made him think.

She'd invited him and Grebe to stay for the summer. He looked out of the window now, with a surge of excitement, half expecting to see Grebe. No. Too early. She wasn't due until mid-day.

Someone tapped on the door and he turned to see William.

'Call for you,' he said, handing him a phone. 'Take as long as you like, since it's your last day.' He smiled.

Fella put the phone to his ear.

'Hello?'

'Fella!' The voice bounced at him.

'Hello, Dr Farl.'

'I was just ringing . . . well, to say congratulations.'

'Thank you.'

'Distinctions in every subject!'

'No, not every subject.'

'All the same, very well done!' said Farl.

'Well, there are some great tutors in here,' he said, 'and Carys has helped a lot. And Grebe.'

'Ah, yes! Greta's done very well too, I hear.'

'Yes.'

Fella waited. Still he felt wrong-footed by this man.

'Well . . . I just wanted to say well done,' said Farl, 'to both of you. It doesn't seem like two years, does it?'

'It does to me!'

Farl laughed.

'Um . . . ' said Fella, 'I need to finish packing . . . '

'Oh yes. Yes, of course,' said Farl.

'Goodbye then.'

William gave him a questioning glance as he handed back the phone. 'All right?'

'Yeah. That was Dr Farl.'

'Ah yes.'

Fella could tell that William was remembering Farl and his evidence at the trial. But he didn't want to think of that today.

'When's Greta coming?' said William cheerfully.

'Twelve o'clock,' said Fella, 'but my aunt Carys has told the press I'm leaving at one from the front entrance, so they'll all be waiting there. That's the plan, anyway.'

'Ah,' said William. 'Well, I'll see if I can do anything to

help her with the diversion. They don't know anything about the wedding, do they?'

'I hope not,' said Fella.

'Well, let's make sure they don't get any clues,' said William. 'Come on, I'll help you finish packing.'

Chapter 76

Grebe turned into the wide street. At the far end she could see the crowd of press people already in place, eagerly waiting for Carys Winton to collect her nephew from the Academy. She indicated right, turning down the side street that led to the back of the building, flinching as the gears graunched. She hadn't had that much practice driving on her own.

In a while, Carys would drive her car to the front gates and give a press statement about Fella and about the changes that were beginning to happen on the Satellite Islands. That would distract the cameras and the reporters so that she and Fella could make their getaway from the back.

She parked and hurried to the little gate in the high brick wall.

As the gate opened she was pleased to see Arthur's friendly face.

'Ah, come on in!' he said. 'Coast is clear at the moment. We've been checking this back road all morning. Oh, I'm going to miss you! I'll miss both of you.'

Arthur chatted away as he led her to Fella's room.

'Twenty-three boxes of books!' he said. 'They'll 'ave to get a lorry, I reckon. Says he wants to take one of the boxes with 'im now, though. Can't be parted from it.'

'Right,' said Grebe, 'then he can carry it himself.'

Arthur chuckled. 'That's right!'

As they reached the door, he turned and held out his hand. 'I'll leave you now and say it's been a privilege to know you. You have a long and happy life, pet.'

'Thank you, Arthur.'

She paused a moment, watching Arthur go. Then she tapped on Fella's door. Her heart was hammering. Stupid. She'd come here almost every day for two years. But today felt strange. Exciting, a bit frightening.

He looked up as she opened the door. His smile burned right into her. And suddenly she remembered the time, long ago, when he had first told her there was a way off the Island.

Chapter 77

I n the car, Grebe felt shaky and awkward. They'd got clear of the Academy but still she kept checking the rear-view mirror.

Now they were heading out of town. No press gangs in sight. She should feel calmer. But she didn't. Neither of them had spoken much. Perhaps Fella was letting her concentrate on the driving. But perhaps it wasn't really that.

'This Milo's car?' he said at last.

'Yes.'

'The one he taught you to drive in?'

'Yes.'

'So . . . how often did you have lessons?' he said.

'We'd try to go out every day, depending on what we were both doing, you know . . . '

'Every day!'

'Yes.'

'For how long?'

'Oh, about three months, maybe four . . . '

'What? It can't be that difficult, can it?'

'Well, yes, actually, it is!'

He made a sort of snorting noise. Grebe snatched a quick glance across at him.

'Are you jealous?' she said.

'No.'

'You are!'

'I'm not!'

'Oh, Fella!' she said. 'Of course I like Milo . . . '

'Yes, of course you do. It's obvious. You're always talking about him.'

'Only cos I thought you'd be interested to hear about the outside world.'

'Well, just lately the outside world seems to consist mostly of Milo and what Milo's doing—'

'Excuse me! What about that Frankie woman? She's been visiting you all the while you've been in there!'

'Yes, with Baz—'

'Not always—'

'*With Baz,* and they were bringing me recordings of all the documentaries they'd worked on. They thought I'd be interested. Anyway, who's jealous now?'

She slewed the car over into a lay-by and tugged at the handbrake.

'Get out of the car,' she said.

'What?'

'I said, *out!*'

She got out herself and strode round to his door. She opened it for him. The sun was searing. They were in lush countryside now and the sweet smell of mown hay hung heavy around them.

He climbed out of the car and stood facing her. He was trying to keep his face serious, she could tell. There was a quivering tension around the corners of his mouth. And something in his eyes that sent a ball of fizzing warmth plunging right through her.

She pushed him back onto the hot metal of the car door.

'I think we need to sort this out,' she said.

Chapter 78

F
ella sat in silence as they drove on into the country-side towards where Josie's wedding was going to take place. Every now and then he looked across at Grebe.

Where had she learned to kiss like that?

But he knew better than to say that. He didn't want another quarrel.

Or perhaps he did.

He looked at her. He knew she could feel him looking.

'Well, at least that stopped you prattling on about Milo,' she said.

And when had she changed? Why hadn't he noticed?

She slowed the car and took the opportunity to throw him a smile that brought back the flooding warmth of that kiss.

'Here we are,' she said.

They turned into a narrow lane with rolling fields and woodland to either side.

'Look up the hill, on the right,' she said. 'That's the house where the wedding's going to be. Beatrice has done all the decorations herself.'

'Oh dear, really?'

'Don't be horrible! It all looks great. And Josie's going to make a beautiful bride.'

She glanced at her rear-view mirror. 'And if you look behind us, you'll see that Carys has caught us up. There's a wild creature bouncing about in the car; that'll be Louis. He's really excited about seeing you. He's been going on about it for days.'

Fella twisted round in the seat and waved in the direction of the rear window. From the back seat of Carys's car a headful of black curls jiggled as a small arm waved frantically back.

They swung round to park on the wide gravelled drive-way of the house. There were people milling around the front door, the women dressed in a fabulous burst of colours, and the brightest plumage, of course, belonging to Beatrice.

They got out of the car and Grebe looked at him across the roof. He held her smile, not wanting to look away. Suddenly a shriek cut across their silence and he turned to see Carys lift Louis from her car and set him down on the gravel.

And now the child was hurtling towards him in a wobbly run, head lolling, mouth wide with grin.

'Fella home, Fella home!' he cried.

Fella picked up his cousin and swung him high into the air, shaking shrieks of laughter down around their heads.

'You're right, Louis. Fella home.'

alison **allen-gray**

was brought up in the wilds of Suffolk. After university (English and Drama at Aberystwyth) she joined a theatre company and set about converting an old cinema into a performing arts centre which hosted many exciting new companies and innovative work. Here she began performing and scriptwriting with a group that included the composer Neil Brand and fellow children's author Lynda Waterhouse.

Alison co-wrote four musicals, two of them for children, whilst also developing her acting career. After having had a musical and a picture book published, she began writing for young adults. She is a member of the dynamic authors' and illustrators' group, Islington Writers for Children, which has given invaluable feedback during her writing career.

Alison lives by the coast in Sussex and one of her many dreams is to design and build her own house. When not dreaming or writing, she enjoys fell-walking, horse riding and going on trips all over the world with her partner in their vintage car. Her first novel, *Unique*, won the Stockport Schools' Book Award, was longlisted for the Carnegie Medal and shortlisted for six prizes, including the Booktrust Teenage Fiction Prize.

Also by alison **allen-gray:**

Unique

ISBN 978-0-19-275576-6

I know the **big secret** now.

The thing nobody wanted me to find out.

I'm **not** an only child. There was someone **before** me.

My brother. He was everything I'm not.

Clever. Funny. Loved. But he's gone.

Now I can't believe a word they say.

Got to get away.

They're after me. They want me to be like him.

Before they find me, I have to find the truth . . .

the whole truth.

'Allen-Gray writes in an easy, readable style, raises stimulating
questions, and offers a plot that keeps you guessing throughout'

Financial Times

Shortlisted for the Booktrust Teenage prize